Mother Knows Best

OTHER TITLES BY KAREN MACINERNEY

Margie Peterson Mysteries

Mother's Day Out

Dewberry Farm Mysteries

Killer Jam

Gray Whale Inn Mysteries

Murder on the Rocks

Dead and Berried

Murder Most Maine

Berried to the Hilt

Blueberry Blues: A Short Story

Brush with Death

Death Runs Adrift

Pumpkin Pied: A Short Story

Tales of an Urban Werewolf

Howling at the Moon

On the Prowl

Leader of the Pack

Mother Knows Best

A Margie Peterson Mystery

KAREN MACINERNEY

THOMAS & MERCER

Published by Thomas & Mercer, Seattle

www.apub.com

Amazon, the Amazon logo, and Thomas & Mercer are trademarks of Amazon.com, Inc., or its affiliates.

ISBN-13: 9781503954830
ISBN-10: 1503954838

Cover design by Cyanotype Book Architects

Printed in the United States of America

To Jessica Park, for leading the way. Without you, this book never would have been written!

CHAPTER ONE

You'd be surprised how hard it is to find a parking spot at a strip club on a Sunday afternoon.

My boss, Peaches Barlowe, and I had been following real-estate maven Marty Krumbacher's red BMW convertible for two hours. Peaches's Buick Regal was in the shop—a client's ex-husband had taken both a Louisville Slugger and a chain saw to it earlier that week—so we were driving my slightly dented Grand Caravan. Peaches, in a bright-orange Lycra dress that matched her hair and dipped perilously low in the front, wasn't in any hurry, but I was starting to fret. Marty needed to wrap up any nefarious activities by three so I'd have time to make it to the new-parent orientation at Holy Oaks Catholic School.

We'd spent the morning sitting outside of Marty's downtown office, drinking black coffee and eating pork rinds (Peaches was on a low-carb diet again) while we waited for something to happen. When Marty shot out of the parking garage at 1:45, I was worried it was going to be another trip to the Milk and Honey Spa for a manicure, but when the red BMW turned north and then pulled into the Sweet Shop parking lot, I began feeling optimistic.

A few days earlier, a blonde woman in Lululemon yoga pants and about five hundred dollars' worth of Nordstrom-counter makeup had marched into Peachtree Investigations in a cloud of lily-scented perfume. Which was a nice change, really, from the smell of melted paraffin and nail-polish remover that permeated our new workplace.

Since the office had blown up a few months back, we'd been subleasing space on the east side of Austin in a Brazilian waxing salon called the Pretty Kitten. I still hadn't adjusted to the near-constant sound of Velcro ripping, punctuated by the occasional scream, and that day was no exception. No sooner had the blonde woman walked through the door than a stifled yelp came from one of the rooms down the hallway.

"What's that noise, Mommy?" my daughter Elsie asked, opening and closing her beloved French-fry phone as I tried to finish up a worker's-comp report. I was relieved to see the fry phone in her hands; unfortunately, she had chosen one of the rarest Happy Meal toys on the planet as her love object. I had lost it on a job six months ago, and since then did twice-daily checks to make sure it hadn't gone missing again.

School hadn't started yet, and my husband, Blake, had client meetings that afternoon, so I'd had to bring Elsie and her younger brother, Nick, to the office with me for the day. Nick, thankfully, was engrossed in building a Duplo version of the Loch Ness Monster, allowing me to focus on the details of Fred Goertz's faked ankle injury while Elsie was finishing up a *Frozen* coloring book.

"It's a kind of beauty treatment," Peaches told her.

"I don't think I want to be beautiful," Elsie said, wrinkling her nose and fingering the rhinestone dog collar she'd taken to wearing a few months back.

"You already are, sweetheart," my boss told Elsie, and as my daughter picked up the blue crayon again, Peaches turned to the blonde. "What can I do for you?" she asked in her slow southern drawl.

The woman looked around, her nose wrinkling. "I think my husband's cheating," she announced as if my children weren't in the same room with us.

"Uh, could you hold on a minute?" I asked. "I'm just going to relocate the kids."

She pressed her lips together into a thin line and gave a sharp nod as I fired up my iPhone, found the *Frozen* soundtrack, tucked the earbuds into Elsie's ears, and ushered both her and her brother into the small back room where we kept the files.

"But I need my blocks!" Nick complained.

"I'll bring them to you," I said, gathering handfuls of Duplos and tossing them into the plastic bin. "This should keep you going for a bit," I told him. "It'll only be a few minutes."

The door to the storage room had barely closed before the woman continued. "I need proof," she said, "but he can't know a thing about it." She looked at the cracked plastic visitors' chair as if it might be contaminated, then perched on the very edge of it, holding her enormous designer bag in her lap. Her words were cold and detached, but I could see that her eyes were red.

"Discretion, then," Peaches said, leaning back in her creaky Naugahyde office chair. "We can handle that. Are you concerned he'll take measures if he suspects you're having him investigated?"

"Damned right I'm concerned. Why else would I come to a place like this?" She swept a manicured hand through the air. Despite the anguish in her blue eyes, which looked like they could have burned holes through concrete, her Botoxed face was as smooth and stiff as a mannequin's. She leaned forward, and the expensive scent of perfume wafted over to me. "If that bastard knows I'm on to him, he'll move every dime we have to a Swiss bank account. I've given him eight of my prime years, and he's not getting out of this without giving me a return on my investment."

"Investment?" I asked.

"Eight of my prime years," she repeated.

"Have you considered moving funds to a separate account?" Peaches asked.

"Of course," she sniffed. "But don't you think that would kind of negate the whole 'discretion' thing?"

Peaches pursed her hot-pink lips. "So we're talking cash."

"I went to the bank this morning. Just tell me how much you need," the woman said, fishing a leather wallet from her bag and pulling out a stack of hundreds. Peaches's purple-lined eyes widened, and by the time Mitzi Krumbacher had pushed through the glass door and marched back out to her cream-colored Porsche Cayenne, Peaches had pocketed a cool thousand bucks and was already running a background check on the woman's potentially wayward husband.

"He's loaded," Peaches said. "Real-estate magnate here in town. Looks like we won't have to worry about rent for a month or two."

"Why was that lady so angry?" Elsie asked as I opened the door to the storage room.

"Sometimes, when people are married for a long time, they run into difficulties, darling," I told her.

"Like you and Daddy?" she asked, making my heart wrench. Peaches raised an eyebrow.

"Not quite the same," I said. At least, I didn't think so. Although it could be. For all I knew, Marty Krumbacher was into sequin-clad drag queens, just like my husband. Blake and I were still living together, but things were what my mother-in-law referred to as "strained." I smiled at my daughter and redirected her attention to the fry phone, then turned back to my report, wondering with a pang of guilt how much psychological trauma my husband and I had inflicted on our children—and whether taking them to a Brazilian waxing salon was compounding the damage.

Since that day, Peaches and I had spent a lot of time tailing Marty Krumbacher around town, but with no success.

Until today, that was. Instead of driving to a steak house, he headed north and pulled in at the Sweet Shop—which sounds like a trendy bakery but evidently specializes in young women who make their living dancing with poles. The sign above the building showed a buxom girl wearing nothing more than a lascivious smile and two strategically placed cupcakes, both of which were topped with enormous strawberries.

"Busy place. Must be the free food," I said, pointing to the neon sign blinking beneath the cupcake lady and advertising "FREE LUNCH."

"Nah. It is a good lunch—I swing by sometimes when billing isn't great—but it's packed because of Whipped Cream Sunday." Peaches pointed to the banner hanging over the entrance.

"Do I want to know what that means?" I asked.

"I think you can figure it out. Big waste of good Reddi-wip, if you ask me," she said as I circled the parking lot looking for a space. "But I'm not their target audience. Hey, there's a guy backing out over there," Peaches said, pointing to a Subaru Forester with a "MY CHILD IS AN HONOR STUDENT AT EANES ELEMENTARY" sticker plastered to the back window. It was easing out of a space marked "Compact" and only narrowly missed taking the bumper of the Corolla parked next door with it.

"I don't know if we'll be able to get the van door open," I said.

"He got into his station wagon, didn't he? Besides," she added, pointing up, "you have a sunroof."

I sighed and squeezed into the open space, putting the van into park. There were about six millimeters between my side mirrors and the cars on either side of me. "I'll wait here for you."

Peaches turned to me and blinked. "What do you mean, wait here?"

"I thought you just needed me for the car."

"You always bring backup when you have it," she said. "Besides, I'm going to let you take charge today. It's good training."

I pointed to my faded Green Meadows Day School T-shirt and my khaki shorts, which sported an enormous hole in the left leg where Rufus, my temperamental Siamese cat, had slashed them. "I can't go in. I'm way underdressed!"

"Underdressed? Margie, you're going into a strip club." Peaches winked, making her heavily mascaraed eyelashes stick together. "Less is more, you know?"

And with a brief prayer that my children would never find out that their mother had taken to hanging out in a strip club, I followed Peaches inside.

CHAPTER TWO

I groaned. "Do we really have to go in? I mean, he's at a strip club. What else do we need to know?"

"If your husband were playing hide-the-tamale with a young woman covered in whipped cream, wouldn't you want to know about it?"

Sadly, I knew the answer to that question. I'd found out just a few months back that my own husband had been having an affair with a young man who favored false eyelashes and sequins.

"Oops. My bad," Peaches said, realizing her mistake. "How's that going, by the way?"

"He keeps telling me it was just a phase."

"A phase?" Peaches asked.

"I know," I said. "But what else can I do?"

"Filing for divorce comes to mind," she suggested.

"He doesn't want to. And I'm not going to bring it up now; it's bad enough that my mother's coming for a two-week visit." My mother was lovely, but she also believed she'd been Cleopatra in a former life and had recently converted to an all-raw vegan diet. Now that I thought about it, maybe spending the afternoon in a strip club wasn't so bad. "Is the liquor free, too?" I asked.

"Nope. Ten dollars for a margarita."

"That's too bad." Though since I was due at the parent orientation at Holy Oaks in two hours, it was probably for the best.

I gestured toward the entrance. "Do they really do . . . well, *you-know-what* in there?" I asked, changing the subject.

"Sometimes," she shrugged. "I never pay that much attention—I'm usually only here for the steak. But there's only one way to find out." She tucked the pork-rind bag between the seats and opened the van door, smacking it into the side of the Corolla. "Oops." She glanced up at the sunroof. "We might need to go to Plan B."

"I do have sliding doors," I reminded her. We crawled to the back and sidled out of the van, squeezing between the cars.

"You might want to get this thing washed," Peaches said, brushing off her spandex minidress and pointing to the giant clean spots we'd made on the side of the Caravan.

My T-shirt now had a big brown splotch in the middle of it, and I was afraid to look at the back of my shorts. "I hope I have time to change before the parent orientation," I grumbled as Peaches adjusted her cleavage and tottered toward the entrance in her cork platform wedges. I followed in my sensible Nike sneakers and battered shorts. Next to Peaches, I was feeling a little like Cinderella in her pre-fairy-godmother phase.

All too soon, we had stepped out of the hot August sun and were facing an enormous, shaved-head bouncer wearing a very tight pair of jeans and full sleeves of the ink variety.

"Hey there, Peaches," he said. "Come for the New York strip?"

"You bet," she said. "They got chocolate mousse today?"

"Nah. Strawberry shortcake," he said, nodding toward the banner. "Theme day, you know?" He squinted at me. "Who's your friend?"

"Business partner," she said, and I gave a feeble wave. "Chewy, this is Margie. Margie, Chewy."

"Nice to meet you," I said, not quite sure of the etiquette.

"First time in a strip club?" he asked, grinning.

"Oh, no," I said airily. "I do this all the time."

"Uh-huh," he said, and waved us on through. "Have fun! And I recommend the Caesar salad."

I had never been in a strip club before, so I didn't know what to expect when we walked around the partition into the main room.

It took a moment for my eyes to adjust; the lighting was low, except for spotlights directed at the stages. There were three of them—a big one down the center of the room, with two smaller stages flanking it. The center stage was currently occupied by a young woman wearing a hot-pink bob, green-and-white-striped stockings, and a very, very small apron.

"Strawberry Shortcake," Peaches said as the woman wrapped herself around the candy-striped pole and then did a series of contortions that would have made the US Olympic gymnastics team jealous.

"Wow," I said involuntarily. "I had no idea pole dancing could be so . . . athletic."

"And lucrative," Peaches said, pointing to the men crowding around waving money. "But someday she's going to need the cash for bunion surgery. Look at those heels," she said, pointing to Ms. Shortcake's six-inch stilettos.

"Ouch."

A few feet in front of Ms. Shortcake and her pole, a gigantic inflatable pool had been set up, and a waitress wearing pink hot pants and a bra with very small cupcakes for cups was selling cans of whipped cream to a line of men.

"You see him?" Peaches murmured.

"No," I said, although, to be honest, I'd almost forgotten I was supposed to be looking.

"Over there," Peaches said, nodding toward the tables close to the main stage. Krumbacher had sat down with two men in white shirts and jeans. "We'll sit a few tables back."

I followed her across the dark club to a table that was painted to look like a peppermint candy, then sat down on the disturbingly sticky chair. *It's just beer,* I told myself, trying not to let my skin make more contact than necessary with the vinyl seat, and attempted a casual pose.

"You look like you're in church," Peaches said, leafing through the menu. "Loosen up a bit."

"Right," I said, slouching a little.

"I said loosen up, not pass out." She handed me a menu. "Here."

"It's hard to relax when we're the only women in here," I muttered.

"What do you mean? There are women everywhere," Peaches said, pointing to the gorgeous African American woman gyrating on the stage closest to us. She wore a pointed foil hat, thigh-high silver boots, and a sultry smile. And that was it.

I turned to Peaches. "Please tell me she's not supposed to be a Hershey's Kiss."

Peaches grinned. "You'll never think of them the same way again, will you?"

The waitress sashayed over before I had a chance to respond. "Can I get you ladies something?"

"Two strip steaks, please, darlin'." Peaches looked at me. "Medium-rare, right?"

I nodded.

"And those two gentlemen would like to buy you each a drink," the waitress added, nodding toward two octogenarians in the corner. They bobbed their heads when I looked.

"Sorry, but I'm driving," I said.

"I'm not," Peaches said cheerfully. "Two Cuervo margaritas, please. And tell them thanks."

"Aren't you working?" I pointed out.

"Supervising," she said. "Besides, it's been a rough week."

"What's going on?"

"Man troubles," she said.

"Tell me about it," I replied. "But not now," I added as Marty and his buddies stood up and headed toward the back of the club. "Where's he going?"

"Why don't you go find out?" she asked. "I'll take care of the drinks. If you need to take a picture, don't forget to turn off the flash!"

I hurried after Marty Krumbacher, trying to look casual and wondering if I might fit in better if I stripped down to my bra and panties. Not enough sequins, I decided. Besides, I already felt like a Budweiser Clydesdale in a roomful of My Little Ponies. Exposing a few extra acres of post-baby stomach wasn't going to do anything to help me look like I belonged here.

I hung back as Krumbacher and one of his friends walked down a pistachio-green hallway and into a room at the far end. I gave them a moment before trotting after them and sidling up to the door, hoping they hadn't closed it. It was open about an inch.

Glancing behind me to make sure no one else was in the hallway, I peeked through the crack in the door.

I don't know what I was expecting—maybe a hot-fudge-and-maraschino-cherry-studded orgy featuring Plum Puddin' and Raspberry Tart—but, despite being in a strip club, Marty Krumbacher didn't look like he was into tarts.

He was sitting at a table with two other men, and they were deep in discussion.

"I told you, it's out of our hands," one of the men said. "We're waiting on a shipment. Without raw materials, there's nothing we can do but wait."

"Find another supplier," Krumbacher said, his voice cold and hard—and remarkably similar to his wife's, now that I thought of it. They made a pretty good match. "I have deadlines to meet."

"But Mr. Krumbacher—"

"The next shipment goes out next Wednesday. Figure it out, or I'll have to send Thumbs to pay you a visit."

I had read about people blanching, but I'd never understood the term until now. The guy Krumbacher was talking to suddenly looked like a vampire had just sucked all the blood out of him.

Whatever was going on here was weird, but not the kind of thing Mrs. Krumbacher was interested in. Would she be happy, I wondered, or sad that her husband wasn't getting it on with one of the bonbons from an X-rated *Nutcracker*?

"Better get going," Krumbacher said, standing up and stretching. "I don't want to miss Shortcake."

I turned to run back to the table. Unfortunately, I bounced off a nubile young woman wearing nothing but a cupcake wrapper as a skirt. She was accompanied by a jeans-clad man who was looking at her like he'd just spent six months on the Atkins diet and she was his first dessert.

"Can I help you?" she asked, eyeing me suspiciously.

"Is the ladies' room back here?" I asked as Krumbacher stepped out of the room behind me. I flicked my eyes to him, and his locked on mine. I gave him a weak smile before turning back to the cupcake woman.

"You're in the wrong hallway," she said. "These rooms are for . . . private dances." As she spoke, the man behind her licked his lips.

"Thanks," I said, and excused myself, hurrying away from Krumbacher.

"How'd you do?" Peaches asked when I scuttled back to the table.

"Not so hot," I said.

"What do you mean?"

"He was meeting with a couple of guys, talking about shipments and someone named Thumbs. Then I turned around and bumped into a cupcake lady, and he saw me."

"He saw you?" Peaches groaned. "First rule of private investigation: don't let them see you." She took a sip of one of the fishbowl-size margaritas that had appeared in my absence and then said, "He's looking at you."

"Great," I said.

"Hi there, ladies!" It was the octogenarians. "Don't mind if we join you," the taller one said, sliding into the sticky seat next to mine. His friend, who was like the little teapot—short and stout, only wearing glasses with lenses so thick I wondered if he'd borrowed them from the Hubble Telescope—pulled up a chair next to Peaches.

"Actually—"

"I've not seen you in here before, sugar," the man next to me cooed, sliding a skeletal hand onto my thigh. "Ooh." He gave my leg a squeeze. "Nice and plump. I like a woman with a little meat on her bones."

I didn't know what to say, so I didn't. Instead, I reached down and pried his bony fingers off my leg, wondering how on earth this man had made it through eight-plus decades of life without learning not to call a woman you wanted to sleep with "plump." On the other hand, perhaps that's why he spent his Sunday afternoons trying to pick up women in strip clubs.

"I like your dress," purred the guy next to Peaches, switching to his reading glasses to get a better look at her cleavage. "I like the way it matches your hair."

"Thanks, hon," Peaches said absently, taking another swig of her margarita.

"How come you're all covered up?" asked the man next to me, who was inching his chair closer and looking like he was considering making another try for my leg. His arm was covered in liver spots the size of Chihuahuas. It was a little alarming, really.

"Have you had that checked?" I said, pointing to one that looked a little like Darth Vader's helmet. "It looks like it could be melanoma. See how the borders are irregular, and it's darker at the top?"

"If you'd like, you can give me a full-body checkup. I've got another one right down here." He reached for his belt buckle and started to undo the clasp.

Fortunately, at that moment the announcer came on. "Gentlemen," she purred, "are you ready to have some fun?"

Liver Spots tucked the tongue of his belt back in, to my relief, and from the whistles and hoots that erupted around me, I was guessing the answer was yes. Even Krumbacher seemed to have forgotten about me; he was handing a wad of bills to the whipped-cream salesgirl and tucking three cans under his elbow. "Well, then, head on down to the pool, gentlemen, and help Strawberry Shortcake and Banana Twirl kick off Whipped Cream Sunday!"

As we watched—evidently the lure of whipped-cream-covered flesh was enough to distract Liver Spots from his campaign to show me his moles—Shortcake and Banana Twirl minced down the runway, their slick lips pushed into provocative pouts. Shortcake slipped out of her heels and peeled off her striped stockings one at a time, leaving her dressed in about six inches of green dental floss.

Banana Twirl had a bit more to take off, and after slowly removing a bright-yellow bikini top and a green scrap of fabric that I was guessing was supposed to be a banana leaf, she took a provocative twirl around the pole, which resulted in howls from the crowd.

"Her signature move," Peaches said knowledgeably as Liver Spots grunted in appreciation.

The two women held hands and jumped into the pool together. "Let the creaming begin!" the announcer declared. The men who'd gathered at the end of the stage put the whipped-cream cans in front of their belt buckles and began squirting the women as they slithered around in the pool.

"Why are they holding them like that?" I asked.

Peaches gave me a look over the rim of her glass.

"Oh," I said, wrinkling my nose. "They really pay ten dollars a can so they can pretend they're . . . you know?"

"Looks like it," Peaches said.

I watched the men holding the cans at their crotches—including our friend Krumbacher, who was right at the front—and shuddered. "Gross. Should we get a photo?"

The men beside us, thankfully, seemed to have forgotten our existence and were staring slack-jawed at the spectacle at the end of the stage. The two women were writhing around together on the bottom of the pool. It looked a little like they were playing Twister, except that they were mostly naked and covered in Reddi-wip. And Banana Twirl's G-string had slipped twice.

"It's not grounds for divorce, but it'll look good in the report," Peaches said. "Show that we're doing something."

"You should go," I said. "He's already seen me."

"First rule of private investigation," she repeated sternly. "I'll go," she said grudgingly, "but wave at me when the steak gets here. I don't want it to get cold."

I agreed and sat back happily, scooting my chair farther from Liver Spots as Peaches headed down toward the pool.

She wove through the crowd of men, tugging her orange dress down over her thighs, and wedged herself into the crowd until she got a ringside seat opposite from Krumbacher; I guess she figured she'd have a better shot of him that way. She had just positioned herself between two men in cowboy hats and pulled out her smartphone when Banana Twirl's head popped up from the tangle of Reddi-wipped limbs, a giant glob of whipped cream hanging from her chin.

"Hey," she said, wiping her eyes and squinting. "I know you." She was looking right at Peaches. "You're the bitch who followed my boy-friend around and took pictures of him at the monster-truck rally last month."

"I don't know what you're talking about," Peaches said, and took a step back.

But Banana was advancing on her.

"You've got the wrong girl," Peaches protested as Banana stepped over the rim of the pool, leaving a dollop of cream on the pink carpet.

Banana wasn't smiling anymore, I noticed. "He lost ten thousand dollars in workers' comp thanks to you!"

Peaches tried to back away, but the cowboys were blocking her escape route. Before she could find another exit, Banana Twirl had grabbed her wrist with a cream-covered hand and hauled her into the pool.

CHAPTER THREE

What happened to the first rule of private investigation?" I asked Peaches as I slammed the van door behind us, almost forty minutes later. It had taken me ten minutes to wrangle Peaches away from the slippery talons of Banana Twirl, and we'd spent another fifteen minutes in the ladies' room rinsing off the Reddi-wip and tending to Peaches's black eye. Chewy had had to hustle us out the back door, leaving our steaks untouched.

"We all have bad days," Peaches said.

"How did she spot you at a monster-truck rally? Aren't there like thousands of people at those things?"

"It's a long story," she said. "I'll tell you over a beer sometime."

I looked at the clock; it was 3:45. "This day is turning out to be a disaster."

"It was just a little whipped cream," Peaches said.

"I have to be at Holy Oaks in fifteen minutes," I reminded her, throwing the van into reverse and just missing the corner of the Corolla. "It's my first time meeting the other parents, and I look like I lost a battle with the Stay Puft Marshmallow Man. Plus, we didn't get a picture, and now Krumbacher's seen both of us."

"More of me than you," Peaches pointed out. She was right; at least twice during the tussle, Peaches had inadvertently mooned the entire club, Marty Krumbacher included. Miraculously, her top had stayed in place, but it had been touch-and-go a couple of times. "Don't worry about it. It's just a little setback, Margie," she said, flipping down the visor and applying a coat of lipstick. "Nothing we can't handle."

A little setback. Peaches was nothing if not optimistic.

I glanced at myself in the mirror. My reddish hair was still streaked with globs of white, and there were powdery patches appearing on my cheeks where the cream had dried. Plus, I was starting to pick up a yogurty aroma from my clothes. "I need to go home and change; there's no way I can show up at the school looking like this."

Peaches shook her head. "If you do that, you'll miss the whole thing. Can your hubby fill in?"

"Blake's in a client meeting this afternoon," I said.

"On a weekend?"

"He's an attorney, remember?" I reminded her. "Anyway, my mother-in-law agreed to watch the kids so that I could go." Normally I could turn to Becky Hale in a pinch, but since Holy Oaks had turned Becky's daughter down and she had written a nasty editorial about it in the *Austin Heights Picayune*, things had gotten a bit chilly between us.

Peaches turned and squinted at me. "It's not really that bad, you know. If you sit in the back of the room, you'll be fine."

"Are you sure?" I asked, stealing another look in the mirror.

"You've got baby wipes, right? Just sponge yourself down with those and you'll be fine. If anybody asks, tell them you were doing an art project with the kids and lost track of time."

"Whipped-cream finger-painting?"

"Sounds good to me," she said.

• • •

We pulled into the last available space of the Holy Oaks Catholic School parking lot at 4:15. There'd been no time to drop Peaches off; she was planning on waiting outside and making some phone calls while I was inside.

I spent another five minutes frantically wiping my hair and body with Huggies Wipes, the end result being that I now smelled like yogurt *and* diapers.

"How do I look?" I asked Peaches.

"Like you just came out of a car wash," she said, squinting at my blotchy T-shirt.

"Thanks."

"Hey. At least you look clean!"

I ran my fingers through my hair one more time and grabbed my purse. "This shouldn't take long," I told her.

"I hope not," she said. "I've got a hot date in two hours."

So did I. Unfortunately, it was with a six-year-old who only ate her food if it was white and I referred to it as "kibble," and a four-year-old whose favorite word was "no." I loved my kids, but there were days when I missed my single life.

Or did I? Despite Blake's assertion that his fascination for men in blue satin was "only a phase" and that we'd "work things out," I was likely looking at being single again. Only this time, with two young kids in tow.

I pushed that unpleasant thought from my head as I hustled through the manicured grounds toward the front entry. I couldn't help noticing that there were not a lot of minivans in the parking lot. And certainly not a lot of minivans with their back bumpers held on with coat hangers. In fact, the lineup of sparkling Porsche Cayennes and Mercedes SUVs made me wonder for a moment if I'd accidentally driven to a luxury-car dealership.

It was 4:25 by the time I reached the front door and slipped into the lobby, which was the temperature of a meat locker. A young woman in a designer dress and sky-high heels glanced down at my outfit, made a poorly concealed moue of distaste, and said, "May I help you?"

"I'm looking for the new-parent orientation," I told her.

"Right there in the library." She waved a French-manicured hand at a set of double doors. I thanked her and scurried over to it, slipping in quietly and heading toward one of the few empty chairs in the back of the large, book-lined room.

My whipped-cream-stained shorts had barely hit the seat when the petite, perky woman at the front of the room said, "And who is *this*?"

It wasn't until the entire room turned around to look that I realized she was talking about me.

I raised a hand and gave a little wave. "Margie Peterson," I said, trying to sound casual. "My daughter's name is Elsie; she's starting first grade."

"Wonderful!" the perky woman exclaimed, the brittle smile never wavering. "We were just discussing the uniform policy. There's a packet of information for you here." She held out a folder with *PETERSON* emblazoned on the front.

"Thanks," I said. "Sorry I'm late." I heaved myself to my feet and traipsed the length of the library, aware of every set of eyes on my whipped-cream-stained backside. It quickly became apparent that I was the only one who favored cream-covered shorts. In fact, I was the only one wearing shorts at all; the women all wore coordinated jogging ensembles or cute belted dresses, and the men had on jeans or khakis and button-down shirts.

I grabbed the folder from the head of the elementary school, who was dressed in a red sheath dress and a scarf with the Holy Oaks logo printed on it in blue. Beside her sat the headmaster, a vague, avuncular look on his round face. He had a fringe of white hair around his bald scalp, blue slacks over which spilled a small gut, and a tie with the Holy

Oaks logo emblazoned on it. Was there a whole Holy Oaks wardrobe available at the school store?

As I turned around, ready to sprint back to my seat, my gaze fell on a familiar face.

It was Mitzi Krumbacher, her eyes boring into me like she was trying to reduce me to cinders telekinetically.

And next to her, with a smirk on his face, was her husband Marty.

. . .

The next hour seemed to go on for days—and not just because I was wearing damp shorts that smelled like yogurt. The woman in charge of the elementary school—Claire Simpson, I remembered her name was—covered the uniform policy, the fundraising campaign for the new buildings, the hot lunch program, the facilities they hoped to add once they'd fundraised for the new buildings, the importance of parent council, and more details on the capital campaign for the new buildings.

I was starting to sense a motif.

She concluded by brandishing a large "Sky High" poster for the capital campaign, looking as if she were showing off Door Number One on *The Price is Right*. "Welcome to Holy Oaks," she told us. "I'm looking forward to seeing your children's shining faces tomorrow morning. And, of course, I hope you'll all pitch in and help Holy Oaks grow deep roots and reach Sky High!"

There was polite applause, and everybody stood up. The young woman from the front office came and opened the double doors to the lobby.

And that's when I heard Peaches, her Texas twang carrying across the empty space like she was talking into a bullhorn.

"I told you, I don't like to use hookers for jobs like this!" she bellowed into the phone. "Their hourly rate is way too high." She was sitting on the bench in the front lobby, her smartphone plugged into an outlet, her orange hair plastered to her head, and her white-streaked orange dress hiked up high on her plump thighs. She looked a little like a Creamsicle.

My eyes flicked to Mitzi. Her jaw had dropped, which, frankly, was more movement than I thought her Botoxed face could handle, and she looked pale beneath her suntan.

"Peaches," I hissed.

My boss looked up, and I noticed her black eye had started to turn purple. "Oh. Hey, Margie."

CHAPTER FOUR

Hookers?" I asked as I tore out of the Holy Oaks parking lot, the information packet wedged between the seat and the console. "You couldn't take that call outside?"

"The timing wasn't great, I'll admit. My phone battery started to die just as we got to the important part, so I had to come inside and plug it in." She shot me a sheepish look. "Sorry about that."

"Maybe you should order the small margarita next time," I suggested.

Peaches gave a little belch. "Probably because I didn't eat. Tequila always goes to my head if I don't eat."

"Well, there's nothing we can do about it now. I'm sure everything will be okay," I said, hoping it was. Elsie hadn't started her first day of school yet, and I'd already managed to scandalize half the parent population.

"Mitzi was there," I said. "So was her husband."

"Yeah, well, it's a pretty ritzy school, and Austin's a small town. Did he mention Banana Twirl?"

"We didn't really get a chance to chat," I said. I'd fled the scene with Peaches in tow, figuring it wasn't the best time to try to explain. I was just hoping it would all blow over. "They both recognized me, though."

Peaches sighed. "We're probably safe. Hubby probably isn't going to want to tell Mitzi we met over a can of Reddi-wip."

"It's going to make it hard to follow him, though," I pointed out as I pulled onto MoPac from Bee Caves Road.

"That's what disguises are for, Margie."

"No dye this time," I said. "It took me months to get that black stuff out of my hair."

"No problem," she said. "I've got a blonde wig that I think will do just fine."

I groaned for about the fifth time that day, wondering—again—why I hadn't gone into makeup sales like my best friend Becky.

• • •

I rolled up in front of my mother-in-law's house about twenty minutes late, which was par for the course. It had taken me longer to get Peaches back to the office than I'd hoped; Austin traffic was growing worse every month.

"Margie, darling," my mother-in-law said when she opened the door. As usual, she was dressed impeccably, in Talbots slacks and a pale floral-silk blouse that had somehow survived four hours with my children. Her smile faded at the sight of my stained T-shirt and shorts; I hadn't had a chance to change yet. "What happened?"

"It's a long story," I said. "Thanks for covering for me; the orientation went fine."

"You didn't attend the orientation wearing *that*, did you?"

I sighed. "I didn't have time to change." If Prue found out about my brief foray into the pool at the Sweet Shop—or, worse, Peaches's phone conversation in the Holy Oaks lobby—she might have a coronary, so

I decided to change the subject. Odds were good she'd hear about it soon enough from her Junior League friends, anyway. "How are the kids?" I asked.

"Oh, doing just fine, I guess."

"You guess?"

"Well," she said, biting her lower lip. "I tried Elsie with a new fork today—I bought one that was silver, with her initials engraved on it— but she still insists on eating directly off the plate."

"Did she at least eat at the table?"

"Umm . . . no."

I grimaced. For the past six months, my formerly cooperative daughter had refused to eat unless we put her plate on the floor. She had her own water bowl now, too, on which she'd painted her Pekingese name in sparkly pink nail polish. I was concerned about my daughter's canine phase, and more than a little worried about her fitting in with the other first graders at Holy Oaks. I'd been in favor of the local public school, but both Blake and Prudence had been adamant about the advantages of private education, and when Prue had offered to pay, I'd given in. "Is she still insisting you call her Fifi?" I asked my mother-in-law.

Prudence nodded. "I'm sure she'll grow out of it," she said. "Blake thought he was a hamster for almost six months. He was always stuffing his cheeks with Cheerios—until he choked and we had to call 911." She smiled brightly. "Maybe she'll choke on something, and that will bring her to her senses!"

I was rescued from having to respond to that comment by Nick, who plowed into my leg. "Mommy!" My leg felt slimy where his cheek had touched it; he'd smeared something that looked like chocolate pudding on my thigh. He wrinkled his nose and stepped back. "You smell funny."

"I spilled something on my shorts," I told him, bending down and kissing his head, savoring his baby-shampoo-little-boy smell. "Did you have a good time with Grandma?"

"Yeah," he said. "It was fun watching her make Elsie eat. She had this funny look on her face the whole time, like she was trying to go number two in the bathroom."

Prue turned a delicate shade of pink. "Speaking of your sister," she said to Nick, "Where is she?"

"She's in the backyard, barking at the fence," Nick said. "I'll go get her."

"Thanks," I told him, and he barreled down the hallway toward the back of the house.

"I'm worried about Elsie," my mother-in-law said as soon as he was out of earshot.

"Me too," I confessed. The curious little girl who used to build fairy houses and give me big, gap-toothed smiles seemed to have disappeared, and I didn't know what to do to bring her back.

"I'm wondering if the cause is some factor I don't know about," she said, looking at me intently with her ice-blue eyes. "How are things between you and Blake?"

"Fine," I lied. "But what would our marriage have to do with Elsie drinking from a water bowl?"

"Stress can cause a lot of issues. I've noticed, the last few times we've gotten together, that there seems to be some distance between you and my son." She held up her hands. "I know, I know. I don't mean to interfere, but sometimes these things are easier to see from the outside," she said with a sympathetic smile that made me want to tell her exactly what was going on in my marriage. "Do you think that perhaps your job is creating a rift?"

My job causing a rift? I opened my mouth, not knowing what to say. Fortunately, she continued, relieving me of the burden of responding.

"Marriage troubles can be hard on children. Are you sure you're giving your husband the support he needs?"

I closed my mouth before I said something I would regret, clenching my jaw as I nodded. "I appreciate your concern," I told her, "but I don't think Elsie's desire to be treated like a dog has anything to do with our marriage." I took a deep breath and plastered on a smile. "Now, I hate to run, but I need to get home and get dinner started. Thank you so much for your help."

"Anytime," she said. "Isn't your mother coming into town this week?"

Oh, God. With all the excitement, I'd almost forgotten. "She's supposed to get here tomorrow," I said. Which meant that I'd have to tidy up and do laundry when I got home. And worse, that I'd be facing a litany of questions about my relationship with Blake.

Although Blake and I had been apart since I discovered his affair with a (now) dead transvestite, my husband hadn't wanted to tell anyone what was going on—or not going on—between us. It wasn't really a shock. On the sin spectrum, he'd been raised to believe being gay fell somewhere between kidnapping nuns and selling your children on the Internet. Not surprisingly, after a childhood of football, soccer, and other appropriately "manly" activities, Blake refused to accept that he was attracted to men and kept telling me he was "working on it." Which I was still struggling to understand. I mean, how do you "work on" not being attracted to men? Was he planning on shocking himself with an electric cattle prod every time he thought of Ricky Martin?

And, of more immediate concern, how were we going to keep our current quasi-marital status quiet while my mother was living with us for a week?

"Margie?" Prue was peering at me with a worried frown.

"Sorry," I said. "I was thinking of all the things I have to do before my mother arrives."

"If you'd like, I could send Graciela over to help out," she offered. Graciela was Prudence's housekeeper. She did an amazing job, as evidenced by the spotless, museum-quality interior of my in-laws' home, but my own house was in such bad shape right now it would be hard for Graciela to find a surface to clean. Plus, I wasn't sure we could afford it.

"Thanks, but I think I'll be able to manage. Besides," I said as Nick ran down the hall with Elsie galloping after him on all fours, "the kids can help. Right?"

Elsie tipped up her heart-shaped face and said, "Woof!"

CHAPTER FIVE

It took a few minutes of cajoling to get Elsie to wear her seatbelt, and as we drove through my in-laws' tony neighborhood, I was glad the van didn't have operable back windows. I had no desire to roll past Prudence's neighbors with my daughter's head hanging out the window, tongue flapping in the breeze.

"I visited your new school today, Elsie," I said brightly. "Are you excited about starting first grade at Holy Oaks?"

There was an ominous growl from the backseat. I had to admit, I kind of agreed with her. If Blake's parents hadn't offered to pay her tuition, we'd probably be at the public school down the street. I wasn't sure she wouldn't be happier there.

"Why does Elsie have to go to a new school?" Nick asked. "Doesn't she like Green Meadows?"

"She liked Green Meadows," I said, stretching the truth a bit—she and the headmistress had not seen eye to eye on a few things, such as wearing a dog collar and biting fellow classmates—"but she's in first grade now, sweetheart. Green Meadows only goes up to kindergarten."

The growling got louder.

"Mommy, Elsie's baring her teeth at me."

"Elsie," I said sternly. "If you bite your brother, there will be no brownie in your food bowl tonight."

"No brownie?" She sounded like I was threatening to take her to the veterinarian for shots. On the plus side, I told myself, at least she was using words. A moment later, she made a sound like a car whose muffler had fallen off.

"I'll tell you what. If you can go without biting or growling the rest of the afternoon, then after supper, you can have a brownie . . . *and* ice cream."

The growling stopped, and when I glanced into the rearview mirror, my daughter had stopped baring her teeth. "Thank you," I said.

"What about me?" Nick said.

"You too," I said. *There goes the Mother of the Year Award,* I thought. Not only had I spent the afternoon at a strip club, I'd had the kids for five minutes and already I was bribing them with food. I would read each of them three stories tonight, I told myself. And make them a healthy dinner with vegetables; all the parenting books said you should keep offering them to your kids, even if they didn't eat them.

"But that's not fair," Elsie protested. "Nick doesn't have to do anything."

"He has to not bite or growl at you, too. That's the way it works. No biting and growling, lots of brownies and ice cream. Okay?"

"Okay," they both agreed, and I turned right, wondering where I was going to come up with brownies.

• • •

Blake's car, a BMW that always looked like it had just been detailed (usually because it had), was already in the driveway when I pulled in and put the van into park. While his car looked great, our house wasn't nearly as spiffy. I tried to ignore the too-long grass neither of us ever got around to cutting, not to mention the large hole in the siding that appeared to have little tooth marks around the edges, but that I kept telling myself was wood rot.

Since I'd started my job at Peachtree Investigations, I'd been too busy working and keeping laundry and dinners on track to worry about the house's exterior, and the neglect had started to show. The front yard was looking more like a pasture than a lawn, with knee-high grass and rose bushes that were encroaching on the sidewalk. In fact, I thought as I walked up to the front door, I should probably get the shears out; it looked like the bushes might swallow a passing pedestrian sometime soon unless I took measures to get them back under control. No notice from the homeowners' association had turned up in my mailbox yet, but I suspected it was coming.

Rufus, our incontinent Siamese cat, yowled at me from behind a dead fern in the front hall as I herded the kids in through the front door. His food bowl must be empty—again.

"Blake?" I called as Nick toddled through the front door, throwing off his shoes. One of them almost landed on Rufus. I tried to catch him and return him to the laundry room, but he streaked away before I could grab him, leaving me wondering where he'd deposit his next offering. Last week it had been my closet. I was hoping this time it wouldn't be my pillow. Elsie turned on the TV to PBS and curled up on the cushion she referred to as her dog bed while Nick started building cars out of Duplo.

"I'm in the kitchen," my husband sang out. I took a deep breath; there was a wonderful smell of garlic and rosemary in the air.

"You're . . . cooking?" I asked as I walked into the kitchen, stunned at the sight of my husband in an apron. He was as handsome as always, with dark hair and chiseled cheekbones, but he no longer made my heart do anything but contract a little bit.

"Why not? It's our anniversary, after all," he said, handing me a glass of chilled white wine.

"Oh. Right." I pasted on a smile, realizing with a rush of embarrassment that I'd forgotten the date. I was surprised Prudence hadn't reminded me. "Thank you," I said, and took a big sip of wine—after the day I'd had, I needed it—and peered into the pan on the stove, where two pork tenderloins were sizzling.

"What happened to your clothes?"

"Oh, yeah," I said. "I spilled something on them; let me go change." I escaped the kitchen to what used to be our bedroom and changed into a fresh pair of shorts and a T-shirt. Not the most romantic getup for an anniversary dinner, but romantic wasn't what I was going for. I took a look at myself in the mirror; I'd gained a couple of pounds over the summer, and I needed a haircut. Maybe when my mother was here I could slip away for a few hours. I tossed my dirty clothes onto the growing pile of laundry, arranged my face into what I hoped was a pleasant expression, and headed back to the kitchen. "What's cooking?" I asked.

"Italian marinated pork tenderloin," Blake said. "I picked it up at Central Market." He gave me one of those breathtaking grins of his, all straight teeth and sparkling eyes. "I figured you could use a break in the kitchen."

"Thanks," I said, taking another sip of wine and hoping this didn't mean he wanted to try to get romantic.

"Becky called, by the way. I told her you'd give her a ring back."

Becky? I felt a surge of hope. Were things looking up? If so, that was the only relationship that had any glint of hope.

I studied Blake as he poked at the pork tenderloin with a fork. Although our first year of marriage had been wonderful, filled with spontaneous trips to the beach, candlelight dinners, and passionate nights, things had cooled quickly and never warmed back up. My funny, dashing husband had morphed into someone who was snippy, intolerant, and very worried about what the neighbors thought of us—particularly of me.

I'd written it off as the stress of having children, whose natural tendency toward entropy was obviously a challenge to someone who kept his socks folded and ordered not only by color, but by shade. About six months ago, though, the underlying reason for Blake's frustration had surfaced when I found a photo of him with a beautiful transvestite in his lap.

Blake had relocated to a hotel room for a week, begging me not to tell anyone what I'd found. He'd then pleaded with me to let him move back in, telling me it was just a phase, and that he had put it all behind him. (I resisted the urge to ask exactly *what* he'd put behind him.)

I'd reluctantly agreed, provided he stayed in his office while we worked things out. After all, I reasoned, I had grown up believing that marriage was a commitment you made for life, and it would be better for the kids to have both parents living in the same house. And I was worried about my sweet daughter, who had been withdrawing from both of us more and more lately, lost in her dog persona. She needed all the support she could get right now; I was on the verge of sending her to the Canine Center for Training and Behavior. Or a psychologist.

At least Blake had been less snippy the last few months, which was nice, and even folded laundry once in a while, a welcome change. Things hadn't exactly been lovey-dovey, though. At first, I found myself questioning every moment of our years together. I had truly believed Blake was in love with me when he slipped that silver wedding band on my finger. How could I have been so wrong? And what else in my life had I misjudged? I thought about today's episode in the pool at the Sweet Shop, then told myself that all private investigators occasionally wound up in compromising situations. Besides, if I hadn't been looking for a job with some excitement, I would have taken Becky up on her offer to sell Mary Kay.

The truth was, Blake and I were more like roommates than husband and wife. We hadn't gone to counseling—Blake hadn't been comfortable with it—so we were kind of in a trapped-in-amber situation. Every once in a while, Blake made an overture toward me. We both seemed relieved when I declined.

I was still angry at the way the marriage and life I had envisioned had been destroyed. If Blake had just been honest all those years ago, I wouldn't be trapped in a bad marriage with two young kids. Could I live this way for the next fifteen years? I wondered.

Blake and I had occupied the same house for months now, barely touching. As much as it pained me to hurt my children, I was beginning to think it was time to start considering divorce. My home life was nightmarish; the tension was terrible, and I was worried it was affecting the kids—Elsie in particular. Would it be better for Elsie and Nick if I soldiered on in a dead marriage, or would it be kinder to them both if we separated? The thought made my stomach churn. How would I support my kids as a single mom? I wasn't making big bucks as a private investigator, to say the least. I had spent many sleepless nights turning things over in my head. Was it worth it to stay? More and more, I was thinking it was time to end things.

Which is why it was so disconcerting when Blake raised his glass and said, "To eight years together, and many, many more."

"Umm . . ." I said, not raising my glass.

His face grew serious. "Margie," he said. "I know the last months have been tough. But I think I've found the solution."

A solution to homosexuality? What, was he going to ask me to dress up in overalls and work boots before hopping into the sack? Or maybe strap on a dildo?

"What do you mean?" I asked.

He thrust a brochure into my hand. "It's called Journey to Manhood," he said, hope burning in his eyes as I stared at the cover of the brochure, which featured a shirtless, muscular young man surrounded by other, equally muscular men standing in an attractive sylvan setting.

I looked up at Blake, confused. "What is it?"

"It's a program that helps men discover their manhood. I'm driving out to Dripping Springs the day after tomorrow. It's a four-day retreat."

"You mean . . . one of those gay-conversion programs?"

He winced. "I'm not gay," he hissed, glancing around to make sure the kids were out of earshot. *Thomas the Tank Engine* played in the background, a strange soundtrack to this conversation. "I just have . . . feelings, sometimes. This will help get rid of them." His handsome face reddened. "Anyway," he said, flourishing a pair of tongs, "your mom will be here, so she'll be able to help with the kids."

I leafed through the brochure, which described the retreat as a "supportive environment for men dedicated to resolving their same-sex attractions," detailing three days of "emotional healing, self-exploration, and catharsis." I turned the page to a description of "father-and-son holding" and "emotional release work," and found myself wondering whether the apparently high level of physical contact had something to do with the whole "catharsis" experience. I just couldn't see how having a bunch of repressed gay men giving each other deep, loving embraces would do anything but exacerbate any difficult "feelings."

"Blake—" I began.

"There's a class for wives, too," my husband rushed in before I could say more. "I'd love to sign you up."

I sighed. I appreciated his desire to keep our marriage intact, but just didn't see how a few days of sharing with other repressed gay husbands could change his attraction to men in dresses any more than a weekend girls' retreat could change my feelings about the scene where Colin Firth emerges from the lake in *Pride and Prejudice*. Now that I thought of it, Blake had always seemed to drift into the TV room when that scene came on. Colin Firth might be the one thing we still had in common.

I looked at my husband of eight years. He sounded so hopeful that I couldn't bear to tell him no. "I guess I could try it," I said, attempting to sound supportive.

"It'll all be different," he said. "I just know it." He put down the tongs and gave me an awkward peck on the cheek.

I finished my wine and poured myself another big glass.

. . .

The pork was a little tough, and Elsie refused to touch it or the salad Blake had made, instead holding out for a bowl full of noodles and a dish of vanilla milk—she was a big adherent of the "all-white" diet. Still, dinner went fairly well, considering the circumstances. I excused myself to get the kids down, picking out the longest books in the house to read to them, while Blake lingered in the kitchen, putting the dishes into the dishwasher.

"Thanks for dinner," I said when I returned to the kitchen a half hour later. "It was delicious."

"My pleasure," he said. "Happy anniversary, Margie." He slid the forks he was carrying into the silverware basket and leaned toward me.

I took an involuntary step back and raised my hand. "Let's talk after your retreat," I said, and he moved away from me, too, something like relief flashing in his eyes. I gave him a strained smile. "Let me know when you're heading out."

"If anyone asks, it's a business trip," he said quickly. "Professional development."

"Of course."

"By the way, how did the parent orientation go?"

"It was . . . interesting," I said, deciding to omit the part about Peaches's hooker conversation and my whipped-cream-covered wardrobe. "The talk was mainly about the building campaign," I said, "although I have the uniform and lunch information, now."

"What's the policy on jewelry?" he asked.

"Just a small cross or stud earrings," I told him. "So the rhinestone dog collar is probably out."

"How are we going to break that to her?"

I sighed. "I don't know," I said. "To be honest, I'm concerned about Elsie, Blake. I think Mrs. Bunn was right—maybe it's time to look into counseling." When the director of Green Meadows Day School had suggested Elsie see a psychologist, I'd thought she was making a mountain out of a molehill, but I had to admit that my daughter's behavior had been growing increasingly . . . eccentric. Despite my efforts to connect with my shy but curious little girl, she had been withdrawing more and more into her dog fantasy world. I was worried about her. Maybe it was a phase, maybe not.

"She doesn't need counseling," Blake said, waving my suggestion away. "It's just a phase. She'll work through it."

Just like Blake is going to work through his feelings for men in shiny dresses, I thought. Right.

"I guess we'll see how it goes," I said, unconvinced. Maybe being surrounded by a bunch of girls in uniforms would help her get past her dog phase. One could always hope.

I yawned; it had been a long day, and there was no point discussing it now. "I'm heading to bed," I said. It was too late to call Becky; I'd have to catch up with her tomorrow. "See you in the morning."

• • •

I was dreaming of giant women wearing tinfoil and pouring chocolate syrup onto miniature Darth Vaders when my cell phone rang. I sat up and squinted at the number: it was Peaches.

I grabbed the phone. "Hello?"

"Margie. I'm so glad you're up."

"I'm not," I said, rubbing my eyes. "Or I wasn't, anyway, until you called."

"I need your help."

I peered at the clock. "It's three in the morning."

"I know," she said, "and I hate to bug you, but I'm in a little bit of a bind here."

"What's wrong?" I asked, wondering if she needed to be picked up from a bar. She'd been hitting the sauce a bit hard the last week or two. In fact, it was probably a good thing her Buick was in the shop.

"You're not going to like it," she said. "But I can explain everything."

"Are you in jail?" I asked.

"Of course not," Peaches said. "Don't be ridiculous. I just need you to help me move a body."

CHAPTER SIX

I sat up straight, clutching the phone. "A *what*?"

"You heard me the first time; don't make me say it again." She rattled off an address. "How soon can you get here?"

"You're kidding me. Right?"

"Nope."

"But—"

"If you leave now, it'll be fifteen minutes—twenty, tops. The faster the better, really, before he gets too stiff to move."

"Too stiff to move?" I rubbed at my eyes. I could not believe I was having this conversation.

"I'll explain when you get here. I promise you'll be home in time to take the kids to school."

"But—"

"Thanks, hon. See you in a few." And she hung up.

I sat in bed for a few minutes, still trying to process the conversation. Move a body? Whose body?

And why?

I got up and threw on a pair of shorts, wondering if Peaches had killed someone. If so, and if I had anything to do with relocating the body, wouldn't that make me an accessory to murder?

But Peaches hadn't said she'd killed anyone. She'd just said there was a body. But if the body had died of natural causes, why would she want to move it?

After tossing on the T-shirt I'd worn that day—if I was going to be moving a dead body, there was no point in putting on something clean—I called Peaches again, but she didn't answer. Cursing under my breath, I entered the address into my phone's GPS, tiptoed out of the bedroom, scrawled a note to Blake, and slipped through the back door and into the sultry Austin night.

The GPS led me past the high-rises of downtown. The streets were virtually deserted except for a few homeless people and late-night strollers—or stumblers, depending on how close they were to Sixth Street. Once I crossed IH-35, the architecture got a whole lot shorter, with a mix of gentrified bungalows interspersed with boarded-up old houses, barbecue and taco restaurants, and neon-colored billboards recommending ways to *Enviar Dinero a México!!!*

The address was in a gentrifying area not too far from the roughest part of town, east of IH-35. There were more people on the street in this area, and I checked the locks on my van as I passed a pack of young men who seemed to be eyeing my back bumper with interest. Were they staring because it was falling off, or because they were considering tearing it off and selling it to a chop shop?

My worries over my bumper receded as I pulled up behind Peaches's Buick. She must have picked it up after I'd dropped her off. The fresh paint job gleamed in the streetlight. Whoever had done the bodywork had done a good job; the baseball-bat-size dents had cleaned up beautifully, and the car was no longer missing large swaths of paint and glass. I checked the address on the GPS and stepped out of the van, locking the door behind me.

To my relief, the apartment was on the first floor. *At least we won't have to drag the body down any stairs,* I told myself as I took a deep breath and tried to imagine what might lie behind the windowless front door.

I knocked lightly, half hoping no one would answer. It was not my lucky day. I'd barely lowered my hand before the door fell open, and I found myself facing a young woman in a leather bustier and a studded dog collar my daughter would have killed for.

"Who the hell are you?" she asked, eyeing me as if I were the one wearing a leather bustier and a dog collar. I kept my eyes on hers; it was too awkward to look anywhere else.

Peaches's voice came from somewhere behind her. "Is that Margie?"

The woman in leather cocked an eyebrow at me, and I nodded.

"Think so," she yelled back, still giving me a speculative look. "I thought you said you were calling some muscle."

"She's stronger than she looks," Peaches said, coming up behind the woman in the bustier. "Beefy."

"Beefy?" I said. Granted, maybe I did have a bit of a chocolate addiction, but . . . *beefy?* "You're not exactly sylphlike yourself, you know."

"Keep your pants on and get in here," she said, waving me inside. I risked a quick glance downward. I did have pants on, but the woman who'd answered the door definitely did not. As I stepped inside and the leather-woman closed the door behind me, I reflected that I'd seen more female flesh in the past twelve hours than I had in the past year.

And I was about to see a dead body, too. Oh, boy.

"So," I said, not sure how to broach the subject of the corpse. "The Buick looks just like new."

"Tony did a good job, didn't he?" Peaches asked, tugging her dress down. "I'm glad I got it back tonight—this isn't the kind of job where you want to call a cab," she said. "Did you bring the van?"

"Of course."

"Good," she said. "Because I don't think we can fit him in my trunk."

"I am not putting a dead person in my minivan," I said, holding up my right hand. "I drive my children to school in that van!"

Peaches sighed. "Let's at least show you what we're looking at."

"What *are* we looking at, anyway?" I asked, wishing I'd never answered my phone.

"We didn't kill him," Peaches said. "Promise. We're just putting him in a place where he won't get Desiree in trouble."

I grimaced, feeling fairly sure that coming here was a really, really, really bad idea, but followed my boss into the living room anyway. The space was tastefully decorated, with light-blue couches and a green-and-blue swirly rug that looked like it could handle all kinds of stains. "Where did you get that rug?" I asked, thinking it would look good in my own living room.

"Isn't it cute?" Desiree said, adjusting the strap of her bustier. "I found it at Pottery Barn last week. End-of-summer sale; it was thirty percent off."

"If you're done with the HGTV highlights, he's in here," Peaches interrupted from down the hallway.

"Oh, yeah. Sorry about that," I said, and headed down the hall to where she stood next to an open door.

If the living room looked like something out of a lifestyle catalog, the bedroom—if you could call it that—was decorated in a style I'd call "Spanish Inquisition." An assortment of whips and flails lined the walls, and a series of complicated-looking leather harnesses hung from a beam in the ceiling. The only thing out of place was the pink-mermaid wading pool in the middle of the floor. And the dead man in it.

"Why is he wearing green tights and a belt?" I asked. He was pale and paunchy, and had fallen so that he was half out of the pool. A big red gunshot wound gaped in the middle of his back, and blood was pooling on the pink vinyl. It wasn't the first dead body I'd seen, and I'd known it was coming, but it was still a shock.

"And goggles," Peaches added.

"He had a thing for water," Desiree said. "He liked me to call him Aquaman."

Peaches sniffed, and I wrinkled my nose. It smelled like the kids' bathroom when we were potty-training Nick.

"Water, eh? You mean, like golden showers?" Peaches asked.

"Yeah." Desiree sounded a little sheepish. "He paid extra for me to pee on him," she said. "I always had to drink two Big Gulps before he came over."

"Please tell me you're joking," I said.

"It's better than the ones who want to pee on me," she told me.

I didn't want to think about that, so I focused on the more important issue. "Who shot him?"

"I don't know," Desiree said. "I cuffed him and left him alone for a few minutes. He usually liked to marinate for a little while."

"What were you doing while he was . . . marinating?" Peaches asked.

"Buying curtains online," she said. "The sale ends tomorrow. Anyway, I was just putting in my order when I heard a gunshot. I came in here, and he . . . he was dead."

"Nobody else noticed the gunshot?" I asked.

She shrugged. "It's a rough neighborhood. You get used to it."

I couldn't imagine getting used to gunshots, but I supposed anything could become normal if it happened often enough. "How did the killer get in?" I asked.

"Patio door," Peaches said, pulling back a red-velvet curtain. The sliding glass door behind it was open. "Forced it."

I looked at Desiree. Despite her Morticia Addams boudoir getup, she looked very young. "I'm sorry," I said. "I just can't tamper with a murder scene this way." I looked at Peaches. "Neither of us should be here."

Tears welled up in the young woman's eyes, and she hugged herself. For a moment, something about her reminded me of Elsie. Maybe it was the dog collar. "I can't have him found here. My parents will disown me, and the police . . . I don't know if they'll believe me. I'll never be able to finish school, and I'll have to do *this* for the rest of my life." She flicked a hand at a rack of whips.

"I'm sorry," I repeated.

"You've got to help me," she said, reaching for my hand. "My parents have no idea this is how I put myself through school; it would kill them if they found out. My mother . . ." She shuddered. "I'd lose her forever."

I sighed. "But it's tampering with evidence. And I can't risk being connected with a murder. My kids have too much disruption in their lives already." I looked at Peaches. "How do you know each other?"

"Desiree helped me on an infidelity case," my boss explained to me, "so I owe her a favor. And all she wants us to do is move him out of the apartment."

"But . . . there's evidence here!" I protested. "If we move him, they might not be able to find out who killed him!"

"We don't even know who he is," Peaches said.

"He called himself John," Desiree said.

Peaches snorted.

"Does he have a wallet with him?" I asked. I looked at the tights; if he did, he hadn't tucked it in there. The tight spandex left far too little to the imagination.

"His clothes are over there," the young woman said, pointing to a chair in the corner. "I've got gloves if you want." She produced a box of latex gloves from a cabinet under the whip display.

"What do you use those for?" I asked.

"Don't ask," Peaches said, fishing out a pair of gloves and pulling them on, then tossing a pair to me. I found my eyes drawn to the dead man in the pool. He had a large, pink bald spot on the back of his head, and his doughy shoulders were dusted with freckles. Did he have a family? I wondered. Was he leaving a wife and kids behind? How would his wife react when she discovered her husband had been found dead in a wading pool, wearing nothing but green tights and a pair of goggles?

"Got it," Peaches said, holding up the man's license. "George Cavendish," she said.

"George Cavendish," I repeated. "Sounds familiar." I'd heard it sometime recently, but couldn't place it.

"Lives on Plato Court," she said, peering at the license. Then she fished a hundred out of the wallet and handed it to Desiree. "I'm guessing he didn't pay you. This should help with the curtains."

"Thanks," she said, waving it away, "but I just want him out of here."

"There's something else here, too," Peaches said, pulling a clipped newspaper article out of his back pocket and unfolding it. "A story about one of those kids who died of that synthetic marijuana stuff."

"Afterburn," Desiree said, and shuddered. "Horrible stuff. One of my friends ended up in the hospital after smoking some of that. She still isn't right."

Peaches shoved the article back into the man's pocket along with the wallet, then folded her arms over her ample cleavage and looked at me. "Are you in?"

I sighed. I didn't want to be involved in this at all. But I was here. And Desiree looked pretty miserable. I guessed it wouldn't hurt if we just pulled him out into the courtyard. "Do we take the pool, too?" I asked.

"I think we kind of have to," Peaches said, "unless we want to get blood and . . . well, you know . . . everywhere."

"We should probably . . . adjust him a little bit," I suggested. He really was in an awkward position. "Before rigor mortis sets in."

"Grab a leg," Peaches said. "I'll take his arm." I put on the latex gloves and wrapped a hand around his spandex-clad ankle. It was still warm. "On three," Peaches said, and at her count, we both pulled up, flipping him over. The bullet hadn't penetrated his chest. If it weren't for his head lolling to the side—and the blood—it would have looked like he was taking a nap in the pool.

"Watch the goggles," Peaches said. They were askew on his head, about to fall onto the carpet.

Desiree reached down to adjust them, and they slid off of his balding head.

I dropped the ankle and stepped back. "Oh my God."

Peaches looked at me. "What?"

"I know him," I said, looking with horror at the round face and fringe of silver hair.

"One of your neighbors?"

"No." I swallowed hard. "He's the headmaster of Holy Oaks Catholic School."

CHAPTER SEVEN

Y ou're shitting me," Peaches said, her mouth gaping as she looked at him.

"He didn't like that, at least," Desiree said, wrinkling her nose. "I have limits."

"What was he doing here?" I asked, trying to reconcile the image of the headmaster in his Holy Oaks tie and blue suit with this goggled man in urine-soaked Aquaman tights.

"I think that's fairly obvious," Peaches said. "But the real question is, how are we going to get him out of here?"

"The patio door, I'm thinking," Desiree said. "Why don't I slip into something more comfortable?"

"Good call," Peaches said. "Those stilettos will trip you up."

As Desiree vanished into another room, I stared at Cavendish. "I can't believe the headmaster got shot in a hooker's apartment."

"He doesn't look like headmaster material," Peaches mused, poking at his leg with her red pump.

"Who would want him dead, though?" I thought about it. "You think Desiree got tired of drinking Big Gulps?"

"Nah. He was just a john. And she wouldn't have offed him in her own apartment, anyway."

"True," I said.

"I'm betting it was one of those private-school moms," Peaches suggested. "Maybe little Madison didn't get into Holy Oaks, and her parents got mad. Remember that cheerleader mom who put out a contract on another cheerleader mom?"

"They don't usually cruise the streets of East Austin carrying howitzers," I pointed out.

"It wasn't a howitzer," Peaches said, running a critical eye over what was left of George Cavendish. "The whole apartment would be gone. Looks more like a small-caliber gun."

I looked down at the headmaster, wondering how he had ended up in this situation. There was obviously more to him than originally met the eye. And I wasn't talking about the limp bratwurst in his tights.

"I guess I could poke around at school," I said.

"Why?" Peaches asked. "It's not our case. The police will look into it."

"I guess, but it bothers me. My daughter's going to Holy Oaks," I said. "I was hoping not to have to have the death discussion before the end of the first week of school."

"I probably wouldn't mention the tights or the urine," Peaches suggested. "But kids are resilient; I'm sure she'll be fine. Besides, it's not like they have a long-term relationship. She hasn't even started school yet."

We stood silently for a few minutes, waiting for Desiree to come back. It was a bit awkward, really, standing by a dead man in a room lined with implements of torture. I tried to think of something to break the silence—something that didn't involve whips and golden showers. "By the way," I said, averting my eyes from what looked like a ball gag, "I got my new business cards."

"Lemme see!"

I took off the gloves and shoved them into my pocket, then fished in my purse for my cards. *Margie Peterson, Assistant Investigator* was emblazoned in black under the words *Peachtree Investigations* and an image of a peach that looked, well, slightly obscene. I hadn't found the right moment to suggest we hire a graphic designer to come up with something a little less . . . graphic.

"Looking good," Peaches said with a smile, handing me back the card. "Now you're a real professional."

I put it on the top of the stack and was about to tuck the cards into my purse when something bit my ankle.

"Ouch!" I jumped, and the cards leaped out of my hands, flying around the room. A ball of black fur streaked toward the open patio door and out into the night.

"Jesus," I said, looking down at my punctured ankle. "It bit me!"

"What is it with you and cats?" Peaches asked.

"I don't know," I said. Blood welled from four little pinprick tooth marks; it looked like I'd been attacked by an elf. I rifled through my purse for a McDonald's napkin and pressed it to the wounds. "Think she keeps the cat around to use on some of her clients?" I thought of my own testy Siamese. "Maybe she'd be interested in taking Rufus, too, now that I think of it."

"Probably not. Hard to get a cat to learn safe words."

I looked up at her. "Safe words?"

"Didn't you read *Fifty Shades of Grey*?"

"It's on my TBR pile," I lied. With two small kids in the house and a husband who wasn't exactly champing at the bit to get me into bed, *Mr. Putter and Tabby Walk the Dog* was about as racy as my reading material got. "What do I do with the cards that fell in the pool?"

"Flush 'em," she said.

With my luck, they'd clog the toilet—and Aquaman clearly wasn't going to be coming to my rescue. I dabbed at the blood a few more times, then folded up the napkin and tucked it into my purse. No need to leave any DNA evidence. "Got any more gloves?"

Peaches handed me a pair, and I pulled them on before trying to round up my cards. One had fallen square in the middle of Cavendish's spandex-clad pelvis, and several others were soaking in the pool. I picked the cards up gingerly, as if they were covered in acid, and tried not to drip on the carpet.

"Where's the bathroom?"

"Across the hall," Peaches told me.

I left the dungeon and headed for the small bathroom, holding the cards in a gloved hand. Like the living room, it was tastefully decorated, with a blue printed shower curtain and a coordinating throw rug. If Desiree decided dominating men in tights wasn't her thing, I thought, she should consider interior design. I flushed the cards, jammed the second pair of gloves into my pocket to get rid of later, took a good look at myself in the mirror, and resolved to buy a new tube of under-eye concealer from my friend Becky Hale the next day. I wouldn't be averse to seeing what other tricks she and Mary Kay had up their pink, flouncy sleeves, either, I decided. I fluffed my reddish hair and opened my green eyes wider, but I still looked like a slightly chunky thirtysome-thing woman with a serious Cheetos habit who hadn't slept in a month.

I gave up on the personal grooming—after all, I was here to move a body, not win a beauty contest—and headed back to the dungeon. Peaches was sitting on the arm of a vinyl chair-like contraption I hadn't noticed before, eyeing the wading pool.

"What is that thing you're sitting on?"

"You don't want to know," she said, and nodded toward the pool. "Think that'll fit through the sliding glass door?"

"I hope so," I said. "If we bend it, it should; it looks pretty flexible. But where are we going to put him?"

"You're sure you don't want him in the van?" Peaches asked.

"No!" I took a few deep cleansing breaths, then wished I hadn't. "I'm worried about this, Peaches. What if we get caught lugging a dead body?"

"It's three in the morning," Peaches said. "Not a lot of people out."

I thought of the gang of young men eyeing my bumper, and decided they weren't likely to call the cops on us. "Let's hope you're right," I said.

Desiree walked back in, wearing khaki shorts and an oversized UT sorority T-shirt. Except for the heavy mascara, she had transformed from Desiree the peeing dominatrix to Desiree the demure coed next door.

"Margie doesn't want to use the van," Peaches said. "Where do you want him?"

Desiree grimaced. "The courtyard would be easiest, but it's probably too close," she said.

"Did anyone see him come in?" Peaches asked.

She shook her head. "I don't think so."

"How about the curb?" Peaches asked.

"What, like you're putting him out for bulk pickup?" I asked.

She arched a tweezed eyebrow at me. "You have any other suggestions?"

"What about his car?" Desiree asked. "Can we fit him in there?"

"It's an idea," Peaches said. "But what do we do with the wading pool?"

"I'm not keeping that thing here," Desiree said, crossing her skinny arms over her Tri-Delt Spring Dance T-shirt.

"Maybe we should just put the pool next to the car," Peaches said. "It's not perfect, but at least it's not at your apartment. How did he get in touch with you, by the way?"

"I have a Gmail account," she said.

"No phone?"

She shook her head.

"They still might track you down," Peaches said. "It's too bad we can't drive him somewhere."

"His keys are in his pants pocket," Desiree said. "We can always stick him in the trunk."

I held up my hands. "Peaches, I want to help," I said, "and I appreciate everything you've done for me. But all I can do is help you carry the body out of the apartment. And I shouldn't even be doing that." I took a deep breath. "I can't be connected to something like this."

"Fair enough," Peaches said. "Just help us get it through the door, and you're on your way." She pulled another pair of gloves out of the box and tossed them to me. "Put these on," she said, "and we'll get it over with."

"Fine," I said, pulling on the gloves and grabbing one side of the pool, trying to breathe through my mouth. Desiree picked a spot next to me, and Peaches took the other side.

"Ready?" Peaches asked, and on three, we folded Cavendish up in his pool like a pink vinyl Aquaman taco and dragged him out into the night.

CHAPTER EIGHT

It was almost five by the time I got home, still convinced I had smudges of bodily fluids all over me. I stripped in the laundry room and tossed my clothes in the washer—hot water, heavy soil setting, sani-rinse—then fumbled my way through the house until I got to the master bathroom, where I spent at least forty minutes scrubbing my skin until it was raw. Then I dressed the cat bite with Neosporin, climbed into bed, and had just managed to fall asleep when the alarm went off and it was time to get up.

I started a pot of coffee in a haze, then went to pry Elsie and Nick out of bed. There was a smell that suggested Rufus had left another nighttime deposit somewhere in the house, but I didn't have time to track it down right then; it would have to wait until after I'd taken the kids to school. I could hear Blake snoring from his cot as I walked by the office and into Elsie's room.

"Wake up, sleepyhead!" I called in my happy-mommy voice, trying to sound like Mary Poppins instead of a body snatcher, and rumpled my daughter's dark, silky hair. She growled.

"It's your first day at your new school," I cooed. "Aren't you excited?"

She pulled up the covers. "Go away."

Well, I told myself, at least she's using words.

"Are you okay?" I asked, sitting down beside her and stroking her back.

After a moment, I felt her relax, and she peeked over the edge of the covers. "I don't want to go to a new school," she said. "I don't know anyone. What if they don't like me?"

"It's scary," I admitted. "But just be yourself."

"Does that mean I can wear my dog collar?"

"Umm . . . I might save that for home, sweetheart."

She pulled the covers back over her head again, and I sighed.

"Why don't you take a few moments to wake up? I'll go make tea and pour you some cereal. I mean, kibble." I kissed her head, feeling butterflies in my stomach; it felt like my own first day of school. Elsie seemed fine now, but I had no way of helping her when she was at school. What if she ate her lunch from the floor? What if she refused to do anything but bark or growl? And what if she bit someone again?

I struggled to quell my anxiety as I stepped into Nick's room next. He was curled up like a pill bug under the covers. "Time to get up, sleepyhead," I said, bending down to kiss his cheek. "Did you sleep okay?"

No answer. I sighed and picked him up, carrying him to the living-room couch, inhaling the scent of his hair—that heart-melting smell of sleepy child. I would bottle it and keep it forever if I could. Elsie was getting too big to carry, but I could still manage Nick, at least for now.

"Cereal or waffles?" I asked as I situated him on the couch and draped the throw blanket over him.

"Waffles," he murmured.

"I'll bet you can't wait to see your friends at Green Meadows," I suggested.

"Too tired," he complained, and curled up like a pill bug again.

I sighed and headed back to the kitchen, narrowly avoiding stepping in a pile of cat poop on the corner of the living-room rug. We had acres of tile and hardwood floor, but somehow, Rufus always managed to hit carpet or upholstery. At least I'd found it before I stepped in it.

I had grabbed a roll of paper towels and a bottle of Nature's Miracle when the doorbell rang. My heart pounded in my chest, and I suddenly felt wide-awake; had the police somehow connected me with the dead body? Had we accidentally left fingerprints or some other evidence on the pool? Were detectives here to question me—or worse, cart me off to jail?

Adrenaline coursed through my body as I reached for the doorknob, clutching the Nature's Miracle to my chest and searching for plausible explanations for my connection to George Cavendish and his Aquaman tights.

I said a quick prayer and opened the door, only to be blasted by a wave of patchouli.

"Marigold!" My mother held out her arms, and I almost fainted into them.

• • •

"You know this cereal is full of GMOs. And food coloring, too, not to mention refined flour and sugar," my mother said as she watched me fill Elsie's bowl with Lucky Charms.

"It's one of the few things she eats, Mom," I told her.

"You just haven't exposed her to enough," she said, opening my cabinets. "Kraft Easy Mac? Did you know I just read an article on this the other day? They can't sell it without a warning label in Europe. It's pure poison."

"I'm sure it's not ideal," I said. "But it's better than nothing."

"I don't know about that," my mother said. "It's a good thing I came. I'll be able to help out with the kids; I know how busy you are."

She picked up a box of Fruit Roll-Ups and tsked. I braced myself for another lecture, but instead she said, "How's the job going? Still enjoying being a private investigator?"

"It's interesting," I said, remembering Peaches's foray into the wading pool at the Sweet Shop. I still wasn't up to thinking about Aquaman. "Gives you a different view of human nature."

"I'll bet," she said. "And how are things with Blake?"

"Fine," I said quickly. "He's been very busy at the office, though. Working late at home, too."

She sighed. "It's all work and no play for him, isn't it? I worry about you two sometimes." As she put back the box of Fruit Roll-Ups, my eyes fell on the Journey to Manhood brochure; it was lying in the middle of the counter, blaring like a billboard.

I made a grab for it, but my sharp-eyed mother spotted it first. "What's that?" she asked.

"Just junk mail," I said. "We get all kinds of brochures." I stuffed it into the recycling bin.

"Hmm," she said as I buried it deep under a stack of expired Box Tops.

"Would you mind going and getting Elsie up?" I asked. "It's her first day of school, and I think she's a little nervous. You know how she is about transitions."

"Does she still think she's a Pekingese?" my mother asked.

"Um . . . yes," I said.

"Have you considered counseling?"

"We're still talking about it," I said. "It's expensive, and we're not sure if it's just a phase."

"Maybe I can align her chakras while I'm here," she said, heading down the hallway to Elsie's room. I braced myself, expecting a flurry of angry barks, but instead heard a delighted squeal. I smiled, relieved to hear my daughter sound happy for the first time in a month.

She and my mother came down the hallway hand in hand, followed closely by Blake, who was tying the belt of a blue bathrobe around his trim waist.

"I found my girl," my mother beamed, looking twenty years younger than her age. "And who's hiding under that blanket?" she asked, looking at where my son was curled up on the couch.

Nick sat up and held out his arms. "Grandma!"

As my mother stood with my children hugging both her legs, Blake walked into the living room. "Good morning, Constance," he said, giving her a polite hug and turning on his client-pleasing charm. "You're here early!"

"I wasn't tired, so I just kept driving," she said, her hands resting on the kids' heads. "I got here a little early, so I stopped at Kerbey Lane for a vegan omelet. I couldn't wait to see my grandkids."

Elsie's rhinestone-studded dog collar glinted in the morning light as she squeezed my mother's leg, her face bright and smiling. It made my heart expand to see her smile again. I only hoped the first day of school would be better than I anticipated. Maybe my mother could convince her to eat with a spoon.

My daughter's eyes lit on me, and the smile switched off. "I don't want to go to school," she announced.

"Let's have breakfast first, before we think about that. Here's your bowl," I said, putting it on the table with a spoon optimistically wedged into it.

Elsie narrowed her eyes at me. Then she marched over to the table, pulled out the spoon, and set the bowl on the floor in the corner of the room. With one defiant glance back at me, she buried her face in the bowl. For a long moment, the only sound was slurping.

"Well, then," my mother said brightly, even though her eyebrows were up around her hairline. The Eggos popped, and I put them on a plate and sprinkled them with dark-chocolate chips before setting them on the table for Nick. "That's breakfast?" she asked.

"They're whole wheat," I said defensively. "And dark chocolate is good for you."

"Mmm," she said. "Have you read about the links between gluten and sugar and—"

"Let's talk about it later," I interrupted. "I've got to get everybody ready for school. Blake, can you get them their vitamins?"

The next half hour was chaos, but by the end of it, both children had their hair and teeth brushed, I'd managed to surreptitiously strip the sheets from the cot in the office, and everyone was fully dressed. (Elsie had agreed to wear the school-prescribed plaid jumper only if I promised her a trip to PetSmart.) My mother had even convinced Elsie to take off her dog collar. "I'll see if I can polish up those rhinestones while you're at school," she told my daughter as Elsie surrendered it reluctantly. I mouthed thanks to her as I herded the kids toward the door, Elsie clutching her fry phone and looking at me like I was Cruella de Vil. "I'll clean up and we can have a cup of tea when you get back," my mother said as the kids filed out the door.

"I've got a parent coffee and another appointment today," I told her. "It's kind of a busy day."

"Why don't we all have dinner at Casa de Luz, then?" she asked. "I've heard great things about it. We can invite Prudence and Phil, too; I'll call her this morning. That way you won't have to cook!"

"They're not really into vegetarian food," I said as we headed out.

"Oh, the food is so good they won't miss the meat!" my mother said cheerily. It wasn't until I'd gotten the kids buckled into their booster seats that I realized I'd forgotten to pack their lunches.

CHAPTER NINE

We got to Holy Oaks only five minutes late, which wasn't bad, considering the fact that I'd had to run back in and assemble two lunches while my mother made a pile of GMO-laden products in the middle of the kitchen table. Still, it was awkward filing past the "Sky High!" fundraising banner into the middle of the opening hymn, which sounded something like a musical limerick about Jesus and flowers and new beginnings.

"Are you sure I can't have my fry phone?" Elsie asked.

"I would hate for you to lose it," I told her, patting my pocket. "I've got it right here. I'll keep it safe."

She gave me a look that suggested she didn't completely believe me. To be honest, I couldn't blame her; my track record wasn't exactly unblemished when it came to the fry phone.

"Promise. And sweetheart, I know you like being called Fifi, but I think that's probably something we should save for home," I reminded her as the door swung shut behind us.

"Don't want to," Elsie said, balking a few steps inside the door and clinging to my leg.

"Your teacher's over there," I said, pointing to a motherly look-ing woman whose brown bouffant hairstyle was straight out of a 1959 *Redbook* magazine. "See? She's saved you a spot." I led my daughter to the empty plastic chair at the end of the first-grade row, conscious of several pairs of eyes on me. I hoped it was only because we were late, and not because the news of Peaches's colorful phone conversation had spread through the population like chicken pox. Still, that was nothing compared to what the headmaster had been up to last night. Had he been identified yet?

I gave Elsie's shoulder a squeeze. She looked up at me as if we were at the owner surrender department of the Austin Animal Center. I handed her her backpack and lunchbox—which I'd filled with leftover Kraft Macaroni & Cheese, mozzarella cheese sticks, and grapes—and forced myself to step away. I knew Elsie wouldn't touch the grapes—they weren't white or artificially colored—but lunch-packing was always a triumph of hope over experience. My daughter whimpered as I stepped away from her, and my heart squeezed. Ms. Rumpole smiled at Elsie, directing her attention to the words of the hymn, which were displayed on a video screen at the front of the room, but while the rest of the room sang about rainbows and sunrises, my daughter bent her head and began sniffing her lunch box. I prayed she wouldn't drop to all fours and start barking.

I drifted to the back of the room, my anxiety growing as I left my dark-haired daughter among the sea of largely blond, singing children. Again the urge rose in me to snatch her up and hustle her back to the minivan, but I tried to ignore it. I couldn't keep her home forever; she had to learn to make friends and figure things out on her own.

When the hymn ended, the woman who had run the parent orientation—the headmistress of the lower school, I remembered now—clicked across the terrazzo floor to the front of the room, beam-ing at us like a spotlight. A big, gold cross gleamed on her bony chest. "Usually Mr. Cavendish would be here to greet you, but he's been, ah, detained this morning," she began. *That's one word for it,* I thought. "Refrigerated" was another. For just a moment, her smile wavered, and she looked as if she wasn't sure how she'd found herself standing in front of a bunch of plaid-encased children singing an off-key tune about Jesus. It was enough to make me wonder if she had some idea, somehow, that the headmaster was on a slab in the morgue this morning, rather than behind the desk in his home office. At least, that's where I was guessing he was; odds were good he was no longer "marinating" in a wading pool on the curb of Chicon Street. Had Peaches and Desiree left his wallet with him? And if they had, had someone stolen it before the police were called? If so, it might take longer to identify him.

"We're excited about all the bright and shining faces here this morning. If this is your very first day, let me be the first to welcome you to a new year at Holy Oaks Catholic School!"

There was polite applause, after which she launched into a description of how wonderful the faculty was and how great the new facilities would be when they were built. "Just think how amazing it will be to have a university-grade science lab and four squash courts!" As I wondered what a squash court was, I glanced around the room, looking for friendly faces. I came up empty.

On the other hand, there were at least a few people I recognized from the newspaper. Leonard Graves, who had made his fortune selling expensive shampoo to women, sat in the back, sprawled over a chair as if he were a lion claiming his territory. It was ironic that he should have made his fortune in hair-care products; his head gleamed like a polished bowling ball. His wife, whom I'd seen in the paper promoting a local reality show about modeling, sat primly beside him, looking like a well-dressed stick insect. Her tan, sinewy arms reminded me of beef jerky, and all of her body fat appeared to have been surgically relocated to her lips.

My eyes moved on, landing on Deborah Golden, who Prudence had informed me was a real-estate agent with a lock on all the million-dollar-plus lake properties in Austin, and made more money in a day than I would in two years. She looked a bit older than the photos I saw plastered on "For Sale" signs in my mother-in-law's neighborhood, but still beautiful, with chiseled cheekbones and dark-brown hair. I wondered which child was hers.

The hair prickled on the back of my neck, and I turned to see Mitzi Krumbacher staring daggers at me, her enormous green earrings swinging menacingly under her impeccably highlighted and styled hair. Peaches had told me she'd gotten an earful yesterday afternoon; apparently Mitzi had terminated our agreement and was demanding a refund. I gave our former client a weak smile and turned away, tugging at my T-shirt hem. I'd had to buy an assortment of plaid and khaki uniform clothes for Elsie, but no one had told me the adults had a dress code, too.

As I stood pretending to listen to the woman with the gold cross drone on, Mitzi edged over to me, smelling like a funeral-home floral arrangement.

"Hello," I said with a polite smile.

"What are you doing here?" she hissed through a clenched jaw. "I fired you."

"I'm here as a parent," I told her. "It's my daughter's first day of school."

"She won't last," Mitzi said, venom in her voice. "I promise you. She's going to be completely out of her league."

"Thanks for the encouragement," I said, my stomach contracting as she stalked off. I hated to admit it, but I was afraid Mitzi might be right. Thank goodness my mother had talked Elsie into leaving the dog collar at home—and I'd managed to confiscate the fry phone. I patted the plastic toy in my pocket, reassuring myself that it was still there.

As the service droned on, I edged toward the door. I maneuvered myself to place a potted palm between me and Mitzi, and I leaned against the back wall as the chaplain led everyone in the Lord's Prayer.

We had just reached the "forgive us our trespasses" part when the glass doors opened.

A man and a woman walked in, both wearing blazers. For a moment I wondered if they were parents, and my stomach flipped over as I recognized the man.

It was Detective Bunsen, and he was staring right at me.

CHAPTER TEN

The last time Bunsen and I had met, he had seemed disappointed that he wasn't putting me behind bars for murder. Something told me his opinion of me hadn't changed much since then. I looked back at the terrazzo floor, mumbling through the end of the Lord's Prayer and attempting to look pious and completely unaware that the headmaster had recently died in a wading pool, looking like an incontinent Aquaman wannabe.

But Bunsen sidled up to me after the "Amen," murmuring, "Ms. Peterson. I'm so glad to see you here."

I did my best impression of startled, and swore to myself never to help anyone move a body again. "Detective . . . Bunsen, right?" I blinked innocently. "I didn't know you had a child here. What grade?"

"I don't have a child here," he said as the music teacher—a woman with a pouf of gray hair and a thin, disapproving mouth—led everyone in a rousing rendition of "Kumbaya." "But I'm pleased to find you here."

"Why?"

"We found a dead man in East Austin this morning."

I swallowed hard. "I'm sorry to hear that. But what does that have to do with me?"

"We'd like to talk to you about your friend Becky Hale," he said.

My mouth turned dry. "Why?"

"There seems to be a connection between your friend and the dead man."

I swallowed again. "She wrote an article about him in the paper a few months ago, but other than that . . ." Too late, I realized I wasn't supposed to know who the dead man was. I'd never functioned well on short sleep.

"Interesting," Detective Bunsen said. "Did you and your friend plan this together?"

"Plan what?" I asked, as if I hadn't just said the stupidest thing possible.

"I think we need to chat," he said with a grin that sent a shiver down my spine.

• • •

"The headmaster of Holy Oaks is dead," I told Becky on the phone as I backed out of my parking space a few minutes later, narrowly missing a Porsche Cayenne. I wished I was done with Bunsen, but I wasn't; when I glanced in the rearview mirror, he was right behind me. We were going to Starbucks so he could interrogate me, unfortunately.

"Wow. Really?" my friend asked.

"It happened last night."

"Usually I'd say 'poor man,' but in this case, I think it serves the bastard right," Becky said. "Although I do feel bad for his wife. He has a wife, right?"

"He does," I confirmed.

"I still don't know why you decided to send Elsie to that school."

I maneuvered out of the parking lot, stifling a sigh. "You've mentioned that." *Practically hourly, for months,* I thought but didn't add.

"It's all about the money for him," Becky said. "One of the teachers told me that's why the board hired the guy. What happened to him? Heart attack? Death by shame?"

"Actually, he didn't die of natural causes."

"What, did some angry parent finally off him?" She snorted into the phone, and I remembered why I missed her so much. "I do feel bad for him, believe it or not, but I'm not surprised. After all, a guy who would give Zoe's spot to that hair-care guy, just because he moved in from California and offered to pay for a building, isn't exactly high on morals!"

"Becky," I said. "I just talked with Detective Bunsen. I don't know why, but the police think you might have been involved in his death."

There was silence on the phone for a moment. "Involved?" she said, sounding confused. "What do you mean, involved?"

"Well, you wrote that article in the *Picayune,* for starters, so they know you weren't fond of him."

"I wrote a letter to the editor on Holy Oaks' admissions policies and said I think the headmaster was selling spots in the school to the highest bidder. That's not quite the same as knifing him in the back," she said. "I haven't seen the man in five months. How did he die, anyway?"

"I don't know," I lied, again banishing the image of George Cavendish's bullet-perforated, urine-soaked body. "Where were you last night?"

"I was at home with the kids," she said. "It was a school night."

"Was Rick there?" I was hoping her husband could give her an alibi.

"No, he's in Houston on business. Why?"

Damn. "Was anyone else there?"

"Of course not. Why would they be?"

I let out a long, slow breath. "Well, the police are going to be in touch with you today. I don't know why, but they think you may be linked with the crime. Be careful."

"They won't find any physical evidence, anyway. Like I said, it's been months since I talked with him."

"You do have that going for you," I told her as I pulled into the Starbucks parking lot a few spots down from Bunsen. "I have to go talk with Detective Bunsen now. I'll call you later."

"Isn't that the guy from the last case—the Selena Sass thing? Why do you have to talk with him?"

Because I'm an idiot who can't keep her mouth shut, I wanted to tell her, but didn't. "I'll . . . it's complicated. I'll catch you later, okay?"

I hung up before she could answer and stepped out of the car to join Bunsen; his partner had remained behind at Holy Oaks, presumably to break the news and talk to the staff.

Bunsen and I stood awkwardly in line. We'd first met over a dead transvestite in the Princesses' room at an Austin bar, and our relationship had never been chummy. Now, as we stood in line at Starbucks, I considered offering to pay for his coffee, but decided that would seem too much like a bribe. Besides, he wasn't a cheap date; he ordered a six-dollar venti quadruple-shot mocha latte. I ordered a small drip, and we retired to a table toward the back of the shop.

"Do you have children?" I asked, to break the silence.

"No," he said curtly as I took a sip of my budget coffee, which I'd doctored with several sugar packets and a good dollop of cream while he waited for his latte. "But you've got a kid at Holy Oaks now. Business must be pretty good."

"It's not bad," I said, which was stretching the truth more than a bit. So what if we only had one case this week? Summer was slow in the PI business. At least, that was my theory. Besides, Peaches had mentioned last night that she had a new job for me.

"Where's your new office? Or did you rebuild the old one after it blew up?"

"It's, um, on the east side of town," I said. I wasn't about to tell him we were sharing it with a Brazilian waxing salon. "How about you?" I asked politely. "Keeping busy?"

"Oh, it's going much better now that I know someone who has information on the case I'm working," he said with a slow smile and pulled an iPad out of his briefcase.

I blinked. "Who?"

He stared at me, stylus poised over the iPad screen. "How did you know I was talking about George Cavendish this morning?"

"I . . . heard a rumor." I took a swig of coffee, burning my mouth.

"Really," he said in a dry sort of tone that didn't inspire confidence in me. "Who told you?"

"I don't remember," I said. "I hadn't had coffee yet." There was a long silence. "Also, I'm a little psychic sometimes."

"Psychic."

"I get it from my mother."

He sighed and jotted a note on his iPad. "Tell me about your friend Becky," he said. "She wasn't very happy with Mr. Cavendish, was she?"

"She didn't like anything about Holy Oaks," I told him. "They booted her daughter to let in the kid of a hair-care magnate who offered to pay for a new building."

"And yet you sent your daughter to the school. That can't have been great for your friendship."

"What happened to Cavendish, anyway?" I asked, feigning what I hoped looked like natural curiosity.

"Why don't you tell me?" he smirked. "You can use your psychic powers."

I took another sip of my coffee and attempted to look innocent. "I'm assuming it must be foul play, since you're involved," I said. "But why are you so interested in Becky? People write letters to the editor all the time, and they don't get questioned by the police."

"We found something at the crime scene," Bunsen said. He reached down and pulled a piece of paper out of his briefcase, then slid it across the table to me.

My heart almost stopped.

It was a copy of Becky's Mary Kay Consultant business card.

CHAPTER ELEVEN

What was he doing with Becky's card?" I asked out loud, even though I knew. When I'd pulled out my new business cards to show Peaches, I must have dropped Becky's card—I always carried a few to help her network. How had I missed it?

"I was wondering the same thing," Bunsen said.

"She gives those cards out all the time," I improvised. "He probably had tons of cards with him."

"No," Bunsen said mildly. "Only this one."

"Maybe he was going to call and offer her a spot at the school," I suggested. "You can't possibly think she did him in and left her card behind. She's not stupid."

"When we found him, he didn't look like he was about to make a phone call," Bunsen said. "I have to ask you again. How did you know the headmaster was dead?"

"Someone said something," I said. "Normally, I wouldn't think anything of it, but he wasn't there that morning, and the elementary-school head seemed uncomfortable. And when you showed up . . ."

"You somehow divined that the headmaster had died in suspicious circumstances," he said. "Right. Did your friend call you last night?"

I hesitated, thinking of Peaches, then realized (duh) that he was talking about Becky. "No," I said. And then remembered that I was wrong. Becky had called me. "Actually, she did," I said. "My husband took the message, but I didn't get a chance to call her back."

"What time was that?" he asked.

"Oh, around six, I think."

He made another note on his iPad. "We'll check the phone records, you know."

Would they? And if so, what would they think of Peaches's call to me at three in the morning? I'd burn that bridge when I got to it, I decided.

Bunsen took a long swig of his giant latte and looked at me as if he wanted to shake the truth out of me. I gave him a bland smile. "I suppose that's it for now," he said grudgingly. "But this isn't over yet. I'm going to find out how you knew he was dead. And I'm going to find out what your friend Becky Hale had to do with it."

My coffee curdled in my stomach as he flipped me a business card. "I'm sure we'll be in touch."

• • •

Things were hopping at the Pretty Kitten when I pulled up to the strip mall a half hour later; three young women and a man with tweezed eyebrows were reading fashion magazines in the waiting room when I pushed through the front door. Unfortunately, things at Peachtree Investigations were a little less frenetic. The only lead we'd gotten that week involved a missing pet, and we'd lost the Krumbacher case. If things didn't turn around soon, Peaches and I might have to consider moonlighting as assistant crotch waxers.

"We've got a problem," I told Peaches when I walked into the office.

"If it's about last night, I'm sorry," she said. "I put my back out doing one of those P90X exercise videos the other day, or I would have handled it myself."

"The cops were at Holy Oaks this morning," I told her in a low voice.

Peaches leaned forward, taxing her zebra-print spandex. "They figured out who he was, then."

"They found my friend's business card on the body," I told her. "I must have dropped it."

A furrow appeared between her eyebrows. "Did she know him?"

"She wrote a scathing letter to the editor about him to the *Picayune* a few months back, and they published it. And I said something about Cavendish being dead, even though there was no way for me to know it was him."

Her eyes got round. "Smooth."

"Exactly."

She fished her e-cig from under a bra strap and took a long drag, blowing out a vapor cloud. Menthol. "Did they interview you?"

"Of course," I said, collapsing on the plastic visitors' chair.

"How did it go?"

I shrugged. "They're going to talk to Becky. I am such an idiot." I slumped in the chair. We'd rescued it from the original office; part of the seat was melted and a little bit blackened. "It's my fault."

"It's going to take a lot more than a business card for the police to charge her with murder," Peaches said. "Does she have an alibi?"

"No. Her husband was out of town last night."

Peaches grimaced. "That's too bad."

"And she called me last night," I said. "My husband answered, and I didn't call her back, but there's no way to prove she didn't talk to me. They think that's how I knew Cavendish was dead."

"But he wasn't dead yet. So that's something." Peaches toyed with her e-cig. "How are things going with your hubby, anyway?"

"He's starting this program called Journey to Manhood," I told her. "He made me swear not to tell anyone. It's supposed to cure gay men."

She barked out a laugh. "What do they do, smack them in the doodad every time they start making eyes at each other?"

"Umm . . . I think there's a lot of group work," I said. "And hugging."

"That should help," she said, her voice dripping with sarcasm. "Hugging lots of men is going to miraculously turn him straight?"

"That's the theory," I said. "There's supposed to be a support group for wives, too."

She stared at me. "A *support* group? What do they do? Suggest ways to look more butch?"

"Hey. At least he's trying."

"How long have you been in separate bedrooms?" she asked.

I shrugged. "About six months."

"You're not getting any younger, sugarplum. You might want to start thinking about the big D."

"I'll give him another month," I said. My stomach wrenched just thinking of it. If I weren't a mother, separation from Blake would be a no-brainer. But I had children; any decision I made would affect them, too. I wanted so much to give them the intact home I'd never had. It killed me that it might not be possible.

Peaches gave me an appraising look. "Nobody knows about him yet?"

"No one but me," I told her. "His parents would probably disown him. And my mother's in town, so he'll have to move back into the bedroom. We're all going to dinner tonight, at a vegan macrobiotic place." I made a mental note to stop by the store for potato chips and earplugs. And maybe a flask.

"Relationships," Peaches said, taking another moody drag. "Not worth the trouble, if you ask me."

"Uh-oh," I said. "Is everything okay with Jess?"

"We broke up," she said, examining her e-cig. "I never thought I'd say this, but I think I like menthol."

"What do you mean, you broke up?" Peaches and Jess had met about six months ago, after he saved me from a particularly unpleasant premature death. I had warm feelings for him, obviously, but sparks had flown between him and Peaches, and they'd been two-stepping every Saturday night since. Last I heard, they were talking about moving in together. "When did this happen?" I asked.

She waved a plump hand. "A couple of weeks ago."

"And you're just now telling me? What happened?"

She shrugged. "We got into an argument, and it just kind of went downhill from there."

"An argument? About what?"

"It doesn't really matter," she said.

"Come on," I said. "I've told you my husband was sleeping with a transvestite named Selena Sass. And you can't tell me what you and Jess argued about?"

"Fine," she said, taking another drag off her e-cig and exhaling slowly before answering. "We argued over ice cream."

I blinked. "Come again?"

"Ice cream," she repeated.

"Ice cream."

She moved to stub out her e-cig, then remembered it was an e-cig and reached into her stretchy top for its plastic case instead. "He said Amy's Mexican Vanilla was better than Blue Bell Homemade Vanilla. I'd had a bad day at work; that was the day the Fischer case fell apart." I remembered it. She'd rear-ended the guy she was tailing, causing about three thousand dollars of damage and blowing her cover. It hadn't been a good couple of months for the office. "He wouldn't let it go," Peaches continued, "so I hung up on him."

"You called him back, though, right?"

"Nope." She opened the plastic case, inserted the e-cig, and snapped it shut. "We haven't talked in three weeks."

"Peaches," I said. "While I completely agree with you on the merits of Blue Bell Homemade Vanilla, that is not a reason to end a relationship with a good man."

"Are you sure?" she said. "I thought we had a lot in common, but then he starts talking smack about Homemade Vanilla. Next thing you know, I'll find out he drinks Chardonnay and eats foie gras." She grimaced. "What else is he hiding?" She jammed the case into her purse. "And if he cared so damned much, why didn't he call me back?"

I was beginning to understand the heavier-than-usual margarita consumption these last few weeks. "Uh . . . you hung up on *him*, not the other way around."

"What? Is chivalry dead?" She stood up. "Anyway, I've got bigger fish to fry now. Like getting your friend out of trouble." She reached for a fresh file folder, scrawled *HOLY OAKS* on the top of it, and opened it up. "Tell me everything you know about our friend Aquaman," she said. "I'll run a background check, and you can see if you can get into his office while you're volunteering at school, dig up some dirt." She sucked on the tip of her pen. "It might not be a bad idea to check out his house, too. Is he married?"

"I think so," I said.

"Maybe you can get chummy with his wife," she suggested. "It's got to be a shock, finding out your husband died wearing goggles and Aquaman tights. Secret life and all." She paused. "Come to think of it, you guys have a lot in common; you should hit it off just fine."

"Gosh. Thanks," I said.

"Don't mention it," she replied, and pulled up the background-check site on her computer.

Peaches might occasionally run into trouble doing surveillance, but she was an expert on finding out about people. Within thirty minutes, I knew more about George Cavendish than I'd imagined possible. His home (a tony address in Rob Roy), his car (red BMW), his marital status (thirty years), his past job history (headmaster of expensive private schools in Massachusetts and Connecticut), and his children (none).

"Nothing about his Aquaman fixation," I remarked.

"Must have been something that happened when he was growing up," she said. "Cape Cod. Lots of water there."

"It doesn't explain the peeing, though," I said.

"Maybe some of his summer-camp buddies peed on him as a hazing ritual," she speculated, "and he decided he kind of liked it. You never know. Human sexuality is a mysterious thing."

"No kidding," I said, thinking of my husband and his penchant for men in tights.

Peaches looked up from her computer and squinted at me. "How much is your husband paying for this Journey to Manhood thing, anyway?" Evidently her mind had run along the same track as mine.

"I never asked," I said.

"And you're all alone for the next few days. Good thing your mother's in town to help out with the kids," she said.

"That's true," I said, "until she tries to feed them on a diet of seaweed shakes."

"Whoever said suburban life was easy never met you," Peaches said, rolling her eyes. "You've got the weirdest family I've ever heard of—and that's saying something."

It was hard to disagree with her.

She pursed her lips and looked at me. "I keep thinking about this Cavendish situation," she said. "We might want to talk to Desiree again. See if she remembers anything."

"Do you know how to get in touch with her?"

"We'll pay her a visit tomorrow," she said. "In the meantime, I'll see what I can find out. No police records that I can see, but I might call a buddy of mine down at the station and see if she's heard anything."

"Do you think the cops will really blame Cavendish's death on Becky?"

"I hope not," Peaches said. "If it comes down to keeping her out of jail, I'll fess up and tell them Desiree asked us to help, and I roped you into it. It will at least help explain how you knew—and why your friend's card was in that pink pool."

"You'd do that for me?"

"I would if I had to," she said. "But I'd rather see if we can figure things out ourselves first. I haven't waitressed in a long time, and if I lose my license I'm going to be slinging drinks down at Coyote Ugly. Just between you and me, I'm getting a little old for that." She took a sip of her Diet Coke. "Also, jail is off the table. I don't look good in orange."

"You wore orange yesterday," I pointed out.

"Yeah. But that was tangerine orange, not jumpsuit orange. Plus, those overall things make my butt look big."

"How do you know?"

"I just know," she said. A long, low moan sounded from next door, accompanied by a ripping sound that made both of us wince. "Desiree hasn't called me, and I'm of the opinion that no news is good news." Peaches reached into a drawer and pulled out a slim file folder. "I've got something to take your mind off things, anyway."

"The missing pet?"

"Little bitty pig, according to the owner. She's pregnant with piglets." While I digested that bit of information, Peaches slid the folder across the desk to me. "Lady thinks her ex-husband stole her and is planning to sell the piglets for big money. She'd go retrieve the pig herself, but she's got a restraining order."

"A restraining order?"

"Yeah. She's not supposed to get within fifty feet of him or his residence."

"Why?"

She shrugged. "I didn't ask."

I flipped open the file. It included the ex-husband's address, along with the pig's identifying features. Evidently the missing porker was classified as "teacup-size" (whatever that meant), had a cocoa-colored coat with a white spot on its snout, and sported a tattoo in the left ear. Something to check in case I thought I might have picked up the wrong cocoa-colored teacup pig. How many pigs could there possibly be in Austin? Then again, the address *was* near South Lamar. I looked up at Peaches. "It answers to *Bubba Sue*?"

"I didn't name her. I just took the case."

I sighed. "I've got to go to a Holy Oaks first-grade-parent coffee," I told her, closing up the file and tucking it into the old diaper bag that I used as my briefcase, "but I'll check it out this afternoon."

"The coffee would be a good place to ask questions about Cavendish," Peaches reminded me. "You might pick up something useful."

As I left, another shriek sounded from behind me. We really did need to find new office space.

CHAPTER TWELVE

The parent coffee was in Tarrytown, a posh neighborhood just west of central Austin, in a sprawling villa that looked like it had been plucked out of Tuscany and plunked *Wizard-of-Oz*-style on top of the three modest homes that must once have occupied the space. I'd left Becky two messages on the way to the coffee, hoping the police hadn't already hauled her off to jail. Would she ever speak to me again? And if so, would we have to chat with a Plexiglas partition between us? I thought of Becky's children, Zoe and Josh. I couldn't bear it if my stupidity resulted in them growing up while their mom made license plates in a state penitentiary.

I left Becky another message and parked on the side of the narrow, tree-lined street, wedging the van in between a Mercedes station wagon and a Porsche Cayenne. I was late—it was almost eleven—but it looked like people were still there. The last thing I wanted to do was make polite conversation with strangers over coffee, but I reminded myself that at least one of those strangers might know something about Cavendish's Aquaman fixation—or, better yet, why someone had shot him. I squared my shoulders and marched up the long stone walkway to the massive arched front door, half expecting to see striped-stockinged legs sticking out from beneath the shrubbery.

The door chime rang like church bells, and a few moments later, the real-estate agent I'd seen that morning answered the door. She wore her long brown hair pulled back, and her cheekbones were so sharp I could have used them to slice apples. I smiled, and she grimaced as if she were expecting me to pitch her a line of cleaning products.

"Can I help you?" Her greeting was frosty.

"I'm here for the parent coffee."

She flicked her brown eyes up and down me as if she wasn't sure she believed me, but stepped back and opened the door anyway. "Of course. Please come in."

"Thanks!" I said, following her through the massive door into the cool, tiled entry. An arrangement of moss balls was artfully displayed on an antique table to my left; above it was a still-life oil painting that included two dead rabbits and a bowl of fruit. "I'm Deborah Golden," the woman said, jolting me from staring at the two lifeless, furry little bodies.

I turned back to the hostess. "I'm Margie Peterson. You have a very nice house."

"Thank you," Deborah said, leading me toward the distant sound of voices. She wore denim capri pants and a filmy white blouse that looked hand-embroidered. She was definitely petite; even in her cork wedges, she was still two inches shorter than me in my sandals. "My husband and I love traveling in Italy, so we decided to create our own piece of Tuscany here in Austin."

"How nice," I said, not knowing what else to say.

"We're in the kitchen, having coffee and pastries. Who do you have starting at Holy Oaks?"

"My daughter, Elsie," I told her as we walked through the cavernous living room, which was well-stocked with couches that must have been built with giants in mind and a coffee table I was guessing might be a cross section of a redwood trunk. Deborah looked like she risked being swallowed by her own furniture if she sat down. On the other hand, I mused, looking at her bony frame, she probably never sat down. "Is this your first year at Holy Oaks?"

She laughed. "Oh, no. We've been at Holy Oaks since the school started, practically." As she spoke, we passed the dining room—the table seated twenty, with high-backed chairs that looked like they were designed for a conclave of cardinals—and into a kitchen the size of my backyard.

The room was filled with slender, tanned women with bright white teeth, along with one man who stood in the corner looking as if he'd rather be somewhere else. The only person who appeared naturally bronze was a young Hispanic-looking woman in an apron, who was scurrying around, retrieving used plates and disappearing with them into another room. I found myself thinking that Holy Oaks might want to work on their diversity mission a bit.

A rack of copper pots that, from their gleaming exteriors, had likely never seen the top of the stove hung over a gigantic granite-topped island. Beneath the pots, there were several trays of muffins and croissants and a crystal bowl filled with fruit salad. A silver coffee urn squatted on one of the other counters, each of which was the length of a runway. I was guessing there was no Easy Mac behind the custom-made mahogany cabinet doors. "Hi, everybody," Deborah announced. "This is Margie Peterson; she's new to Holy Oaks this year."

"Hi!" everybody responded, almost in chorus. I noticed a few eyebrows rising, and was sure the episode with Peaches and her cell phone would shortly be a topic of conversation. In fact, it probably had been already.

"Help yourself," Deborah said, gesturing toward the seemingly untouched array of food. "Plates are over here."

"Thank you," I said, reaching for a dainty plate rimmed with poppies. I selected a chocolate-chip muffin and a croissant, added a few chunks of watermelon, and turned to make my way across the vast expanse of hardwood floor to the coffee urn, where I filled a hand-painted cup and loitered by the counter.

I'd barely sipped my coffee before an industrious-looking woman with a strawberry-blonde bob and a pair of faded mom jeans accosted me. "Hello," she said. "I'm Kathleen Gardner. My daughter's Catriona, and she's in Ms. Rumpole's class. Who is your child?"

"Elsie," I said. "She's in the same class."

"My daughter's name is Catriona," Kathleen said a second time, taking a sip of her black coffee and nibbling on a piece of sliced pineapple. "She's really excited about starting Holy Oaks; we've been reading a book a day all summer so that she's fully prepared academically. Of course, it's been hard to fit it in around her dancing schedule, particularly now that we're starting with math tutoring."

"I can imagine," I said, glancing over her shoulder for somebody else to talk to. Preferably somebody who didn't make me feel like I was standing on the target end of a firing range. I might have imagined it, but I thought the lone man in the corner gave me a pitying look.

"Anyway," she continued, "I'm the room mother for Ms. Rumpole's class, and I'll be organizing the volunteering. It's so important to be involved in our children's lives, don't you think? It really shows them that they're a priority." She adjusted the Peter Pan collar of her pink blouse. "What activities is your child involved in?"

"Umm . . . she's thinking about taking a musical instrument." Elsie had, after all, had a brief obsession with the kazoo she'd gotten at a Blazer Tag birthday party.

Kathleen beamed at me, exposing a line of slightly yellowed teeth. "Studying a musical instrument is so important for academic development. Particularly in math, although of course we've been working through the second-grade workbook, just to stay fresh. Catriona has been playing violin—Suzuki Method—since she was two. She is so talented—her teacher suggested we take her to New York to study with one of the concertmasters there. Of course, we had to decide where to put her energy, so we're having to cut back on violin to four times a week now that she's in the advanced tap classes."

"Wow," I said without thinking. "You certainly stay busy."

"Of course," she said. "It's all part of creating a well-rounded child." She took another sip of coffee. "I do hope your daughter—Elsie, is it?—will sign up for Girl Scouts. I promised Catriona I would be the troop leader, and I have lots of enriching activities planned."

"How will you have time?"

"Oh, we always make time for our priorities," she said.

"Speaking of which," I said, searching for a polite exit strategy, "I didn't have time for breakfast, and that watermelon was delicious. If you'll excuse me, I think I'm going to grab a bit more."

"So, can I count you in for the Scouts?" she asked.

"I'll ask Elsie," I told her as I attempted to wrench myself out of her orbit. "Thanks for telling me about it!"

She had glommed on to someone else by the time I refilled my plate, and I edged toward two women with Jennifer Aniston hair and wedges. One of them, a buxom woman with a plunging neckline and a dress that reminded me of Peaches's orange Lycra number—only several sizes smaller, and lime green—was regaling a wide-eyed woman in capri pants about her divorce. "And would you believe the judge ruled in his favor? At least I got full custody of the twins."

"That's a relief," her rather less-endowed companion said feebly, taking a half step backward.

"But I have to get creative to give them the education they need. I'm appealing the judgment, of course, but in the meantime . . ."

I started to back away, but the woman in the tight dress had spotted me. "I remember you," she said.

"Have we met?"

"Not officially," she said. "I just remember you and your . . . friend," she said, her mouth quirking up in a little bit of a smile. "From the new-parent meeting yesterday."

"Um . . . she's a coworker, actually."

The thin woman in capri pants peered at me. "What line of work are you in?"

"I'm a private investigator."

"How interesting," the thin woman replied, her smile brittle. "Was your . . . coworker working on a case, then?"

"Must have been," I said. "Anyway, is this your first year at Holy Oaks?" I asked, anxious to change the subject.

"Yes," the buxom redhead answered. "Both of my children are starting today; I was so lucky to get them both in. Private schools are so competitive these days, aren't they?"

"I know. And they work so hard to build diversity," the thin woman said, her eyes flicking to me. "What does your husband do, Margie?"

"He's an attorney," I said.

"Oh?" The suspicious look faded a fraction. "What firm is he with?"

"Jones McEwan."

"My husband's an attorney, too," the thin woman said, looking more at ease. "I'm Melissa Truluck."

"Margie Peterson," I said.

"And I'm Cherry Nichols," said the buxom redhead. "So great that we all get to know each other. We're so lucky to be at Holy Oaks, don't you think?"

I sipped my coffee and took a shot at steering the conversation toward the topic I was interested in. "I'm kind of surprised the headmaster wasn't there this morning."

"Me too," the redhead said. "He was probably out fundraising for the new building campaign. I hear that's the main thing the board wants from him."

Before she could say more, someone behind me said, "New to the school?"

I turned; it was the man I'd spotted earlier—and the only other person wearing shorts. His were khaki, and he wore a polo shirt with a small constellation of bleach stains around the hem. I was encouraged.

"Yes," I said, smiling. "How about you?"

"I have a new first grader, but I've got a third-grade daughter, too." He stuck out a hand. "Kevin Archer," he said.

"Margie Peterson," I said, shaking his hand. "Do you like it at Holy Oaks?"

He gave me a strained smile. "It's an interesting place."

CHAPTER THIRTEEN

I looked at Kevin with renewed curiosity. "Interesting?"

"Let's just say that, although it's a Christian school, the meek—not to mention the less well-heeled—haven't exactly inherited the earth at Holy Oaks, if you know what I mean."

Kevin and I exchanged notes for a few minutes; we were both public-school kids, and both had married professionals—me an attorney, him a dermatologist. But whereas I spent my child-free time running around in a van spying on adulterers, he spent his playing shuffleboard on the international circuit. I wasn't sure which activity was more unusual.

"But I want to hear more about Holy Oaks," I said after a few minutes. "What do you think of the school overall?"

He glanced over his shoulder, then said in a low voice, "It's been a tumultuous couple of years, to be honest. Cavendish is the second head in three years, and the emphasis seems to be more on the building campaign than the academics." Evidently, Kevin had no idea the school was about to be on its third headmaster.

"Why do you stay, then?"

"Victoria likes the teachers, and she's made a good friend," he said. "I hope Elsie has the same experience. It can get crazy around here."

"What kind of crazy?"

"Umm . . . Well, here's an example. One of the first-grade girls had a birthday party," he said, glancing around again to make sure no one was listening. "They sent a limo to pick up each girl, and then brought them all to a spa for mani-pedis and makeovers."

"In first grade?"

He nodded.

"Wow," I said, then remembered my real purpose was to find out what exactly had happened to Aquaman. "So the parents can be a bit over-the-top. What do you think of the headmaster?"

"George? He's been here two years. The board is happy with him— apparently he's made a lot of money for the capital campaign." He leaned forward and spoke in a low voice. "I probably shouldn't tell you this, but it's best if you know what you're getting into. If one of the big donor families doesn't like you, you may find your daughter out on her ear."

It wasn't surprising, based on what had happened to Becky's daughter, but I felt my stomach turn over. What had I let Prue get me into? "Money talks, eh?"

"Money rules," he said darkly.

"Who should I watch out for?" I asked.

"The Krumbachers and the Goldens," he whispered. "And—"

"Kevin! I haven't seen you all summer!" It was Mitzi Krumbacher. She shot me a nasty look as she inserted herself between us, then turned to Kevin with a smile that showed off all her veneers.

My new acquaintance took a step back, looking surprised by the attention and maybe a little guilty. "Mitzi," he said. "How are you?"

"Just back from a trip to the South of France," she said, waving her hand and distributing a cloud of expensive perfume. "How about you?" She grinned in what I surmised was supposed to be a flirtatious manner, but the facial paralysis made it hard to tell. "Have you been taking home any more national titles?"

"Not this summer. The next tournament is in October," Kevin said. "Mitzi, have you met Margie?"

I stuck a hand out and applied a polite smile. "Yes, we've met. You have a first grader?"

"Violet," she bit out. "Anyway, Kevin, there's someone I want you to meet. If you'll excuse us . . ." Without waiting for an answer, she hooked his arm and led him off.

I watched as she pulled Kevin over to another corner of the vast kitchen, then I drained my coffee and refilled it so that I wouldn't fall asleep standing up. I listened to the conversations around me as I sipped my coffee, hoping to hear something related to the headmaster, but the primary topics seemed to be lakeside real estate, exotic summer vacations, pedicures, and after-school enrichment activities.

I was about to go back for another muffin when Deborah Golden's phone burbled from a few feet away from me. She hurried over and picked it up, looking irritated by the interruption. Then her eyes widened, and she excused herself from the kitchen. I abandoned my pastries and followed her.

Her voice floated down the vast hallway, and I slipped behind a column that looked like it had been looted from a Florentine church. "What do you mean, he's dead?"

So someone knew. Who was on the other end of the line? I wondered. At least I could probably cross Deborah Golden off the list of suspects.

"Shit," she said, which kind of surprised me. "That creates all kinds of problems. But it'll be a while till we get an interim, so we have time. Have they been through his office yet?" There was silence for a moment. "Do what you can. I've got half the first-grade parents here. I'll call you back when it's over."

Uh-oh. No time to escape. I edged around the column as Deborah Golden's wedges clip-clopped toward me, but either the column needed to be wider or I needed to be skinnier.

"Can I help you?"

Deborah Golden's voice was cold, and her face bore no trace of the fake smile she'd greeted me with.

"Yes, actually," I said. "Lovely pillar, by the way," I added, stroking the antique marble and feeling like a total idiot. "Where's the bathroom?"

"Just to the left of the front door," she told me, still sounding distinctly unfriendly. "Were you hoping for a secret button, or a passageway?" she asked, with a pointed look at the column.

I gave what I hoped was a light laugh, but it sounded more like I was gagging. "Of course not. Just admiring your beautiful house," I said, and drifted off toward the jumble of antlers hanging in the living room.

It was almost noon by the time I managed to extricate myself from Little Tuscany, thankful to be back in my derelict minivan. It had been an interesting morning. Was Deborah Golden worried about the police finding something in Cavendish's office? I wondered as I put the van in drive. And what kind of "problems" did his death create?

• • •

My mother was in full swing when I stopped by the house to pick up the cat carrier and grab a sandwich. My first clue that she was doing something industrious was that all the windows were open. Which is not ideal at noon on an August day in Texas.

"Hello, darling!" she called out as I cautiously stepped through the front door into the sauna that was my house. There was some kind of chiming music coming from the kitchen, and Rufus had retreated to the top of the television, which was no longer in its customary location against the wall. He hissed when I reached to pet him.

"Mom?" I called. "What are you doing?"

"Just doing a little space clearing," she said. I followed her voice to the kitchen, where the entire contents of my cabinets and pantry had been disgorged onto the table. My mother balanced on a stool, reaching for a jar of applesauce. She wore a long, flowing, tie-dyed skirt and a tank top, and her hair was pulled up into a loose bun. I couldn't help noticing the sweat stains on the tank top.

"You mean pantry clearing," I said.

"Well, that's part of it," she said. "I can't believe how many refined food products you have. No wonder Elsie is having trouble."

"Who said she's having trouble?"

"Well, she does seem a bit . . . stressed," my mother said. "I thought maybe if we did an elimination diet, it might help."

"Eliminating what?"

"Well, white foods, of course. White bread, pasta, sugar . . . refined junk." She held up a box of Kraft Easy Mac—Elsie's sole concession to the color orange. The music coming from the stereo system chimed, and my mother hummed along as she tossed the box into an open trash bag.

"You mean a starvation diet," I said.

"Starvation diet?" She laughed. "Not at all! Children have very flexible palates. I know it seems harsh, but after a few days, I'm sure she'll surprise you. Kale can be absolutely delicious if you roast it with a little olive oil and salt. She'll be begging for it."

"Hmmm," I said, feeling a sudden strong urge for a nice glass of Chardonnay. I couldn't, though; I still had to kidnap a teacup pig, stuff it into a cat carrier, and pick up my kids. And somehow procure a turkey sandwich. "How about we just try cutting back a few things first, instead of getting rid of everything? She's starting a new school this week; isn't that stressful enough?"

"Don't be silly, Marigold. I'll bet nutrition is a big part of the problem, and the vitamins will do her a world of good. In fact," she beamed, "we'll start tonight at Casa de Luz. I've included Prudence and Phil, of course. And Blake told me this morning that he'll come. By the way, is someone sleeping in the office?"

"I was just setting it up for you," I said quickly.

"But Blake's things are in there."

"You know how closet space is," I said. "And he does sleep there sometimes—he has a snoring problem."

"Probably gluten intolerance," she sighed, tossing a box of Fruit Roll-Ups into a trash bag. "It's a good thing I came when I did."

My phone rang. It was Becky.

"I have to run, Mom," I said, heading to the garage. I didn't want to pick up until I was out of earshot.

"See you this afternoon!" she said as I closed the door to the house behind me. I stabbed at my phone and thrust it to my ear.

"Margie, they think I killed him."

CHAPTER FOURTEEN

What do you mean?" I asked, feeling my entire body deflate. I leaned up against the wall and waited for Becky to answer.

"The cops just left my house. I don't know why, but they think I had something to do with George Cavendish's death."

"Becky—"

"I'm a mess, Margie. What do I do if they arrest me? If only I hadn't written that stupid article. Or even applied to that stupid school—"

"Becky. There's something I have to tell you."

There was a clicking sound. "Damn. That's the other line; it's probably Rick. I'll call you later."

She hung up before I could tell her I was the one who had dropped her card.

I hit Peaches's number; she answered on the second ring.

"The police think Becky killed Cavendish," I told her. "It's all because I dropped that damned card. I have to tell Detective Bunsen what we did."

"Hold on there, buttercup," she said. "If you do that, we're all in the soup. You, me, Desiree . . . They'll haul us all off."

"But I can't let Becky go to jail to protect us! I have to tell the police the truth."

"And wind up in jail while the murderer runs free? Think about it for a minute," she said. "Somebody is responsible for what happened to Aquaman, and we're in the best position to find out who."

"More than the police?"

"We're investigators, remember? People pay us to do this stuff. Plus, we know more about the crime scene than the police do."

"Only because we illegally moved the body," I pointed out.

"So? You put a murderer behind bars a while back, didn't you? And rescued a bunch of folks from Mexico. Right?"

"Well . . ."

"This is a piece of cake compared to that," Peaches said.

"But it's not ethical," I said, leaning up against the overloaded garage shelves and dislodging a plastic sand bucket. It rattled to the floor, disgorging a pair of sandy shovels and distributing a good portion of the Galveston beach onto the garage floor. "Peaches, I have to tell the police."

"I know you're trying to do the right thing, kid, but if you do, I could lose my license and we may both go to jail," Peaches told me. "You won't see your kids for years."

"But Becky will go to jail if I don't," I said. "I can't do that to her."

"You're right," she said. "You can't."

"So I'll call."

"Call if you have to. But can you give us a week before you do it?" Peaches asked. "We've got access to the school, his associates . . . We can figure this out."

I poked at a shovel with my toe. "You think so?"

"I know so," she said. "We'll go talk to Desiree and find out everything she knows, and I'll bet you've already got a few leads."

I thought of Deborah Golden's odd conversation at the coffee. It wasn't much, but it was something.

"And if we don't figure it out," Peaches continued, "I'll call Detective Bunsen myself and tell him I strong-armed you into it, and that you and your friend had nothing to do with it."

"Promise?"

"Promise."

I took a deep breath and wondered if I was insane. "Okay," I said.

"I'm working on digging up dirt online. You have time to go to Holy Oaks this afternoon? Think you can talk them into letting you volunteer?"

I glanced at my watch. "I was about to pick up Bubba Sue, but that shouldn't take too long."

"Get the pig, stick it in your laundry room, and see if you can get into his office."

I took a deep breath. "What do I tell Becky in the meantime?"

"Tell her whatever the hell you want," Peaches said. "But unless they're hauling her off in handcuffs, don't say anything about what happened last night."

"Okay," I said.

"While you're at Holy Oaks, I'll call Desiree and set up a time to go talk to her."

"I'm still not sure I shouldn't call—"

"One week," Peaches repeated. "Now, stop worrying and go get that pig."

• • •

Bubba Sue's address was on the south side of town, not too far from South Lamar. Although the developers seemed intent on turning the area into a monument to concrete, there was still a lot of eccentricity to be found, and the address listed in the file was no exception.

Becky was still in the back of my mind as I cruised past the house. It was a faded green bungalow with watermelon trim. A giant dinosaur that appeared to have been constructed from hubcaps and discarded lounge chairs squatted in the middle of the unmowed front yard, and a 1980s-era pink couch sagged on the front porch. There was no car in the driveway, and boxes showed through the clouded garage windows; it looked like no one was home. An overgrown Turk's-cap bush obscured what looked like a gate to the backyard, which was a bonus— less chance of being spotted by neighbors.

I parked the minivan down the street and walked down the tree-root-buckled sidewalk, trying to act like I often went for a stroll with an empty cat carrier. A few new modern houses had sprouted up like mushrooms among the aging bungalows, their grassy front yards replaced by swaths of designer pebbles or glass, but most of the street was still old-Austin funk.

When I got within a few houses of Bubba Sue's temporary residence, thankful that I seemed to be the only one out for a walk, I heard a low grunting. I glanced around to ensure I was alone, then waded through the overgrown bush blocking the gate in the privacy fence.

The grunting grew louder as I jiggled the rusted latch, trying to free it. The grunting seemed awfully low for a teacup pig. On the other hand, I had never met a teacup pig.

I was about to, though.

After a couple of thwacks, the latch came free and I managed to push the door ajar; it had fallen half off of the hinges and was wedged into the ground. The mounds of freshly dug earth piled up against the gate proved a challenge, too, but I managed to squeeze through.

Although there was still grunting, mixed with the occasional *oink*, there was no teacup pig in sight. There was, however, evidence of the pig—either that or a drunken sprinkler-system installer. The entire side yard had been dug up, leaving only a few islands of weedy grass and a distinctive livestock aroma.

I shoved the gate closed behind me and opened the door of the cat carrier. "Bubba Sue!" I crooned, clucking a few times. "Here, girl!" I unwrapped a cheese stick, tossed it into the cat carrier, and backed away, hoping I wasn't stepping in pig poop. "Here, Bubba Sue!"

There was a loud oinking, coupled with a few menacing grunts. I took another step back. "I brought you a snack!"

I heard an ominous thudding—Bubba Sue had an awfully heavy tread for a teacup pig—and then, from around the corner of the house, loomed a sow the size of a small refrigerator.

She might have been cocoa-colored, but it was hard to tell, since her entire bristly coat was covered in dried mud. I thought I could make out a white spot on her snout, but when she curled back her lips, exposing two rows of white, piggy teeth, I stopped paying attention to her snout.

I froze as the beast snuffled a few times and stepped toward the cat carrier, eyeing me warily with her little piggy eyes. Which were the only things little about Bubba Sue. There was no way she was fitting in that carrier. In fact, I wasn't sure she could get her *head* into that carrier.

That didn't mean she wasn't going to try, though. As I watched in horror, she snuffled some more, trying to identify the source of the cheesy aroma. She approached the carrier, and I edged toward the gate. Maybe she'd get the cheese stick out and I could reclaim the carrier and slip out the gate without bothering her. Maybe I could find a vet who would prescribe piggy Valium, and I could drug her and somehow truss her up and drag her out in a piggy sling. Maybe I could get out of here without being trampled or gored.

She poked an exploratory snout into the cat carrier. I had tossed the cheese to the far back, so it wasn't easy to get. She leaned in farther, and I could hear a smacking and grunting noise that indicated she had located her prize.

I waited for her to pull her head out and amble off, maybe in search of a few blades of grass she hadn't yet uprooted—something to complement the cheese. And she did back up after a moment. Unfortunately, the cat carrier backed up with her.

If I thought there was a lot of grunting before, it was nothing compared to what was happening now. There were grunts—low, menacing grunts—as she swung her head around, trying to dislodge the cat carrier. Unfortunately, she managed to thwack the carrier into the side of the house, which only pushed it down farther.

Then the grunting stopped, replaced by loud, human-sounding squeals. She rocketed around the side yard like an angry bull, the cat carrier clunking as it rammed into the siding, and the fence, and then the siding again. And then suddenly, the cat carrier was pointed at me.

There was a snuffling sound, and a loud braying noise, and she rocketed toward me. I darted to the side, reaching for the gate, but she backed up and charged me again, hitting the boards of the fence with a sickening thud. One of the screws came out of the cat carrier, opening it up a few inches and giving her a better view of her prey. She pawed the ground once and hurled herself at my knees. I jumped up, clinging to the top of the fence, my feet balanced on the wooden crossbar as the fence shuddered beneath me.

She backed up and took aim again. I heaved one leg up over the side of the fence, discovering reserves of gymnastic ability I hadn't known existed, and pulled myself to the top just as Rufus's carrier connected with the rotting wood—right where my legs had been. I had worked my other leg over, congratulating myself on my quick reflexes, when there was a sliding sensation from my left pocket, and a clatter against the fence.

I looked down in horror.

Elsie's fry phone had slipped out of my pocket, right into a pile of pig manure.

CHAPTER FIFTEEN

It was almost two o'clock by the time I finally gave up on retrieving Elsie's fry phone. Bubba Sue was still hurling herself against the fence, grunting furiously, the cat carrier still attached to her head. With a stab of guilt over my broken promise to Elsie, I wiped my sneakers as clean as I could on the grass and climbed into the minivan. I thought about stopping home to change, but that would mean I would have to face my mother, so instead I steered the Grand Caravan toward Holy Oaks. I wasn't assigned to any volunteer work today—my first library shift wasn't until Thursday—but I was hoping to find a way into George Cavendish's office.

And maybe, I thought with a flutter in my stomach, check and see whether Elsie is holding up okay.

As I pulled past the manicured front entrance to Holy Oaks, which was decorated with the school's symbol—a big blue H in a triangle with a banner over it that looked more like a coat of arms than a logo—I again had the unsettling feeling that I was entering into a different world. A world that involved custom golf carts, second homes on the Riviera, and cosmetic-surgery bills that rivaled my mortgage payment.

Even if Elsie could keep her canine fixation under wraps, would she be able to find any common ground with her schoolmates?

My mother-in-law thought so, but I had some serious doubts. I paused at the gleaming plate-glass windows by the entrance, checking myself in the reflection. My hair was brushed and relatively clean, but nothing about me said "couture." In fact, other than wedges and belted dresses, I wasn't sure what constituted "couture" these days; instead of keeping up with glossy magazines, I spent most of my spare reading time devouring books like *When Your Husband Stops Wearing the Pants in the Family* and *Toughing It Out*. Neither of which, frankly, had been helpful.

My thoughts strayed to Elsie; I hoped she was having a good first day. She was a shy girl and had always had difficulty making new friends; she and Zoe had been best friends for the past few years, and she hadn't really gravitated toward anyone else. She could be bright and lively once you got to know her, but I was afraid no one would give her a chance.

The police were gone when I stepped into the chilly lobby, but the perky front-desk woman was still ensconced in the front office. "Can I help you?" she asked in that friendly robotic way that made me suspect she had been programmed.

"Yes," I said. "I had a few hours free," I lied, "and wondered if you needed any help in the office."

"It's your child's first day, isn't it?" she said with a look of pity.

"Um, yes."

"Well, I'm sure she's doing just fine, and to be honest, we don't need any help in the office today," she said, smoothing back a strand of stick-straight blonde hair. "There's a lot going on." At that moment, Kathleen Gardner rounded the corner, carrying a stack of library books and wearing a look of determination.

"You're the new mom from the coffee, aren't you?" she asked when her pale eyes lit on me. "Mary, isn't it?"

"Margie."

"Margie," she repeated, pronouncing it with a soft *g* like *margarine*. Ah, well.

"Do you need some help with that?" I asked, pointing to her stack of books.

"No," she said. "I have it under control. But we could use a little help erasing pencil marks in the SAT prep books, if you're interested."

"Sounds great," I said, surprised she wasn't more concerned about the headmaster's demise. The school must still have been keeping George Cavendish's current medical condition under wraps.

"Well, then," Perky Desk Girl said, relieved to have me dealt with. "Have fun!"

I smiled and trailed Kathleen out of the office and into the library, wincing as I remembered the whipped-cream walk of shame I'd taken just the day before. She settled me at a table in the corner, next to a giant stack of thousand-page books. I had about a hundred things to do that were more pressing than library volunteer work, but I pasted on a fake smile anyway. Should I mention the headmaster's death? Would it help me get any inside info? Probably not, I decided. If this was Kathleen's first year here, how much could she possibly know?

"Now then," Kathleen said, "all we do is open the book, find the pencil marks, and"—she attacked a stray check mark with the pink end of a pencil—"voila!" She smiled at me as if I were a mentally deficient three-year-old. "Does that make sense?"

"I think I've got the drift."

"Great. There's a whole jar of pencils on the desk if you need more erasers. And I'm here if you have any questions."

I couldn't imagine what questions I would have, other than asking if there was a straight razor in the desk I might use to slit my wrists, but I grimaced and set to the task at hand, trying to come up with some reason to get back to the office and snoop.

• • •

The next hour was, to say the least, uneventful. On the other hand, by the time I'd made it through the first two SAT books, I had been treated to the entire biography of Kathleen's daughter, from her twenty-eight-hour birthing process and the details of her favorite breakfast (oatmeal with bananas and walnuts—no sugar, of course) to the trophies she'd garnered, apparently weekly, since she was old enough to crawl. The only thing Kathleen didn't mention was Catriona's father. I gathered from the absence of a wedding ring on Kathleen's square hand that she'd either gone the artificial insemination route or run the poor guy off.

Or perhaps, I reflected as Kathleen droned on about the wear patterns on her daughter's ballet shoes, he'd committed suicide.

"So," she said, straightening the chairs around the tables for the fourth time that morning—the librarian, I couldn't help noticing, had scurried into her office and was, I suspected, hiding behind a filing cabinet—"what colleges are you thinking about for your daughter?"

I paused, my eraser suspended over a particularly tricky problem involving triangles. "Colleges? Isn't it a bit early to think about that?"

"It's never too early to start planning," Kathleen advised me, her graying, no-nonsense bob swinging emphatically with each word. "We're looking at the Ivy Leagues, but that would mean we'd have to move to the Northeast, and I don't care for winters. Still, I'll do what I need to, to support her." She pursed her lips. "She would consider the Plan II program at UT, of course, but UT doesn't quite have the same cachet, does it?"

"Umm . . ." I erased an incorrect addition scribble—whoever had used this book last had clearly missed the "'Rithmetic" part of the three Rs—and realized Kathleen had just given me an opportunity.

"Will you sign her up for the Acorn Scholars program?" I asked.

"Of course," she said. "It's expensive, but so worth it."

I flipped the page and erased another set of pencil marks. "What exactly does the program do?"

"Everything," she said. "The headmaster just started it last year."

"Did he?" I asked, wondering if perhaps the program had something to do with his untimely demise in a pink vinyl wading pool. I was fairly desperate.

"They offer specialized tutoring, help in advanced classes, SAT coaches . . . They even have a professional writer help them craft their essays."

Help them craft their essays? I thought. Or "craft" essays for them?

"How much does it cost?" I asked, wondering if Prudence would insist we sign Elsie up. On the other hand, since she was generously covering Elsie's tuition, I couldn't complain. I sent yet another prayer up that my daughter had left her Fifi identity in the minivan and would at least meet one potential friend on the playground. When was recess, anyway? Maybe I'd take a peek—from a distance, of course. Just to check.

"I'm not sure how much the program costs," Kathleen said, pulling me out of my worried thoughts, "but I know it's in the thousands. Still, ten out of twelve got accepted to at least one Ivy this year, and their SAT scores went up hundreds of points." A small, smug smile played across her ChapSticked lips. "Just think of how good Holy Oaks' reputation will be by the time our daughters are applying!"

"I can only imagine." I erased another check mark. "I wonder where the headmaster was this morning?" I said idly.

"I don't know," Kathleen said, "but I'm sure he was gone on important business."

"I heard something happened to him," I said as I erased a penciled-in *GEOMETRY SUCKS* from the top of a page.

"Oh, I'm sure they would have said something about that," Kathleen said dismissively. A babble of voices in the hallway outside caught my attention; Perky Desk Girl was escorting what appeared to be a potential student and her family down the hall toward the elementary wing. I put down my pencil, grabbed my purse, and stood up. "I'll be right back."

Kathleen's pale-blue eyes darted to me. "Where are you going?"

"Bathroom," I said.

She pointed toward the librarian's office, where Ms. Jones was still in hiding. "There's one next to the office."

"I don't want to disturb the librarian," I said. "Besides, I need to stretch my legs a bit." Without waiting for her to reply, I headed toward the door to the main hallway, trying not to look as if I were fleeing.

With Perky Desk Girl gone, the office was deserted. I glanced back toward the library, half expecting to see Kathleen watching me—thankfully, she hadn't followed me to the door—before darting into the main office.

The place was empty. There were three doors behind the reception desk. Two were open, and belonged to the heads of the lower school and upper school, but unfortunately, the third—which, according to the nameplate beside the door, belonged to the headmaster—was closed. I hurried over and tried the knob, but it was locked. How was I going to get in there—preferably before Deborah Golden's associate managed to cover up whatever needed to be covered up?

Frustrated, I looked around the rest of the office, wondering what else I could discover. There was a big filing cabinet on the back wall. I opened it; there were files on each family, including Becky's. I grabbed hers and leafed through it. Zoe's application was there, along with the admissions notes. *Financial aid requested* was scrawled in red on the top of the file, along with a big red *X*. I tucked it into my purse and scanned the rest of the files, recognizing the Goldens and the hair-care magnate. I added them to the file in my purse—I'd make copies and return them tomorrow, I rationalized—and then grabbed the Krumbachers' file, to boot. I slid the drawer shut and looked through the others, but there was nothing but office supplies. My eyes moved to the wall of mailboxes. The cubby labeled *CAVENDISH* was almost full; could there be something in there that would point me in the right direction? With a quick glance at the main door, I grabbed the stack of mail and flipped through it.

Lots of brochures for building supplies and school products, which was no surprise. A missive from the alumni association of Holy Cross. Two letters from the admissions offices of universities in Boston and New Hampshire. A fat envelope that looked like a financial statement from a firm called Golden Investments. And two hand-addressed letters, both postmarked in Austin.

I held the stack in my hand and glanced over my shoulder. Taking these letters would be a federal offense—I knew that from my investigative training. It would be illegal to do anything but put the letters back.

On the other hand, how else was I going to figure out who had killed George Cavendish? As I hesitated, my phone burbled in my purse. I pulled it out to silence it, and my stomach turned over: it was the Austin Police Department. At that moment, I heard the sound of footsteps in the hallway.

"Did someone leave a phone in the office?" I recognized Perky Desk Girl's voice.

"I don't know, but there really shouldn't be anyone in there," said another female voice—the head of the lower school, I realized. I muted the call and jammed my phone into the diaper bag. Then, almost without thinking, I stuffed the mail in after it and hurried out of the office, almost slamming into Perky Desk Girl as I rounded the corner.

Her brow furrowed at the sight of me. "Can I help you?"

"I was just looking for the bathroom," I said, holding the bulging diaper bag closed and hoping she didn't have X-ray vision.

"Down the hall to the left," she said. She and the head of the lower school stared at me suspiciously.

"Thanks," I said, my heart pounding as I hurried down the antiseptic-scented hallway, past a photomontage of blond, smiling children surrounding a lone Asian girl. Once in the bathroom, I locked myself in the stall and pulled the letters out of my purse. I couldn't believe I had just stolen a dead man's mail.

Borrowed, I told myself. *Not stolen.* I would return it, after all. And it might keep Becky—and me—out of jail. I pulled out one of the handwritten letters first, holding it up to the light. The creamy linen envelope was too thick to see through, unfortunately.

I ran a fingernail under the flap, but it was sealed tight. Could I steam it open and reseal it? I wondered, stifling a flush of guilt at the thought.

If I was going to do that, I needed to go home. And maybe schedule a karma-adjustment appointment for my mother so she wouldn't be around to ask me why I was steaming mail open with a teakettle.

I tucked the mail back into my purse and exited the stall, heading back for the library. As I walked down the hall, a string of first graders filed by. It didn't take long for me to identify Elsie's dark head among the line of jumpered girls. Most of them were smiling, already whispering confidences to one another. My heart squeezed when I saw my daughter, though. Instead of chatting gaily with new friends, she stared at the floor, drifting behind her classmates.

I knew I wasn't supposed to, but I couldn't resist. "Elsie," I murmured as my daughter passed.

She looked up, her big eyes wide and startled.

"Did you come to take me home?" she asked, her face lighting with hope.

"Not yet," I said, and her shoulders sagged as the rest of the class skipped by. "Did you have lunch?" I asked brightly.

She shook her head.

"Where are you headed now?"

"Playground," she mumbled.

I looked behind me; the rest of the children had already turned the corner. "You'd better catch up," I said, then stooped and gave her a hug, folding her small, sweet body into my arms. I had an impulse to gather her up and run out of the building with her, but I stifled the urge. School was part of life; she'd learn to adjust.

Wouldn't she?

"I'll see you in a few hours, pumpkin," I said, and watched as she slumped down the hall after her classmates, glancing back at me forlornly before turning the corner.

At least she hadn't barked, I told myself, my heart feeling like somebody had trampled it with soccer cleats.

CHAPTER SIXTEEN

I spent another twenty minutes erasing SAT books and worrying about Elsie before excusing myself to go pick up my son. Becky's van was already in the Green Meadows parking lot when I pulled in next to her. She was sitting in the driver's seat, staring into space.

I got out of the car and tapped on her window. She jumped and rolled it down.

"Are you okay?" I asked.

"I'm not great," Becky told me. The sight of her pale, makeup-less face made me feel sick to my stomach.

"Did the police say anything else?"

"They found my business card on his . . . his body," she told me, twisting the bottom of her Green Meadows Day School T-shirt. Which was another worrying sign: Becky didn't usually wear T-shirts.

"Lots of people have business cards," I said, leaning against her van and trying to keep my face from looking too terribly guilty. "Did they really think you'd leave a business card if you had something to do with his death?"

She gave a hollow laugh. "I know, right? But they told me they want me to stay in town," she said. "They know about the letter I wrote in the *Picayune*." She took a deep breath. "I'm pretty sure I'm the top suspect right now."

It was on the tip of my tongue to tell her it was my fault, but I remembered what Peaches and I had agreed to. One week. "Did they say anything about what happened to him?"

She shook her head. "Obviously he didn't die of natural causes, though. They wouldn't tell me anything, but they wanted to know where I was last night." She swallowed. "And they asked if I had any firearms."

I sucked in my breath. "You're right. That doesn't sound good."

Becky pulled at her T-shirt again. "Do you think that means he was shot?"

"I don't know," I lied. Which felt absolutely awful. I took another deep breath and said, "Actually, Becky, I do know."

Her eyes widened. "What?"

I glanced behind me to make sure nobody was in earshot. "I think I'm the one who dropped your business card on George Cavendish," I confessed.

"You mean . . . *you* killed him?" Her hand leapt to her chest. "You did that for *me*? I never wanted him dead . . ." She paused for a moment, thinking about what I said, and her forehead wrinkled. "And why did you leave my business card?"

"No . . . I didn't kill anyone! I just . . . helped move the body."

"Why?"

I glanced over my shoulder again. "Peaches called me."

Becky looked confused. "Peaches killed him? But she doesn't even have kids!"

I took a deep breath. "We don't know who killed him. He was in a young woman's apartment, wearing . . . well, not very much."

"He had a mistress?"

"Sort of," I said. "Anyway, somebody broke in and shot him while she was in the other room buying curtains."

My friend blinked at me. "Buying curtains?"

"She's into interior design—she's pretty good, actually. Anyway, Peaches called me to help her move the body, so that the young woman wouldn't be connected with his death and her parents wouldn't find out how she pays her college tuition."

Becky's eyes got even rounder. "So she's a . . . a prostitute!"

"I think so," I told her. "She's got a whole dungeon and everything, and some kind of weird sex chair . . . Anyway, I messed up, and I'm sorry."

"Jesus, Margie. Why did you do it?"

"I don't know," I said. "When Peaches called, I didn't really understand what I was getting into. And the girl was nice—I felt bad for her. I can understand why she didn't want her parents to know about . . . well, how she paid the bills."

"So you helped move the body. But how did you manage to drop my business card? I'm always looking for new business, but hookers and dead men aren't my usual target market."

"It was an accident." I told her about showing Peaches my new cards, and the attack of the renegade cat. "I guess one of them must have gotten wedged in the pool."

She blinked again. "The what?"

"He was in a pink vinyl pool when he died."

"What was he doing in a pink pool?"

"Um . . . marinating in pee, evidently. Wearing Aquaman tights and goggles."

Becky looked horrified. Then she giggled. "Aquaman tights? Seriously?"

"It smelled even worse than it sounds," I said, and started giggling with her. Soon, we were doubled over laughing and wiping our eyes. When we were gasping for breath, I said, "I'm sorry I didn't tell you right away. I talked to Peaches this morning, as soon as Bunsen showed me a copy of your business card. She wanted me to stay mum for a week before talking to you, so that we could solve the case, but I'll call Detective Bunsen right now if you want."

"Wait," Becky said, putting a hand on my arm. "Wouldn't that mean you and Peaches might go to jail?"

"We did move a murder victim, so there's a good chance of it."

"But the kids . . . with everything going on between you and Blake, and Elsie's issues . . ." She looked at me. "I don't know, Margie. Do you really think we can figure this out on our own?"

I glanced back at the minivan, where I'd stashed the diaper bag and its contraband contents. "I grabbed his mail and a couple of files from the Holy Oaks office today. It's a start."

She bit her lip. "I think Peaches is right," she said slowly. "We should at least try to figure this out on our own."

"Are you sure? I can call the police and clear this up right now."

She nodded. "If I get arrested, we'll talk. We can at least see what we can find out. What *did* happen, anyway?" She was already looking better, I noticed. Still pale, but that was to be expected when she wasn't wearing her signature Cherry Blossom blush.

"Somebody broke open the sliding glass door and shot him, then took off. We're going to talk to Desiree to see if she saw anything else."

"Desiree?" She snorted. "Was that really her name?"

"I doubt it's on her birth certificate, but that's what she goes by." I sighed. "It's been a pretty shitty twenty-four hours, all in all. And to top things off, I dropped Elsie's fry phone next to an angry pig."

"A pig?"

"It's the only case in the office right now," I said, wondering how I was going to get Elsie's fry phone back. I'd swung by the house again on my way to Green Meadows, but evidently Bubba Sue remembered me; I hadn't even gotten to the gate before she was battering the cat carrier against the fence. I was going to need to resort to a pig tranquilizer—or hiring a bull rider from a rodeo.

"A case involving an angry pig?"

"A pignapping. Ex-husband took the momma and is planning to sell the piglets," I explained. "The pig's name is Bubba Sue. She's supposed to be teacup-size, but she's about the size of a Fiat."

"I thought it was bad enough with your mother coming to town."

"Oh, my mother got in first thing this morning—when she rang the bell, I thought it was the cops. She's emptied the cabinets of edible food and replaced it with organic sawdust," I told her, "and she's invited Blake's parents to join us for dinner at Casa de Luz tonight."

Becky grinned. "The vegan macrobiotic restaurant down by the lake?"

I nodded. "And you haven't even heard about Blake's new Christian anti-gay program. Journey to Manhood. He wants me to go to the wives' support group: Warrior Wives."

"Have you considered divorce?" she asked. "Maybe from your entire family? Except for the kids, of course."

"When would I have the time to file?" I sighed. To be honest, the prospect made me feel sick to my stomach. The familiar thoughts churned through my head. I hated the idea of destroying my children's home . . . And how would I be able to make it as a single mother? I pushed the thoughts away; I couldn't afford to think about my marriage right now. "Is Rick still out of town?"

"Till Friday."

"Can I come over and steam open some envelopes tonight?"

"Call me when the kids are down," she said, getting out of her van. Together, we walked through the Green Meadows gate to retrieve our children, giving Mrs. Bunn—whose distinctly authoritarian leadership style had earned her the nickname Attila the Bunn—a quick wave as we hurried past the office.

Things might not be going great, I told myself.

But least I hadn't accidentally dropped off pictures of dead Aquaman for the school newsletter.

• • •

The kitchen table was no longer piled with packaged food when I stepped through the door at 4:30 that afternoon, both kids in tow. The windows were now closed, and the air conditioning was huffing as it attempted to return the interior temperature to a habitable range. We'd stopped at Subway so the kids could eat something substantial before facing my mother's version of an after-school snack. Not to mention "dinner" at Casa de Luz.

"Wow," I said, opening the fridge and blinking at the glass jars of green juice that now lined the interior. "You really cleaned us out."

"Not at all!" my mother said, her earrings tinkling as she swept across the kitchen on a wave of patchouli. "I simply replaced what you had with higher-prana food."

"I know what pranas are," Nick said. "Mommy got some when we were in Galveston. They're big shrimps!"

My mother laughed. "No, Nick," she said. "Prana is life energy. You want to taste some?"

"Sure!" he said. Elsie, who was older and wiser, stood in the corner adjusting the buckle on her dog collar. She hadn't said anything about school yet, but I hadn't heard from the teacher, either. I was operating under the assumption that no news was good news.

"I'll pour you a big glass so you can really taste it," my mother said, grabbing one of the jars of green liquid from the fridge and pouring him a healthy glob.

"What do I do with it?" he asked, tipping the glass from side to side and watching the contents climb up the sides of the glass. It reminded me of those lava lamps from the sixties.

My mother squatted down and grinned at him, her earrings tinkling. "You drink it, silly!"

He eyed her with suspicion. "But it looks like frog water."

"No frogs," she said. "Just lots of good growing things."

"Like mold?" he asked. "Mommy had to throw out two peanut-butter-and-jelly sandwiches last week because the bread was furry."

I grimaced. Embarrassing moments got very hard to sweep under the carpet once you had children.

"Not mold," my mother said, sounding somewhat less chipper. "Fresh fruits and vegetables. Good things like cabbage, and kale, and apples."

"I like apples," he said. "But cabbage smells like bathroom."

"Try it!" my mother encouraged him, her smile looking a little tight. "Just a sip."

"Okay," he said with a quick glance at me. I kept my poker face on as my son took a small sip and scrunched up his nose. "Gross."

"Be polite, Nick," I reminded him.

"Okay." He looked up at my mother. "I don't care for any more green slime, thank you."

My mother was still smiling, but her face had a set look that worried me. "I'll just drink this up," she said, tipping the glass up and taking a swig, then smacking her lips as if she were drinking a chocolate milkshake. "I've got another recipe I think you'll like better."

"Is it green?"

"We'll see, won't we?" she said vaguely, finishing the drink and tucking the glass into the dishwasher. Elsie had walked over to the pantry and stood staring at the largely empty shelves.

"Where did all the food go?" she asked.

"What do you mean?" My mother hurried over to the pantry. "There are rye crisps, and seaweed snacks, and even some fruit leather."

"Where's my Easy Mac?"

"I dropped it off at the food bank, darling," she said.

Elsie turned in horror. I could only imagine how she'd react when I broke the news about the fry phone. "The food bank? Can we get it back?"

"We don't need it back! We've got lots of other things that are just as yummy—and much healthier for you!"

"Like green slime?" Elsie asked.

I stepped in between my mother and my children. "Why don't we get our homework done before dinner?" I asked in a bright voice. "Kids, why don't you get your backpacks and we'll work together at the table!"

"I don't have homework," Nick said.

"Well, then," I said. "You can read a book or go outside and play."

"Can I watch TV?"

"Um . . . I seem to have disconnected something when I moved the television," my mother said.

I sighed. "How about Duplos?"

He crossed his chubby arms. "But I'll miss *The Clone Wars*!"

"I'll get a copy at the library tomorrow," I said.

"But they don't have the new ones!"

"Just go," I said, more sharply than I meant to. He shot me a dark look and trudged down the hallway to his bedroom. Elsie, meanwhile, had taken the opportunity to skulk out into the backyard, where she was squatting in the doghouse she'd made out of an old refrigerator box. Occasionally she'd throw herself a tennis ball and fetch it.

"They're going to need some serious nutritional retraining, Margie," my mother said. "But I think you'll see a real shift in their behavior problems."

I blinked at my mother. "Their behavior problems?"

She looked out the window, where Elsie was crawling back to the refrigerator box with a tennis ball wedged in her mouth.

Perhaps she had a point. But I didn't see how kale-and-garlic smoothies were going to help.

CHAPTER SEVENTEEN

B lake was running late, so he was planning on meeting us at Casa de Luz. I'd detached the tennis ball from Elsie's canines, wiped most of the dirt off of her knees, and surreptitiously slipped each child a cheese stick to tide them over through dinner. My mother had put on a glittery sari-like thing and refreshed her patchouli oil. As we pulled out of the driveway, I switched the minivan's AC from "Recirc" to "Fresh."

Casa de Luz was in a low-slung building at the back of a New Agey complex close to Lady Bird Lake. It was beautifully landscaped, but the look veered more toward untamed tropical rainforest than country-club golf course. Prudence and Phil had already arrived and had stationed themselves near an outdoor Japanese teahouse area that was ringed by bamboo and covered with some kind of aggressive vine. As we pulled up, a couple with matching dreadlocks and Hula-Hoop-size holes in their ears sauntered by while my in-laws pretended not to notice. Phil looked very out of place in khakis and a golf shirt, and Prudence looked like she might already be sweating through her cashmere twinset. There was no sign of Blake.

"Prue!"

I could see Prudence recoil as my mother launched herself at her in a wave of patchouli-scented batik.

"Constance," she said, giving my mother an awkward pat on her cotton-clad back.

"Call me Connie," my mother said. "All my friends do!"

"Right," Prudence said, then bent down to hug the children. "How was your first day of school, sweetheart?"

Elsie turned away, fingering her dog collar.

"It seems to have gone okay," I answered for her.

Elsie looked up at me. "Can I have my fry phone?"

"It's, uh, at the office, honey," I said. "I'll get it tomorrow."

She narrowed her eyes and growled.

Prue straightened, smoothing her cashmere sweater just as Blake walked up, looking lawyerly in a button-down shirt and pressed khakis. "Blake!" She enfolded him in a hug and pecked his cheek. "You look terrific."

"Thanks," he said. Phil gave him an awkward hug, slapping him on the back a few times and then stepping back as if embarrassed by the contact.

Prudence looked around. "Where's the restaurant?"

"Back this way," my mother said. "I'll show you!"

"What kind of food is it, again?" Phil asked as we followed in her wake, passing classrooms advertising chakra-balancing and shamanic-journeying workshops. "Do they have good steak?"

"Oh, no steak," my mother answered. "Everything's macrobiotic."

"Macrowhat?"

My mother waved a bangled hand. "Healthy and delicious. You'll see!"

My in-laws exchanged worried glances as we walked into Casa de Luz, which looked more like a commune cafeteria than a restaurant. There was a decidedly earthy aroma in the air, and the room was lit in part by icicle lights dangling from an overhead beam. The kitchen was in one corner of the low-slung building, divided from the dining room by a Formica countertop. The benches at the maple-wood tables were dotted with a mix of refugees from the 1960s and young, colorfully clad twentysomethings with lush patches of armpit hair. I thought Prudence seemed a bit pale, but it could have been the reflected glow of the icicle lights.

"What do we do?" she asked, looking as if she had been deposited on Neptune.

"Oh, we pay ahead of time, here at the front desk. The salad and soups are self-service"—my mother pointed to the low counter, which featured a soup warmer and a metal bowl with tongs sticking out of it—"and they bring your food to you."

"Where are the menus?" my father-in-law asked.

"There aren't any," my mother said. "They make a delicious daily plate, and they bring it to your table." She whipped out a beaded wallet. "Go get some salad and find a table. My treat!"

Normally my in-laws would have fought her for the bill, but they were so bewildered that my mother managed to finish the transaction before Phil and Prudence realized what was happening. My mother shepherded my in-laws to a large table in the corner, next to the dreadlocked couple, and said, "Would you like some tea?"

"Earl Grey?" Prudence said in a hopeful tone.

"It looks like twig tea today," my mother said, craning to look at the label on the urn on the counter. "They have hibiscus iced tea, too."

"Chocolate milk?" Nick asked.

"Just tea," his sari-clad grandmother said, smiling down at him like a benevolent angel. "It's delicious tea, though. So good for your digestion!"

"Mmm," my mother-in-law said, her lips pressed together so hard they'd almost disappeared. "Maybe I'll just have water."

• • •

Dinner was not a triumph. Elsie did not put her plate on the ground to eat, but that was only because there was nothing on it she deemed edible. Nick seemed to view the food as multicolored modeling clay. We stopped him from forming a line of vegan train engines with his fingers, but he spent the remainder of the meal flicking kidney beans at his sister and giggling when she growled. Prudence picked at her plate, eating the greens dressed with sunflower oil and a bite of mashed squash, but avoiding the mushroom-tamari sauce and the stewed kidney beans. My father-in-law simply insisted he wasn't hungry, which would have been easier to believe if his stomach hadn't rumbled through the entire meal.

"So," my mother said, smiling brightly at Blake, "how did you and Margie celebrate your anniversary?"

"He cooked me dinner the other night," I said. "Pork tenderloin," I added in a low voice, so as not to offend the neighboring vegans. "It was great."

"What? No oysters?" My father-in-law nudged my husband, who forced a smile. "Maybe we should take the kids while you two have a romantic weekend!"

Romantic weekend? I felt my face flame. The last thing I wanted to do was spend a whole two days with just Blake. Though if we never spent any time together, how was our marriage going to survive until the kids grew up? My heart ached as I looked over at Elsie and Nick. I wondered, was it the right thing to keep our marriage going, for their sake? Even if it meant I was married to a man who couldn't love me back?

"Or I can watch them while I'm in town!" my mother suggested, taking a swig of twig tea.

"No," Blake and I barked in unison. The kids looked up, startled.

"I mean, I've got a business function this week," Blake said. "But I'm sure Margie would appreciate your help while I'm away."

"What kind of meeting?" Phil asked, leaning forward.

"It's a . . . networking event," he said.

"It would be great if you could help out while he's gone, Mom," I said quickly. "I've got lots of cases I'm working on."

"Speaking of cases," my mother said, her earrings jingling as she turned to me, "did you ever get that pig?"

"Not yet," I said. Although I welcomed the change of subject, I couldn't help regretting that I'd told her about my most recent assignment. "It was . . . a little bigger than I was led to believe."

"What pig?" Prudence asked.

"It's confidential," I said, and turned to my husband, who was looking at something behind Elsie. He jerked his eyes away when I said his name. My eyes followed his to the young man who was bending down at the waist to pick up one of the kidney beans Nick had launched.

"Well, then," Prudence said. "I think we're about done here, don't you?"

I looked around at my family. All the plates but my mother's were still full, but no one was holding a fork. "Looks like it," I said, gathering my purse.

"But what about dessert?" my mother said.

I glanced at the bakery case. Sugar-free date-walnut pie and coconut-avocado custard. "I think we're good, Mom."

"Wasn't dinner delicious?" my mother asked. "It's amazing what they can do with a pot of beans."

Nick began making retching noises, but I shushed him. "Thanks so much for coming to join us," I said, giving each of my in-laws a polite hug. "We'll see you soon, I hope!"

"Next time we're going to Austin Land and Cattle," Phil said, and glanced at his watch. "In fact, how late are they open?"

"Phil," Prudence said in a stern voice. Although my father-in-law was usually mild-mannered, something about my mother's caftans and patchouli scent seemed to bring out his inner troglodyte.

"See you at home, Blake," I said, heading toward the van with my mother and two hungry children in my wake.

CHAPTER EIGHTEEN

I never thought I'd be anxious to head out for a second encounter with Bubba Sue, but compared to an awkward evening at home with Blake, my mother, and two underfed children, wallowing in the mud with an angry sow sounded like a spa getaway. By the time 8:45 rolled around, I'd cut up apples for both kids, snuck them each a package of contraband Goldfish, read *Thomas the Tank Engine's Big Lift* three times, supervised toothbrushing, and played two games of fetch with Elsie in an attempt to get her to forget the fry phone, which she'd started asking for when we were halfway home from dinner. When I emerged from the back of the house, leaving a bouncing four-year-old and an inconsolable six-year-old behind me, Blake was on his back under the TV trying to get it re-hooked-up, and my mother was moving the battered recliner back and forth across the living room in six-inch increments, trying to maximize the room's "chi."

"I have to go out," I announced, grabbing the car keys and half running toward the door, clutching the diaper bag. My plan was to retrieve the fry phone, then take my Holy Oaks contraband over to

Becky's house. I hadn't had a moment to look at the files since I'd left the school that afternoon.

"So soon?" my mom said. "I was hoping we could have a nice chat over a cup of tea."

"Maybe tomorrow," I said. "I feel terrible that I've hardly been around since you got here, but things have been really crazy." I did feel horrible abandoning my mother when she'd been so sweet to come and visit, but I knew I needed to help Becky out of the mess I'd gotten her into. "I have a really big job."

"Is it that pig?" my mother asked.

"Sort of," I said, realizing I was so focused on the fry phone, I'd forgotten I was supposed to get the pig, too. I made a mental note to grab some rope and Google *hog-tying*. "Don't wait up," I said. "I may be late."

"I understand. I've got it under control, but I still worry about you."

"I know," I said, giving her a kiss on the top of the head. "Thank you."

"Stay safe, honey," my mother called, squeezing my hand before I headed for the door.

It was just after nine when I cruised past Bubba Sue's house. The streetlight showed a beaten-up Range Rover parked in the driveway, and there was a light on in the house. Not ideal, but I still hadn't recovered from yesterday's late night, so I wasn't going to wait for the client's ex-husband to go to bed. I wasn't interested in Bubba Sue tonight, anyway; I'd have to figure out hog-tying before I made another go at her. All I wanted was Elsie's fry phone.

Assuming Bubba Sue hadn't eaten it.

I parked the minivan, slipped my keys and phone into a secure, buttoned back pocket, and headed toward the little house. I glanced around, thankful that the street was deserted, and darted across the darkened yard to the gate.

There was no grunting this time. There was also no sound of plastic being battered against hard surfaces, so I assumed Bubba Sue had gotten out of the cat carrier. And, thankfully, there was no snuffling sound. I hoped Bubba Sue might be inside with her owner—or at least asleep in a pig house somewhere.

I lifted the latch as quietly as I could and pulled up on the gate, holding my breath and praying no one heard the slight squeak of the hinges. When it was open enough for me to squeeze through, I scanned the dark side yard, listening for pig noises. It was quiet, which was good, but it was also so dark I couldn't see anything.

I squeezed in through the gate toward the location I'd last seen the fry phone, then started feeling around with a sneakered foot. I found the bottom half of the cat carrier and the metal door, but there was no sign of anything resembling a French-fry phone. After about a minute and a half of feeling around with my feet, I unbuttoned my back pocket and pulled out my real phone, switching it to the flashlight app.

Although I'd hoped the red plastic fry phone would be lying right where it had fallen, it was nowhere to be seen, although the cat carrier—or what was left of it—was strewn all over the side yard. Could I write off a cat carrier as an expense? I wondered as I grabbed a stick and probed at the ground, hoping the fry phone had just been buried by Bubba Sue's efforts to shred the carrier. After five minutes of searching, I started losing hope. Had she carried it to another part of the yard? Or—God forbid—eaten it?

I inched down the side yard, scanning the ground as I walked, until I reached the edge of the house.

Finally, just as I was about to give up, I saw a bit of something red reflecting the flickering blue TV light from the back windows. I squinted my eyes; it looked the right size, and I could even make out a bit of yellow that might be the French-fry antenna.

Unfortunately, I could also make out Bubba Sue. Her substantial body was lying a few feet from the fry phone, stretched out in a pile of muck she seemed to have fashioned into a sort of earth mattress. Her dirt-streaked side rose and fell slowly; she appeared to be asleep.

I slipped my cell phone into my pocket and took a deep breath, then tiptoed toward the fry phone, glancing back and forth between the house and Bubba Sue. I could see the TV flickering from somewhere inside the house, but the windows were so dirty I couldn't see much else.

Hope flared in me as I closed on my target. I could identify it now; the familiar, if dirty, golden arches on the front, the blue buttons . . . it was almost in reach, even if it was covered in pig manure. I was within two steps of it when my right pocket lit up, blaring "It's a Small World After All," and Bubba Sue woke up.

• • •

We both froze; my eyes locked onto Bubba Sue's beady ones. Until I reached for my pocket to turn off my phone, and the movement jolted her into action.

Bubba Sue rose to her piggy feet with a wavelike motion, then let out a squeal that sounded like someone was skewering her alive. Which, to be honest, would have been okay with me right then.

As she rounded on me, a floodlight flicked on behind me, giving me a full view of her 150-pound porcine frame. From behind me, I could hear the sound of the glass door sliding open, and a man calling, "Bubba Sue, baby?"

The sound of her name galvanized her. As I sprinted toward the gate, she barreled after me, squealing with every step. I considered opening the gate, then glanced back and changed my mind; her open mouth was only two feet from the backs of my knees. In a stunning reprise of the afternoon's gymnastic feat, I leaped onto the fence, clawing at the top and attempting to hurl myself over it. Sharp teeth grazed my ankles, and I jerked my leg away, yelping.

"Bubba Sue! Where are you, girl?" I looked over my shoulder to see a man silhouetted in the floodlit yard.

He was carrying what looked like a shotgun, and I heard the distinctive sound of a gun being cocked.

"Shit," I whispered as I slung my leg over the fence and fell into the bushes on the other side.

I hadn't gotten out of the yard before my phone rang. The problem was, it was on the other side of the fence, which, from the sound of it, Bubba Sue was now battering with her piggy snout. I felt in my pocket, but I already knew it was gone.

As my fingers closed around my keys—thank God those were still there—there was a grunting sound, and then the sound of "Small World" became oddly muffled before fading away. I swore under my breath as I trotted to my dented Grand Caravan.

Unless I was mistaken, Bubba Sue had just swallowed my iPhone.

CHAPTER NINETEEN

I t was almost ten when I pulled up outside Becky's house.

"Do you have tequila?" I asked when she opened the door. She looked much better; her cheeks were their customary cherry-blossom pink again, and she'd traded in the T-shirt for a linen blouse.

"Of course," she said, looking me over. I glanced down at myself. Becky might be looking better, but I had taken a definite turn for the worse. My shorts were streaked with a suspicious-smelling brown substance, and my socks—I'd bagged my sneakers and tossed them into the back of the minivan—were equally filthy. "I got the kids down a half hour ago, so it's just the two of us," Becky told me, wrinkling her nose. "What happened to you?"

"I tried to get Elsie's fry phone back from Bubba Sue."

"How did that go?" she asked as I peeled off my socks in the front hall and followed her to the kitchen, where she wet a paper towel for me and pulled a bottle out of the under-sink cabinet.

I sighed as I dabbed at my shorts. "She ate my iPhone."

Becky almost dropped the bottle of tequila. "She what?"

"It fell out of my pocket as I was climbing over the fence. I saw the fry phone, and I almost got to it, but my phone rang just as I was reaching for it . . ." I waved my hands. "She woke up and started squealing. It was a nightmare. Then the guy came out of the house with a shotgun, and . . ." I let out a long burst of air. "It's been a day."

"No kidding." She poured me a juice glass full of Cuervo, then a smaller shot for herself. "What are you going to do?" she asked after I'd taken a burning swig of the stuff.

"I'm going to tranquilize her," I said. "I'm not sure how—Benadryl, maybe?" I sighed. "At least the phone was in a waterproof case."

"Do you think that will stand up to a pig's digestive system?"

"Here's hoping," I said, and downed the rest of what was in the juice glass. "I'm more worried about the fry phone. I can replace an iPhone, at least." The last time I'd lost Elsie's fry phone, I'd scoured the Internet for a replacement and come up empty; apparently the French-fry phone had only been included in Happy Meals for about twenty minutes a few years back. I pushed thoughts of Elsie's disappointment from my head. Staying out of jail, after all, was my first priority. "Now," I said, feeling like the lining of my esophagus had been sanded off, "let's take a look at Aquaman's mail."

I opened the diaper bag and pulled out the stack of files and mail.

"What's this?" she asked, reaching for the folder with *Hale* printed on the tab. She opened it, and as she read the note about financial aid, her mouth turned to a thin line. "She aced the tests. I know she did." She flipped through the pages to the admissions test. She was right: Zoe had scored above the ninety-fifth percentile in every category. "Even the interview went well," she said, stabbing a manicured finger at the page. "See what I mean? The only reason she was denied was that we requested financial aid. Where's the Graves file?"

As she pawed through the files, I reflected that it was a good thing Detective Bunsen couldn't see Becky right now. If George Cavendish hadn't already had a bullet in his back, I was pretty sure Becky would have happily strangled him. She located the file and ripped it open. "See?" she said, pointing to Ashley Graves's test scores. "Fifteenth percentile in math. Fifteenth! And none of the rest of them are above the fiftieth percentile."

"Maybe the interview . . ."

She flipped to the handwritten page. "'Polite. Shy. Plays with her hair a lot.'" Becky turned another page. "Aha!" she said. "They did deny her admission. But here's a letter from Leonard Graves offering a 'generous donation for the fine-arts building.'"

"How generous?" I asked.

She blinked. "A million dollars," she said.

"Hard to turn that down," I pointed out. "A million dollars goes a long way toward remedial tutoring."

Her jaw set. "But it's not right," she said. "Why deny my daughter the opportunity for a great education just because this mediocre—no," she said, flipping through the pages, "*substandard* kid is loaded?"

"I don't know. I'm beginning to think Elsie might be better off at Austin Heights with Zoe, to be honest," I said.

"What do you mean?"

"Never mind," I told her as I dabbed at an aromatic brown stain on my shorts. There was no point going into it now. Besides, it was only the first day of school; what did I know? Elsie might turn things around and make loads of school friends. And stop playing fetch with tennis balls. And forget about her missing fry phone. I tossed the damp paper towel into the trash and turned to my friend. "Do you have a teakettle so I can steam open the envelopes?"

"The kettle's in the cabinet under the stove," Becky said, still engrossed in the Graves file. "Look at this," she said, stabbing at a page with her finger. "She can't even spell *read*. I can't believe they passed over my daughter for this kid." As I retrieved the kettle and filled it with water, it occurred to me Peaches's disgruntled-mother theory might be worth considering.

"What about the Krumbacher file?" I asked. "Anything in there?"

My friend was still obsessing over the Graves file. "'Hobbies include manicures and spa visits' . . . Really?"

"Becky!"

She looked up, startled. "What?"

"We're trying to find a murderer, not analyze the admissions committee's standards," I reminded her. "Check out the Goldens and the Krumbachers."

"Oh," she said, reluctantly closing up the file and setting it aside. "Right. What am I looking for?"

"I don't know," I confessed.

"That's helpful." She picked up the files and leafed through them. "Neither family asked for financial aid," she said.

"Did they both make donations?" I asked.

"Yup," she said. "Although they don't say how much."

I didn't bother asking about the test scores.

I returned to the table and glanced through the files. Becky was right; there wasn't anything superhelpful in them. Those kids' test scores weren't as bad as the Graves kid's, they were reasonable, and I saw nothing to indicate a motive for killing George Cavendish. The kettle whistled as I pushed the files aside and reached for the stack of mail.

"Ready?" I asked Becky.

"Which one should we do first?" she asked.

"How about this one?" I asked, picking up a linen envelope addressed in a jagged hand. "No return address."

"Let's have some more tequila first," she said. "I hate to break federal laws sober."

• • •

Both Blake and my mother were sitting at the kitchen table when I walked in two hours later, still musing over what we'd found in

Cavendish's mail and regretting the large shot of tequila. It had taken forever for the liquor to wear off enough for me to drive home, and my throat felt as if I'd spent the day practicing a fire-eating routine. Now that I thought of it, maybe running off to the circus might be a good second career option.

Blake's hand cradled a glass of scotch, and my mother was drinking something minty-smelling out of a mug. When my mother saw me, her bangled hand leaped to her throat. "Margie! Where have you been?"

"And what happened to your clothes?" Blake asked, staring with distaste at my blotched shorts. It had not been a good week for my wardrobe.

"I had another go at the pig," I told them, setting the diaper bag with its contraband contents on the kitchen counter. "Why are you both still up? Is everyone okay?"

"You tell me," Blake said, taking another swig of his scotch. "The police called—that Detective Bunsen again. He wants to talk to you about Becky and the headmaster of Holy Oaks."

"They tried your cell phone, but you didn't answer," my mother added helpfully.

"I was busy," I said, feeling my stomach tighten. It was probably Bunsen's call that woke up Bubba Sue. What did he want? Had they found something else—something that tied me to the body? Had I left my fingerprint on Becky's card?

"You never mentioned that the headmaster was murdered," Blake said.

"It didn't seem like a terrific topic for dinner conversation," I pointed out. "Especially with the kids there."

"Poor man," my mother murmured. "On the other hand, maybe being murdered paid his karmic debt."

I doubted Becky would agree with her.

"Why are the cops asking about Becky?"

Despite my tequila-scorched esophagus, I poured myself a bit of Blake's scotch. "They found Becky's business card on him."

He blinked. "They what?"

"Relax," I said, taking a swig of scotch and trying not to choke. "She didn't kill him."

"Well, that's a relief," my husband said.

"He must have had lots of business cards on him," my mother said. "Why are they singling your friend out?"

"It's probably just a routine questioning," I lied.

"Then why are they calling you at night?"

I sighed. "You know how busy the police are these days; Bunsen's probably working overtime. I'll give them a call tomorrow." Then I smiled and changed the subject. "How are the kids?"

"Elsie's waiting for her fry phone," Blake told me.

"I, uh, didn't get a chance to pick it up," I said, remembering Bubba Sue's beady eyes. I was going to have to pick up a new cell phone tomorrow, which was going to put another dent in my budget. It was a shame French-fry phones weren't so easy to come by. "Anyway"—I faked a yawn—"I'm going to head to bed." I escaped, scotch in hand, and managed to be faking sleep by the time Blake came to the bedroom a half hour later.

Unfortunately, it didn't make a difference.

"Margie," he hissed. When I didn't respond, he poked me. "Margie!"

I heaved a sigh and sat up, squinting at him over the pillow wall I'd erected in the middle of the bed. "What?"

"Why are the police really calling you?"

"I told you," I said, "it was because the headmaster had Becky's card on him when he died." I pushed my hair out of my eyes. "She must have given it to him when they were interviewing at Holy Oaks."

"Why are they calling *you*, then?"

The same question had occurred to me, but I didn't tell Blake that. "I don't know. I'll call him in the morning. I'm sure it's nothing, though."

"Is that why you were out so late?" he asked.

"I was chasing the pig," I told him.

"For two hours?"

"It took a long time for the house's owner to go to bed."

"Isn't pignapping illegal?"

"He stole the pig from his ex-wife. Technically, I'm retrieving stolen property." Being married to a lawyer could be irritating sometimes. "Since when is it your business where I am when I go out, anyway?" I asked. "If I recall correctly, it wasn't me who was off gallivanting with other men. Besides," I pointed out, "I wasn't exactly dressed for a night out on the town."

"I'm sorry," Blake said, looking embarrassed. "I didn't mean to suggest that. It's just . . . It's upsetting when the police call at night. And then I couldn't reach you on your cell phone." He paused. "Where is your phone, by the way?"

"I . . . dropped it."

"It's broken?"

"Sort of," I said.

"If you give it to me, I can take it to the guy who fixed mine," he suggested.

"When I get it back, I will."

"What do you mean?"

"Well . . ." I took a deep breath. "I think the pig ate it."

"The pig ate it?"

"Yup. Like I said, when I get it back, you can take it to the repair guy. Hopefully he has some experience dealing with digestive juices."

My husband stared at me.

"Anyway," I said, pulling the sheet up around me and changing the subject, "are you packed for your retreat?"

"Digestive juices?" he repeated.

I sighed and turned over. "We'll talk about it in the morning. I didn't get much sleep last night."

"Why not?"

Because I was moving the dead headmaster out of a hooker's apartment, I thought. "I was worried about Elsie," I said. "I'm not sure Holy Oaks is the right place for her."

"She'll do fine," he said. "I learned to fit in at Catholic school."

And it worked so well in the long haul, I thought, thinking of our sham of a marriage. "We'll talk about it tomorrow," I said.

"I'm leaving for the retreat tomorrow."

"Well, then, when you get back," I said, faking a yawn. "Good night."

CHAPTER TWENTY

My mother was in full force the next morning, offering up a tofu-kale scramble that even I couldn't choke down without gagging. Nick was cheerful and ready to go, but Elsie spent the morning walking around in a pink nightgown, clutching her dog collar to her chest and refusing to speak or get dressed.

"Why don't you want to go to school?" Nick asked her as he poked at the brownish-green mass on his plate.

"The girls aren't nice," she said, turning the collar over in her hands.

I perked up, glad to hear words instead of barking. She'd barely spoken since I picked her up the day before. "Who isn't nice?"

"People," she growled, and pushed her plate away.

"Don't you want some of your omelet?" my mother crooned. Today she was wearing a pink caftan-like thing with strings of crystals that clacked together when she moved. Blake, thankfully, had packed and left early for his retreat, but I could tell by the way my mother was eyeing me that she wanted to talk about something. Maybe it was just the kids' nutrition.

"No omelet," Nick said, pushing out his lower lip. "It looks like dog poop."

I couldn't contradict him, so I just picked up the plates and reached for my coffee, which I'd had to doctor with soy milk and stevia. I took a sip, then put it down and added a trip to Starbucks to my list of morning errands.

"Margie, I was thinking of picking up some wooden toys for the kids," my mother began. "There are so many chemicals in plastic."

"Maybe for birthdays?" I suggested, looking at the living room, which was littered with Thomas trains and dog leashes and had been rearranged so that it was impossible to see the television without sitting in the hallway. "Things are pretty crowded in here right now as it is." I turned to the kids. "Why don't we get going?" I suggested, bundling Elsie's uniform under my arm.

"But they haven't eaten a thing," my mother protested. "And what about lunch?"

"I'll pick something up," I said airily. "Let's go, kids!"

Elsie pushed out her lower lip. "No."

I squatted down and smoothed her dark hair out of her eyes. "Honey, we have to go to school."

"Not going."

"Did something happen yesterday?" I asked. She crossed her arms and turned away.

"I'll take her to school," my mother volunteered. "We can stop and pick up something for lunch on the way. Would you like that?" she asked Elsie.

My daughter turned toward her and nodded.

I hesitated. What about lunch? There was no way Elsie was going to eat the dried seaweed snacks my mother had tried to tempt her with. "Thanks," I said, handing my mother the jumper. "But—and I know your feelings about processed foods—would you please make her a peanut-butter-and-jelly sandwich?"

My mother heaved a sigh.

"Please? I'm willing to think about making some changes, but today, I need her to eat something."

"I guess I can pull something out of the bags I haven't taken to the food bank yet . . ."

"Thank you," I said, relieved. "We'll talk about nutrition later." I kissed my daughter on the head and hurried Nick out to the minivan, glad to have avoided a showdown with Elsie. Maybe today would go better for her. I hoped so, anyway. "Please remind her to take her dog collar off!" I called over my shoulder.

"I'll take care of it," my mother said as the door to the garage closed behind me.

• • •

I got to the Pretty Kitten around nine, after dropping Nick off and stopping for a Starbucks coffee and a gluten- and sugar-filled chocolate muffin. I still hadn't gotten around to calling Bunsen yet, and since, as far as I knew, my iPhone was still lodged in Bubba Sue's intestines, there was no way to know if he'd left a message.

Peaches was on the phone when I walked into the office. I popped the last bit of muffin into my mouth and sat down across from her.

"I'll have her call when she gets here," she was saying, adjusting her stretchy top and eyeing me.

The muffin stuck in my throat. I took a big swig of coffee to wash it down and nearly choked. "Who was that?" I wheezed when Peaches hung up.

"Your buddy down at the police station," she said. "You're not returning your phone calls."

"I can't. Bubba Sue ate my phone," I said, still coughing.

Peaches blinked, and her eyelashes stuck together. She was wearing makeup today, I noticed, and had upgraded to a slinky pink spandex dress that hugged her curves. Things must be looking up for her. Which made one of us. "Bubba Sue what?" my boss asked.

"She ate my phone," I repeated. "And that pig is not teacup-size. She's the size of a refrigerator, and she's mean. I was out there three times yesterday, and so far I'm down a fry phone, an iPhone, and a cat carrier."

"She ate the cat carrier, too?"

"No. She got her head stuck in it and bashed it to pieces against the fence."

Peaches winced. "What happened to the fry phone?"

"The fry phone still seems to be intact, but I can't get to it without being charged by a giant pig."

"Ouch. How'd Elsie take it?"

"She doesn't know," I said. "I told her I left it at the office; I'm just praying I can figure out how to get it back."

"Well, at least nobody saw you."

I sighed. "Actually . . . that's not entirely true."

Peaches stared at me.

"Bunsen called when I was in the backyard last night. The ringer woke up Bubba Sue, and she started squealing, and the guy came out into the yard with a shotgun," I told her grimly. "If you could research pig tranquilizers, that'd be great."

"Maybe a bottle of Benadryl in a cupcake?" she suggested.

"I want to knock her out, not kill her," I reminded Peaches. "Besides, she's pregnant—too many drugs would be bad for the piglets."

"You're worried about the piglets?"

"She's a mom," I said. "A bitchy mom, but she's still a mom." I took another sip of coffee. "Oh, and I told Becky what we did."

"Jesus H. Christ, Margie." Peaches rocked back in her chair. "What happened to our deal?"

"I couldn't lie to my best friend. If she went to jail because I made a mistake and didn't tell her what I'd done, I'd never sleep again."

"You're killing me." Peaches reached in her pink dress for her e-cigarette and took a deep drag. "What the hell happened to the 'one week' thing?"

"We've still got a week. Becky's okay with it. In fact, she helped me steam open Cavendish's mail last night."

"You steamed his mail open?" Her eyes glinted. "You're a quick study, girl. But I wouldn't mention that to Detective Bunsen."

"I wasn't planning on it."

"Maybe it's a good thing Bubba Sue ate your phone. What did you find out?"

"Holy Oaks has a ton of money invested in a firm that belongs to one of the board members," I told her, "and the investment returns are like fifty percent a year."

Peaches grabbed a pen. "What's the name of the company?"

"Golden Investments," I told her. "Their biggest holding is something called Spectrum Properties, according to what the statement says."

She jotted the names down. "I'll see what I can find out. Anything else?"

"A letter from an admissions office, and an angry note from a mom who paid big bucks for the Acorn Scholars program and didn't get her kid into the school of his choice. She wanted a refund."

"See? I told you we should look at the parents," Peaches said sagely. "Maybe you can go interview her after we talk to Desiree."

"When are we meeting with her, anyway?" I asked.

She glanced at her watch. "We're supposed to meet her at a coffeehouse near campus in half an hour."

"We should head out, then."

"I'll drive this time," she said. I eyed her critically; she didn't look as if she'd had anything to drink that morning. In fact, she was looking pretty chirpy, which was a nice change of pace.

"How are things with Jess?" I asked.

"No change," she said, "but I'm meeting a guy from Honkytonk Honeys.com for lunch."

"You've got to be kidding me."

"He's cute. Blond hair, blue eyes, looks good in a western-style shirt, loves to go dancing . . ."

"Sounds a lot like Jess," I said. "You should call him, you know."

She scowled at me and grabbed her purse. "You might want to figure out your marriage to Mr. Twinkle Toes before you start dishing out the relationship advice."

I sighed and followed her out to the Buick, wincing as a woman shrieked next door.

CHAPTER TWENTY-ONE

Desiree looked completely different without the dog collar.

When we walked into the Coffee Bean she was sitting at a table in the corner, looking about twelve years old. Her blonde hair was pulled back into a ponytail, she wore a pink T-shirt with khaki shorts, and an enormous textbook was open on the table in front of her.

"Can we get you a coffee?" Peaches asked as she pulled up a chair next to her.

Desiree darted us a nervous smile and pointed at her iced tea. "No, thanks," she said, and I was guessing from the expression on her face that she regretted agreeing to talk to us. I could see why; we were the oldest people in the coffee shop by about twenty years, and Peaches's tight pink dress wasn't what you'd call inconspicuous.

"Margie?" Peaches asked.

"Just a small coffee," I said, and Peaches lumbered off to flirt with the barista.

"What are you working on?" I asked Desiree.

"Cognitive psychology," she grimaced. "I've got an exam tomorrow."

"Is psychology your major?"

"Yes, but I'm kind of leaning toward interior design. I might do a masters in it."

"You've got a knack for design, but I'll bet psychology comes in handy in your . . ." I almost said "profession," but ended with "line of work."

"Not really," she said, turning slightly pink. Dominatrix by night, shy sorority girl by day; it was an interesting combination. "Most of them just want someone to listen to them," she continued. "If you just nod and sound sympathetic, they keep coming back for more. I've got a lot of regulars."

"Did . . . Mr. Cavendish talk much?" I asked.

Her brow wrinkled. "Who?"

"Aquaman," I prompted.

"Oh. Yeah, right. I keep forgetting his real name." She chewed on the end of her pen with pearl-white teeth. "He talked a lot, but I didn't pay too much attention. They all complain about their wives."

"What did he say about his wife?"

"The same as the rest of them. Didn't ever have the time to listen, too busy with her book club and her running group to pay attention to him, wore granny panties to bed. Just like every other married woman in Austin." As she took another sip, I did a personal inventory. I had to own up to granny panties, but I'd never belonged to either a book club or a running club. It was true that I'd been a bit preoccupied with the kids the past few years, but considering my husband's sexual proclivities, I doubted even a dog collar and bustier would get things going in the bedroom again. Desiree let out a small, superior sigh. "If I ever get married, I'll know what to do, that's for sure."

I stifled both a snort and the urge to tell her to call me in ten years. Instead, I said, "How did you and . . . Aquaman . . . meet up, anyway?"

"I used to work at a strip club," she said. "He was a regular, and when I started doing private work, he was one of my first clients."

"Which strip club?" I asked.

"It's called the Sweet Shop, over by the old airport."

"That's how we got to be friends," Peaches said, sashaying back to the table after placing her order. "I met her when I was in for the strip steak a few months ago, and she agreed to do some work for me. She's an awesome honeypot."

I felt my own cheeks turn a little pink as I remembered the time Peaches had tried to get me to be a honeypot—a woman who lures a straying man to cheat. The guy I was trying to lure turned out to be gay, and I'd accidentally ended up participating in a drag-queen contest. It hadn't been one of my better days.

"Do you know Marty Krumbacher?" I asked, anxious to change the subject.

"Oh, I know Marty, all right," she said. "He was a client for a while."

"Really?" Peaches asked, leaning forward.

"He was big into domination. He was really into those leather collars, and the ball gags."

Ball gags? Peaches and I exchanged glances. Mitzi would have loved to know that, but since we were no longer working for her, there was no reason to tell her. Even though I did feel a stab of pity for her. No woman wants to find out her husband is sleeping with another woman. Or man. Particularly when there are ball gags involved. "Was he a regular at the Sweet Shop?" I asked.

"I think he was a part owner of the place, or something. He was always with the manager. They'd have meetings in the back room, without any of the girls."

I remembered the meeting I'd seen at the Sweet Shop a few days ago. "What was he involved in?"

"There were a bunch of shipments coming into the place," she said. "There's a storage room in the back; there'd be big deliveries a few times a week."

"Did Cavendish say anything about his job?" I asked.

Her smooth brow furrowed. "I think so," she said. "Something was bothering him. Some investment thing."

"Did he mention what the trouble was?"

She gave the pen another nibble. "He wanted to get out of it, but he couldn't. He was having some kind of moral crisis."

Which was ironic, I thought, considering he was confessing to a prostitute. "Why?"

"There was something wrong with it. I'm not sure what."

"Why couldn't he get out of it?"

"Something about a board," she told me, shrugging. "I wasn't really paying attention." She reached for her iced tea and tucked the straw into her mouth as Peaches retrieved our drinks from the bar—a small mug of coffee for me and a giant milkshake-like drink for herself.

Peaches sat down again and crossed her legs, which made her skirt ride up another few inches. I resisted the urge to tug it down for her. "So," she said, looking at Desiree. "Did he mention anything else he was worried about? His wife, maybe?"

"He did mention a woman he'd been sleeping with."

"Oh, yeah?" Peaches said. "What'd he say?"

"He was having second thoughts about her, too. He'd done her a favor, but wanted to back out." She sipped her tea. "Said it was too late, though."

"Too late for what?"

"I don't know. I put the pacifier in, and that was, like, the end of the conversation."

I blinked. "A pacifier?"

She shrugged. "Only on his bad-baby days."

"Bad-baby days," Peaches repeated.

"Oh, yes. I had to put him in time-out a lot. I always kept a box of Depends for him."

Peaches let out a long, low whistle.

I chose not to find out more about bad-baby days. "So he didn't mention a name?"

"He did, now that you mention it. Something flowery. Lily? Rose?" She shrugged. "I don't remember."

"What was the favor?" I asked as Peaches sucked on her straw.

"He didn't say." She sipped her tea again and let out a long sigh. "I still can't believe he died in my apartment—it's been a really shitty week. First that, now this test tomorrow." She sighed again. "Do they know who killed him yet?"

"No," I said.

"I'm just hoping the cops don't trace him back to me. They would have by now if they could, wouldn't they?" she asked, toying nervously with her straw.

"I don't know," I said, thinking of my deal with Becky. If we didn't find out what had happened soon, Peaches and I were going to have to talk with Detective Bunsen, and the cops were going to know exactly where George Cavendish had been when somebody put a bullet in his back.

"Why are you so interested in his personal life?" the young woman asked, then narrowed her blue eyes. "Did the cops figure out you were involved?"

"They found something of ours at the scene," Peaches said. "We're trying to figure out what happened so we don't have to spill the beans on where it all went down."

Desiree's eyes got big. "You wouldn't tell them where you found the body, would you?"

"We might have to," I said. "Now, are you sure you don't remember anything else?"

"But . . . you promised you'd keep it quiet!"

Peaches shrugged a pink-clad shoulder. "We're working on it," she said. "The more you can tell us, the better the odds we can keep it on the down-low."

"Shit," Desiree said, and bit down hard on her pen. "Let me think. I told you about the investment thing, and the chick named Lily or Rose or whatever."

"Did you see anything unusual that night?" I asked.

"Not really," she said.

"Any cars on the street that were different from what was usually parked outside?" Peaches prompted. "Anyone new walking around the neighborhood?"

"I don't remember anyone," she said, then straightened. "Wait. When I closed the curtains just after John . . . I mean, Cavendish got to my apartment, I noticed there was a car outside I don't usually see."

Peaches leaned forward, almost spilling out of her dress. "What was it?"

"It was a Lexus," she said. "It was bright red; that's what caught my eye."

"What kind?" I asked.

"I don't know," she said. "Not an SUV or anything. Four doors, I think."

"I don't think I saw a Lexus when I got there," Peaches said, and turned to me. "You?"

"Where was it parked?" I asked.

"Behind Cavendish's car."

"I don't remember it. And it wasn't there when we took the . . . pool out of the apartment," I said, glancing around to see if anyone was listening. Best not to mention dead bodies in public places.

"It's worth checking into," Peaches said. "Margie, can you poll the parking lot at the school?"

"I'll look today," I said. "You didn't catch a license-plate number, did you?"

She twirled a lock of blonde hair. "Nope."

"Well, it's something," Peaches said, taking another slug of her coffee-milkshake concoction. "So. We know he was sleeping with someone with a flowery name and having second thoughts about it, and we know he wanted to get out of an investment, but the board didn't want him to jump ship."

"And that a red Lexus was parked outside her apartment before . . . the incident," I added.

"Got anything else?" Peaches asked.

Desiree shrugged. "If I think of anything, I'll call you," she said. "But please . . ." She reached out and grabbed Peaches's hand in an iron grip. "Don't tell the cops what happened. I'm begging you, Peaches."

"We'll do the best we can," Peaches said, trying to wrench her hand out of Desiree's manicured clinch. "Seriously, though, anything you think of—anything at all—you call us. Got it?"

Desiree nodded vigorously as we stood up to leave. Peaches was inspecting her hand for fingernail grooves as we headed toward the door. I glanced back at Desiree. The young woman was still staring at her psychology textbook when we left, but she didn't look like she was taking much in.

• • •

"Poor thing," I said as I pulled the door of the Buick Regal closed behind me. My car smelled like French fries, old chicken nuggets, and now my mother's patchouli oil, so we took Peaches's car whenever we could.

"What? Desiree? Sheesh." Peaches massaged her hand. "That girl's got a hell of a grip."

"I hope she doesn't have to tell her parents about what she's been doing for money," I said. "Maybe this will make her rethink her part-time job."

"It'd be hard to make that kind of money slinging burgers," Peaches said.

"Yeah, but she could get an internship with a designer, and that would be so much better for her career. And she wouldn't have to . . . well, you know."

"Pee on people?"

"Yeah," I said.

"At least we got some good info out of her," Peaches said as we pulled away from the Coffee Bean. "We should probably find out more about that Golden Investments."

"You think that was what Cavendish was talking about—the one the board didn't want to let him out of?"

"That's the one that was making fifty percent annually, right?" she asked.

"And Golden's on the board. That's suspect right there. If Aquaman was getting his panties in a wad about it . . . not that he was wearing panties, but you know what I mean."

"I'll see what I can do," Peaches said.

CHAPTER TWENTY-TWO

B y the time I made it to the front door of Holy Oaks, I'd identified three red Lexuses in the parking lot, but only two sedans. I jotted down the license-plate numbers and left a message for Becky to see if she could pick up Nick for me; I was hoping to hang around Holy Oaks for pickup so I could see how many other red Lexuses belonged to school parents. On the other hand, if the owner of the Lexus outside Desiree's apartment was a parent whose kid had been turned down, they weren't likely to show up in the Holy Oaks parking lot. Honestly, though, would a parent really kill someone for not admitting a child to a school? I was about to dismiss the idea until I remembered Becky's face as she pawed through the admissions files. It was not outside the realm of possibility.

The office was buzzing with people, including Perky Desk Girl. I clutched the diaper bag to my chest; there was no way I was going to be able to slip those files back into their cabinet, much less shove Cavendish's mail back into its cubby. I was still a little worried about the condition of the envelopes—they looked like they'd spent a few weeks in a tropical rainforest—but it couldn't be helped.

After loitering for a moment in the lobby, I headed into the library, slipped an SAT book out of the box behind the desk, and positioned myself with a view of the front-office door. Fortunately, only five minutes passed before a clump of people left the office, their wedges clip-clopping down the hallway. I waited a moment, then stood up and headed for the office door, one hand clutching the mail in the diaper bag, trying to look casual.

I was in luck; even Perky Desk Girl was gone.

All of the doors to the inner offices were closed, including Cavendish's. Although I could hear murmurs from behind one of them, no one was in the main area. I grabbed the mail from the diaper bag and stuffed it into Cavendish's empty mailbox, then opened the file drawer and jammed the files in, not taking the time to put them back in order. I was about to close the drawer when there was a *thunk* behind me. I turned to see the custodian standing at the door, a broom in his hand, watching me. I shoved the drawer shut behind my back. "Hello," I said.

He stared at me with dark, appraising eyes. There was a little scar to the left of his eye, and a corner of a tattoo peeked out from under his T-shirt sleeve. His hands on the broom were enormous, with fingers that reminded me of bratwursts.

"Just doing some filing," I said, giving the filing cabinet an affectionate pat.

The custodian nodded and gave me a long, hard look before drifting away down the hallway. The man gave me the heebie-jeebies. Was it the scar on his face, or just the fact that he'd caught me doing something I shouldn't be doing?

Heart pounding, I hurried toward the office door. I was just about to round the desk when I noticed a set of keys on the corner closest to Perky Desk Girl's chair. I hesitated a moment. Would Cavendish's office key be among them? I grabbed them and shoved them deep into the diaper bag, then headed out the office door, where I almost knocked over Deborah Golden.

"Oh. Sorry about that," I said, clutching the diaper bag to my chest.

Once she regained her balance and registered who I was, Deborah's eyes narrowed; she looked behind me to the empty office. "What are you doing here?"

"I'm, uh, here to volunteer," I said. "Thanks again for hosting the coffee; your house is gorgeous. At any rate," I said with a bright smile, "I'd better get back to the library!" I hurried past her without giving her a chance to ask another question and hoped Perky Desk Girl wouldn't notice her missing keys for a while. I glanced over my shoulder as I slipped through the door to the library; Deborah was glaring at me as if I were a scullery maid who had cracked her favorite hand-painted Moroccan teacup.

I raced back to my spot in the library, where I was idly erasing answer bubbles when the gaggle of office staff reappeared.

Moving dead bodies, stealing mail, and grabbing other people's keys . . . I was turning into a real paragon of virtue, I thought glumly as I stared down at a geometry problem involving six angles and a dotted line. Over the past seventy-two hours, I had broken a number of laws.

What kind of example was I setting for my children?

Before I'd had Elsie, I'd envisioned a Pottery Barn Kids childhood for my children, with tidy, attractively decorated bedrooms, regular snack times, and myself hovering somewhere in the background, wearing stylish clothes in single-digit sizes and holding a tray of organic milk, homegrown carrot sticks, and whole-grain, date-sweetened oatmeal cookies. My (straight) husband would be watching admiringly as our spotless, white-clad children finger-painted a family portrait, with our beautifully decorated and remodeled house in the background.

Dead bodies and husbands sleeping with transvestites hadn't entered into the picture at all.

I looked down and stared at an algebra problem. I was doing the best I could, considering the situation, I told myself. It would be a disaster for my kids if I ended up in jail. And I hadn't murdered anyone;

I had just been trying to help a college student stay out of trouble. So what if she was a college student with a fully equipped dungeon in her apartment? She was still following her dream.

Unfortunately, I doubted Detective Bunsen would see it that way.

I turned a page in the SAT book and erased another mark, acutely aware of the purloined keys in my diaper bag. If Perky Desk Girl hadn't discovered their disappearance yet, she'd certainly figure it out when she wanted to go home. Would Deborah Golden tell her I'd been in the office? And what was I going to do about Detective Bunsen?

I flipped to the next page and wondered how many messages he'd left. The more I thought about it, the happier I was that Bubba Sue had eaten my phone. At least I had a good excuse for not getting back in touch with Detective Bunsen.

"Oh, there you are." I looked up: it was Kathleen Gardner.

"Hi," I said weakly.

"Did you hear about Mr. Cavendish?" she asked. "Such a tragedy . . . I'm guessing he worked too hard and had a heart attack."

"Mmm," I said.

"The memorial service is tomorrow," Kathleen said.

"Where?" I asked.

"At Saint John's Catholic Church," she said. "I hope there's enough room for everyone."

"I heard a rumor it wasn't a heart attack," I said. I was guessing Kathleen wasn't in on the gossip circuit, but she was more familiar with Holy Oaks than I was; maybe she knew something that would help me figure out who had killed him. "The police were here the other day."

She blinked at me. "Don't you think that was just routine?"

"I don't know. You don't know of anyone who might have wished him ill?" I asked.

"Well, of course there are all the parents of children who didn't make the cut," Kathleen said. "Holy Oaks is a very competitive school."

"Unless you have money," I said lightly.

"Oh, no," Kathleen said. "The admissions process is entirely based on merit."

"You don't think the fundraising campaign might affect who gets in?" I asked. "Somebody's got to pay for the new squash courts."

"I seriously doubt it," Kathleen said. "Holy Oaks is all about caring and doing the right thing. And academic excellence, of course." She looked at me. "Have you given any more thought to the Girl Scouts?"

I gave her a strained smile. "I have to talk with Elsie about it."

A shadow passed over Kathleen's face. "Your daughter is quite . . . unique, isn't she? Not very socially integrated, it seems to me. Still, I'm sure if I had a chance to work with her, I could make some progress . . ."

I could feel my hackles rise. "What do you mean?"

"Well, Catriona told me she only eats white foods, and that she walks around her chair three times before she sits down. And on the playground . . ."

"What about the playground?"

"Well, I'm sure she's struggling with the adjustment." Kathleen gave me an intent look. "Have you considered having her evaluated?"

"I appreciate your concern, but I'm sure Elsie will be just fine," I said, snapping the SAT book shut. Although my anxiety over Elsie was hitting new all-time highs, I couldn't stand to be in the same room with this woman another moment.

"But—"

"I've got to go," I said, grabbing my bag and heading blindly out of the library. If I hadn't, there was an excellent chance a second homicide case would be opened at Holy Oaks.

CHAPTER TWENTY-THREE

The church parking lot was overfilled when I arrived at Saint John's Catholic Church for George Cavendish's memorial service the next day. I was still brooding over Elsie. She had been uncommunicative the night before, so I hadn't tried to ask about what Kathleen had told me, but I was worried. I had gotten donuts for both kids before school, hoping that starting the day with a little sweetness would help improve their mood. Even though she had the morning off because of the headmaster's funeral, Elsie still growled when I mentioned Holy Oaks.

Now I was cruising around the Saint John's parking lot and looking for Lexuses, but I only spotted one, and it had also been at Holy Oaks. I reminded myself to check with Peaches to see if she'd found out who owned it.

The narthex was stuffed with well-dressed people wearing a smorgasbord of colognes and perfumes. Pulling my pre-pregnancy black cardigan around me—it didn't quite meet in the middle these days, but I was hoping no one would notice—I inched my way over toward the open coffin. I barely avoided running into an earnest Kathleen Gardner, who was regaling another hapless person with her daughter's ballet accomplishments. "She's been asked to do the *Nutcracker*," she was saying as I sidled by, her strawberry-blonde bob bouncing as she spoke. "It's a big sacrifice for her in terms of time—her violin lessons are suffering now that she's only getting an hour a day to practice—but even though her background is in tap, the ballet mistress said the production just wouldn't have that sparkle without her. Besides," she said, "it will look so good on her college application . . ."

Mitzi stood in a corner of the narthex, talking with another woman who was her sartorial twin: they both wore belted black dresses and tall, high-heeled boots. Beside Mitzi was Marty, looking bored in a sober charcoal suit, his short dark hair slicked back. He caught me staring at him, and his mouth quirked up in a half smile. I could feel my cheeks warm, but I responded with my own awkward smile, trying to forget that he'd had a ringside seat as I'd wrestled Peaches away from a cream-covered Banana Twirl just a few days ago, and I looked down—right at the late headmaster.

He looked pretty good for a dead guy. They'd de-goggled him before packing him into the casket, which was a tasteful mahogany, lined with a sober blue silk that matched his pinstriped suit. I found myself looking for goggle marks on his forehead, but the makeup team had erased any dents that might have remained. No sign of blood or urine, either. I tried not to imagine him with a pacifier in his mouth.

"Pretty shocking, isn't it?"

I turned to see Kevin standing behind me. "It is," I said as we moved away from the casket. "Did they ever find out what happened to him?"

"I don't know, but I don't think it was a heart attack," Kevin told me in a low voice. "The police were in the front office this week. There's lots of talk, but nobody's really saying anything." He glanced over his shoulder. "They've already named an interim head."

"Who?"

"Deborah Golden," he said.

I looked over at Deborah Golden, who wore a black sheath dress and almost disappeared when she turned sideways. "But she's a real-estate broker!"

"I know," he said. "I thought it was weird, too. I hope they get someone qualified in there soon. The board's keeping everything really hush-hush right now, though, so there's no way to know."

No wonder, I thought. It wasn't going to help Holy Oaks' reputation if it got out that the former head had been found half-naked and dead in a urine-filled wading pool. If they ever discovered he'd died in a dominatrix's dungeon, Kathleen Gardner would yank her little angel out of Holy Oaks and send her to boarding school—if she didn't succumb to a fit of apoplexy first. As I watched her bear down on another first-grade parent, I briefly toyed with telling her.

"Did you know him well?" I asked.

He shook his head. "No more than anyone else at the school. He was pretty cozy with the board members, but he just glad-handed the rest of us."

"So sad," I said. "His poor wife." I scanned the room, looking for a grieving widow. "Is she here?"

Kevin nodded toward a petite, short-haired woman in a black pant-suit. She looked a little like Nancy Reagan, even down to the little string of pearls, and did not look particularly grief-stricken. Then again, I reflected, some people were like that; grieving looks different for different people. She was surrounded by a throng of mourners. "He didn't have kids, did he?"

"No, it was just the two of them."

"What's his wife's name, again?" I asked, watching her accept a hug from an older man with a cane.

"Cressida."

"She looks like she's holding up okay." Particularly considering the circumstances of her husband's death. Had they told her about the wading pool? Had the Aquaman tights been a surprise? Or had she already known—or seen them when she shot him? I thought about the mysterious red Lexus, and made a mental note to find out what kind of car she drove.

"She's not the dramatic type," Kevin said. "Stiff upper lip and all."

"What does she drive?" I asked, but before he could answer, Kathleen Gardner materialized, looking dour in a black, sack-like dress.

"It's just terrible, isn't it?" she asked. "I just can't think what it'll do for the school's reputation. Catriona was traumatized when I broke the news to her. She's such a sensitive child . . ."

"Did you hear anything about what happened to him?" I asked.

"Just that it was very sudden," she said, glancing over at him. "Oh, look. They even put him in his Holy Oaks tie." I followed her eyes to the coffin. Cherry Nichols, the voluptuous mom of twins, was hovering near the coffin, dabbing at her eyes. Behind her was Cressida Cavendish. Her face went tight for a moment at the sight of Cherry near her late husband, and just for a millisecond, a look of pure venom crossed her features. Then someone touched her arm and the brittle smile was back in place.

Desiree had said Cavendish was having an affair. Was Cherry his lover? Desiree had mentioned his mistress being named after a flower. A cherry wasn't exactly a flower, but a fruit wasn't far off. And if Cressida knew they were having an affair, did she also know what Cavendish had been up to on the night he wound up with a bullet in his back?

"Cherry seems awfully upset about the headmaster's death," I said, nodding toward the curvaceous mother as she sashayed away from the casket, drawing the glances of many of the men.

"They seemed to be good friends," Kathleen said. "It always seemed a bit surprising—I mean, she's hardly the academic type."

"No," Kevin said. "I think she's got other talents."

I glanced at him, my eyebrows rising, and his mouth quirked up into a grin. "Kathleen," he said, pointing to the other side of the narthex. "There's the music teacher. Did you ever touch base with her about Catriona doing a violin solo in the fall musical?"

Kathleen's bobbed head swiveled. "Oooh, there she is. I never did get a chance yesterday; every time I went to talk with her, she somehow disappeared on me." She adjusted the neckline of her dress and turned toward the hapless teacher with a determined look on her face. "I'm going to go talk to her now," she said, and marched off with a sense of purpose that made me pity the poor teacher.

"There's a rumor," Kevin said, leaning down to murmur in my ear, "that Cherry Nichols's kids didn't get in on academic merit."

"You mean . . ."

He nodded. "Someone saw her with Cavendish at the W Hotel this summer," he said.

"Wow," I said, and my heart went out to Cressida Cavendish. The photograph I'd discovered of my husband with another woman still haunted me. Well, with a man dressed as a woman, anyway. I wasn't sure you ever got over something like that. "Does Mrs. Cavendish know—or at least suspect?"

"Did you see the look she shot Cherry a moment ago?"

"Yeah," I said. "So probably she did."

"That's my guess," he said.

Before I could ask another question, the organ started up, and we filed into the sanctuary. I sat down next to Kevin in the back of the room, glancing at the program the usher had given me.

A Celebration of the Life of George Ronald Cavendish, it read, along with a long list of accomplishments. He'd been head at about five Catholic schools, I read, and—at least according to the program—was a man of impeccable morals and strong values. I snort-coughed and looked up, watching as the mourners filed into the church.

The board members were clustered together near the front of the church: the Krumbachers sat next to Deborah Golden, who was accompanied by a tall, spare man with a fringe of white hair around a shiny pate that reminded me of a mottled beach ball. Frank Golden?

It was at least an hour before we all filed out into the narthex again, where a cluster of mourners gathered around Cavendish. I watched Frank Golden from afar. He glanced at his watch several times; after a few minutes, he stepped a few feet back from the casket, where he was joined by Marty.

Kevin had gone to the restroom, so I sidled over to where they stood, a few feet from Cavendish.

"Is everything under control?" Marty asked.

"It is," Golden said. "Is everything clear down at the shop?"

"We've moved most of the boxes out," Krumbacher said. "Do we stop selling it?"

"We'll finish up this shipment and revamp the formulation," Golden said.

"How long do I have?"

Before Golden could answer, Kathleen materialized in front of me like a ghoul at a haunted house. I startled and took a step backward.

"Have you thought more about having your daughter evaluated?" she asked loudly. I pulled away from her and stole a glance at Krumbacher and Golden, both of whom were now staring at me.

"What?" I asked, taking another step back.

"I really think you should. Also, I've been looking for a cookie coordinator, and thought that might be a perfect way for you to support your daughter. It's a big job, but so vital to the troop, and I really think having her mother in such an important position would be a big help to your daughter socially."

"I'll think about it," I told her, looking around for Kevin. "Like I said, I'll talk with Elsie about it."

"Isn't it really the parent's decision?" Kathleen asked. "Children need guidance at this age." She advanced again, like a pit bull who had scented a hot-dog stand. I stepped back another foot, and my hip ran into something hard, making me stumble. My heel turned sideways as I tried to balance, and I instinctively grabbed something to steady myself.

Unfortunately, what I grabbed was the top corner of George Cavendish's casket.

The next five seconds seemed to last about six hours. The casket lurched to the side, and there was a collective intake of breath. I reached out with my other hand, trying to steady the casket, but somehow all that seemed to do was add to the momentum.

The huddle of mourners leaped out of the way as the mahogany coffin crashed down sideways on the green carpet. The lid that had covered the bottom half of George Cavendish sprang open, and he rolled out onto the narthex floor, giving everyone in the church an unobstructed view of his thong-clad buttocks.

There was dead silence for a few moments, with every eye trained on those two pale mounds of flesh. Then there was a strangled cry, and Cressida Cavendish fainted, following her husband to the floor.

CHAPTER TWENTY-FOUR

I t took four of us, including the undertaker, to stuff him back into the coffin. We straightened him up as well as we could—thank God the thong stayed in place—while another group carried Cressida Cavendish and laid her out on a pew. Some of Cavendish's pancake makeup had come off, smudging the carpet, and his mouth had fallen open, giving him a disturbingly vacant look. I tried to push his jaw back into place, but it wouldn't budge, so instead I straightened his tie and stepped back, wishing I could melt into the floor.

An icy silence greeted me as I stepped away from the coffin. I was heading for the front door when Kevin reappeared, looking confused.

"What happened?" he asked.

"I just knocked over the coffin," I mumbled.

Kevin glanced over toward Cavendish. The mourners had not reassembled; either the sight of Cavendish's buttocks had put them off it, or they were afraid the casket might fall over again.

"He was wearing a thong," I added.

Kevin let out something between a laugh and a cough. "You are something else. And I still want to know what was going on with your shorts at the new parent meeting."

"You wouldn't believe me if I told you," I said, glancing over my shoulder. Everyone immediately turned away, as if they weren't staring at me. "I think I'd better go," I said. "When Mrs. Cavendish comes to, will you tell her how sorry I am?"

"Will do," he said as I slipped through the enormous front doors. I'd never in my life been so happy to get out of a church.

On the plus side, I told myself as I climbed into the minivan, at least Kathleen had stopped bugging me about the Girl Scouts.

• • •

My mother had agreed to take Elsie to school for me that afternoon, so I cruised by Bubba Sue's house on the way to the Pretty Kitten, my mind flashing between the horror scene I'd accidentally created at Cavendish's funeral and Elsie's fry phone. *Who the hell puts a corpse in thong underwear?* I wondered as I turned onto South Lamar. Was that one of his "last will and testament" requests? It could have been worse, I told myself. He could have still been wearing Aquaman tights. Still, if Kathleen was right, I hadn't done my daughter any favors in the social department this morning. The least I could do for her was to get the fry phone back.

Unfortunately, the client's ex was mowing the lawn as I drove by. He didn't have a shotgun, but there was a Weedwacker nearby, so I lowered my head and kept driving. Besides, I wasn't exactly dressed for pig wrangling—and I hadn't figured out the whole sedation-and-hog-tying thing, either.

Peaches's Buick wasn't in the parking lot when I pulled up outside the Pretty Kitten. The waxing salon was doing a booming business that morning; the chorus of shrieks and moans reminded me of the haunted-house ride at Disney World.

The answering machine was blinking, but I was afraid to check it; the less I heard from Detective Bunsen, the better. Instead, I sat down at my desk, Googled "sedate pig," and spent the next fifteen minutes trying to estimate Bubba Sue's weight. I didn't want to hurt her, but I didn't want to be gored by an angry teacup pig, either. I was just finishing up my calculations when the door opened and Detective Bunsen walked in.

"Um . . . Hi!" I said.

"You're tough to get in touch with," Bunsen said, hitching up his pants.

"A pig ate my phone," I told him.

"Pardon me?"

"I lost my phone," I said, closing my laptop. If I told him what really happened, I'd sound like an idiot. Besides, I didn't want to be cited for trespassing. Or attempted pignapping. "What can I do for you?" I asked, steepling my hands in an attempt to look cool and professional.

"Your fingerprints turned up on your friend's card," he said. "I was wondering why."

I shrugged, attempting to look nonchalant, although what I was thinking was, *Could this day get any worse?* "I have no idea," I lied.

I gestured for him to take a seat in the plastic visitors' chair. He sat down, and we both pretended to ignore the moaning from next door.

"Where were you on the night Cavendish died?" he asked once the moaning had turned into a whimper.

"At home," I said.

"Do you have anyone who can verify that?"

"It was three in the morning," I said, then resisted the urge to clap a hand to my mouth.

He sat up and leaned forward, looking like a pointing dog who's spotted a wounded pigeon. "What was at three in the morning?"

"I don't know," I said. "Was there something at three in the morning?"

The door opened again, and we both swiveled to look. It was Peaches, resplendent in a zebra-print pantsuit. "New client?" she asked, winking at me.

"This is Detective Bunsen, actually," I said. "Detective Bunsen, Peaches Barlowe."

"I think we've met before. Always a pleasure," she said, extending a plump hand.

Bunsen stood up and shook it. "I couldn't reach your investigator," he told her, "so I thought I'd swing by." In the silence that followed, a loud shriek sounded from next door. Peaches and I both winced involuntarily. "Interesting office space," he remarked.

"We get discounts," Peaches said. "Tell them we sent you, and they'll give you half off."

"I'll be sure to tell my wife," he said.

"They're good with back hair, too," she said. "Just so you know. But I'm guessing you're not here for waxing services." She strode around her desk and slung herself into her chair. "What can we help you with?"

"We found something belonging to one of Ms. Peterson's friends at the scene of George Cavendish's death."

"So you're thinking it's homicide?" I asked.

"That's the working theory," he said. "Considering the circumstances."

"What were the circumstances?" I asked.

"I was hoping you would tell me that," he said while I tried to look innocent.

Peaches crossed her legs. "What was the object in question?"

"A business card," I supplied. "He showed me a copy of it at Starbucks the other morning."

"Whose card?" she asked, looking genuinely interested. It was impressive.

"Becky Hale," Bunsen answered.

"She must have given it to him at some point," I supplied.

"That's one explanation," Bunsen said. "But something tells me it's not the one I'm looking for."

"What happened to him, anyway?" I asked, as if I had no idea he had been killed by a gun while marinating in urine. "He looked pretty good in the casket this morning."

"Again. I was hoping you would tell me that."

I was saved from answering by the sound of gunshots.

Both Peaches and Bunsen hurled themselves under the desk, ending up in a ball of zebra print and khakis. "Get down, Margie!" Peaches hissed, reaching out and yanking at my leg. I fell backward, landing on the floor just as another flurry of gunshots sounded.

As I crouched behind a chair, I heard the click of a gun being cocked, and Bunsen crawled out from under the desk, creeping toward the window. Tires screeched from the parking lot just as he got to the window.

"What's happening?" I asked.

"They're gone," he said.

"Did you get the plates?" Peaches asked.

"No. Not even the make. It was a red car."

"What kind?" I asked.

"Midsize," he said, still peering out the window. "Maybe a Camry, or a Lexus; it turned the corner before I could tell."

"Is everyone okay?"

"No one seems to be hurt," he said, surveying us. "But what kind of car do you drive?"

"A Dodge Caravan," I said.

"I thought so." He stood up, brushing off his khakis, and reached for his phone.

"Why?"

"I hope your tires are still under warranty," he said.

• • •

It wasn't just the tires that were in trouble. We filed outside and stood staring at my perforated minivan as sirens sounded in the distance. Shattered glass glittered on the pavement—the rear window was blown out—and I counted ten bullet holes in the back of the van. Two of the four tires were flat.

"Somebody must have a thing against minivans," Peaches said as Bunsen squatted to inspect the bullet holes.

"Or private investigators," Bunsen suggested. "Any idea who might have done this?"

"I can't think of anyone," I said, feeling cold despite the heat radiating off the pavement. Was someone trying to send me a message? And if so, who? I glanced at Peaches, who shook her head slightly.

"What kind of gun did they use?" Peaches asked.

"It was a semiautomatic," he said. "Not something to mess around with." He walked around the car. "Somebody doesn't seem too happy with you. What investigations have you been working on?"

"We did have an infidelity case recently, but that client isn't with us anymore."

"I can't imagine why not," he said dryly. "Any reason the client might want to shoot you?"

"Not that I know of." I cleared my throat. "We're also working on a pignapping case."

"Pardon me?"

"Missing pig," Peaches clarified. "Ex-husband stole a breeder. We're recovering it."

Bunsen cocked an eyebrow. "Is this the pig that ate your phone?"

Fortunately, at that moment a police car pulled into the parking lot, so I didn't have to answer. Wanda Schwarz, the manager of the Pretty Kitten, walked over to us, her high heels clopping on the pavement. "What happened?" she asked. "I was in the middle of a Brazilian, so I didn't get to see."

"Someone shot up Margie's van," Peaches said.

Wanda's French-manicured hand leaped to her necklace-draped throat. "That's terrible! It's a good thing they didn't hit the store windows." She glanced at Peaches. "I didn't realize subletting the office would be so dangerous. My clients were terrified."

"Sorry about that."

"Well." She crossed her skinny arms. "Is this a regular occurrence?"

"Oh, no," Peaches said. "First time."

At that moment, one of the policemen ran a hand over the hood of Peaches's Buick. "Vinnie did a great job. The bat marks are all gone; it looks like new."

Wanda looked at Peaches. "Bat marks?"

"I was in a bad part of town," Peaches said. "A mob attacked me; nothing I could do. Anyway, I've got loads of client calls," she told Wanda, retreating toward the plate-glass door. She turned to the cop. "Let us know what you find out, okay?"

"Will do, Peaches. I'm sure we'll see you soon," he said, and his partner barked out a laugh.

My boss gave a half wave and disappeared into the building, leaving me with Bunsen and the two patrolmen.

"I hope you're not impounding my van as evidence," I said. "I've got two kids to pick up this afternoon."

"You can keep the van, but I don't think you're going anywhere anytime soon," Bunsen said, pointing to the ruined tires. "Does your insurance cover rentals?" he asked.

I sighed. "I guess I'm about to find out."

CHAPTER TWENTY-FIVE

I did have rental-car insurance, which was a plus. Unfortunately, however, the only vehicle left on the lot was an electric car the size of a shoe box.

"Don't you have anything a little bigger?" I asked the attendant, a young man with the irritating habit of ending every sentence on an up note. I kept feeling like I was expected to answer a question.

"Big convention in town!" he sang. "You're lucky we've got this one!"

I opened the door of the tiny car—a Nissan Leaf—and peered inside. "Assuming I can fit the booster seats in, where do I put the backpacks?"

"Oh, the trunk is ample," he said, popping the back hatch to display six cubic inches of storage space.

I sighed. "You're sure there's nothing else?"

"Only other thing I have is a Hummer, but it'll cost you a hundred extra a day."

I contemplated the car's dollhouse-scale trunk. If I did manage to get Bubba Sue, she'd have to sit in the backseat; there was no way I could stuff her into the rear of the car. "I guess this will have to do," I said, and ten minutes later I was heading toward Holy Oaks, the engine roaring like a sewing machine. If I needed to sneak up on anyone, I reflected, this was the car to drive.

If I felt out of place in a minivan, driving a subcompact electric car made me feel like an alien. Despite Austin's environmentally friendly reputation, the parents of Holy Oaks largely leaned toward the Hummer end of the car spectrum. Luxury Hummers, that is.

I pulled into the carpool line, feeling dwarfed by the Porsche Cayennes and Cadillac Escalades growling like giant, expensive beasts around me. When I inched my way up to the front door, Elsie wouldn't budge until I waved at her.

"Where's the van?" she asked after she'd wedged herself into the booster seat, her backpack on her lap. *Words!* She was using words. I put on my best mom smile.

"I had an . . . accident this afternoon. It's being repaired."

"What about my fry phone?"

"I'm working on it," I told her lamely as we pulled away.

"I want my fry phone," she said. She crossed her arms and kicked the back of the seat. "I hate this car. I hate Holy Oaks. I want to go back to Green Meadows."

And then she burst into tears.

• • •

My mother wasn't at the house when we got home. *Went to food bank—dinner in oven!* was scrawled on a note on the kitchen table. *Back before 6.*

Elsie had stopped crying but still wasn't what you'd call happy. She wouldn't tell me anything about what was going on at school, so I sent a quick e-mail to her teacher and then started scouring the cupboards for snack options. It was a short and unsuccessful search.

"Where's Grandma?" Nick asked as I cut up an apple. Thank goodness apples were still on the approved list. I made a mental note to stop by the grocery store and stock up on nonperishable edibles like Ritz Crackers and Fruit Roll-Ups. I couldn't fit them in the trunk, but there might be room in the glove compartment.

"She had an errand to do," I told him.

Elsie, whose eyes were still swollen from crying, wrinkled her little nose. "What smells bad?"

"What do you mean?" I asked, as if I hadn't noticed the sulfurous miasma wafting from the oven.

"It smells like bathroom again," Nick announced through a mouthful of apple.

"Maybe Rufus missed the litter box again," I suggested. Speaking of Rufus, I hadn't seen much of him since my mother arrived. Maybe he was as traumatized by the pantry clearing as I was—or maybe my mother had tried doctoring his food with kale chips. Was there such a thing as vegan cat food? I wondered. "Anyone have any homework?" I asked.

Elsie—who had her pink collar back on and was curled up on the sofa cushion she liked to call her dog bed—growled.

"Well, if you do, it needs to be done by bedtime," I said. No response. I sidled over to the oven and cracked it open, releasing a wave of distinctly cruciferous hot air. There was a brownie pan on the middle rack, but the gooey green substance it contained bore no resemblance to brownies. I slammed the oven shut quickly and stepped away, tempted to open a window despite the heat.

"What is that stuff?" Nick asked.

"Let's go see if the TV is hooked up," I said, ushering him away from the kitchen. Once he settled down with his trains and an episode of *Thomas the Tank Engine*, I tossed Elsie her favorite rope toy, headed to the kitchen again, and grabbed the phone.

Becky answered on the third ring.

"It's Margie," I said as I retreated to my bedroom.

"I've been trying to reach you all day!" she said.

"Sorry about that; I don't have my phone. Is Bunsen bothering you?"

"He called me this afternoon and asked me a lot of questions."

"He stopped by Peachtree Investigations this afternoon." I told her about the events of the day—including the memorial service fiasco and my shot-up car.

"Thank God you weren't in the van at the time," she breathed. "Margie, this is getting scary."

"I know."

"Somebody's getting nervous, sounds like," she said. "Thank God they shot up your van at the office, and not at your house."

I shivered at the thought. "But why shoot it at all?"

"I'll bet there's something somebody doesn't want you to know about going on at Holy Oaks. They've seen you eavesdropping and nosing around, and they're telling you to drop it."

"I have the key to the school's front office," I said. "I was thinking I might go and investigate tonight, after my Warrior Wives meeting."

"Your what?"

"It's that Journey to Manhood support group for wives of men who . . . well, men who are trying not to be gay," I said. "Blake wants me to go."

"Wow. Want company tonight?" she asked.

I sat down on the end of my bed. "Is Rick hanging out with transvestites, too?"

"Not at the meeting, silly. The school."

"You just want to go through those admissions files again, don't you?"

"No. I want to find out what that school is up to and write another letter to the *Picayune*. Of course I want to go through the admissions files—largely because a certain individual left my business card on top of George Cavendish's tights, resulting in multiple visits from the police."

I sighed. "The meeting is from seven to nine."

"Pick me up when it's over," she said. "How are things going with your mom, by the way?"

"She's been a huge help with the kids," I said, "but the food thing is getting to be a bit of a problem. She took just about everything I had and gave it to the food bank. I'm having to sneak the kids fast food just to get some calories into them."

"How long is she staying?"

"A week. I'm not sure I can make it that long. At least Blake isn't here, so we don't have to share the bedroom, but what if he comes back and wants to get . . . romantic?"

"How do you feel about it?"

I shuddered. "I think I'd rather sleep with an orangutan."

Becky sighed. "You're going to have to deal with this at some point, you know. You can't live like a nun for the next twenty years."

"I know," I said. "But I told him I'd give it a try, and I will. I hate the thought of what divorce would do to the kids."

"You have to take care of yourself, too," she reminded me. "Besides, you won't be young and pretty forever."

I glanced up at myself in the mirror. Young and pretty? I had bags under my eyes that were big enough to hold groceries, and some mornings I wished I could send out a search party to locate my waist. "Really, Becky?"

"My brother thinks you are," she said suggestively.

Michael. I got a little flutter just thinking about him, but quickly quashed it. I didn't want to be having this conversation right now. I had more important things to deal with. Like getting the bullet holes in my minivan patched and convincing my daughter to eat with a fork. Not to mention keeping Becky, Peaches, and me out of jail. "I'll go to the support group, and then we'll go break into Holy Oaks." I got up from the end of the bed and opened the closet door, wondering what one should wear for an evening of support-group sharing followed by burgling. "Let's just figure out who killed Aquaman, and then we can talk about my personal life."

"Touchy," she said.

"I'll call you when it's over."

"You don't have a cell phone," she reminded me.

I groaned.

"I'll see you at 9:20, then," Becky said. "Give or take a few. I'll tell Rick you need to go get a drink."

"You won't be lying," I said before hanging up.

• • •

The Journey to Manhood "Warrior Wives" group turned out to be in the fellowship hall of a Baptist church on the south side of town. I closed the door of the tiny car behind me and adjusted my black cardigan—I'd decided dark was good for burgling, and besides, it was the nicest thing I owned. So what if it was still almost ninety degrees in the parking lot?

As I headed for the metal double doors, bracing myself for what was to come, I reflected that it might be better than being at home with my mother and children. The broccoli–brussels sprout casserole had not been a resounding success; even my mother had deemed it inedible, and to my relief, she relented and let us order pizza. (Plain cheese, no sauce, on Elsie's, of course.)

"What kind of meeting is this, Margie?" my mother had asked when I came back in from taking the trash bag with the casserole's contents out to the curb. The smell was so strong the plastic bag didn't have a chance. "Is this about Elsie's . . . dog fixation?" she whispered.

"Actually no," I said. "It's . . . just about relationships," I added lamely.

"I'm really worried about her," she told me. "I know nutrition must play a part, but I'm not sure that's all there is. Are you sure this school is the right kind of place for her?"

"She's only been there a couple of days," I said.

"But it sounds like there's no opportunity for self-expression." She pushed the bangles up on her arm. "Plaid jumpers, navy polo shirts . . . is it any wonder she's wearing a dog collar as an accessory?"

"She wore that before school started," I reminded her.

"Yes, but the stress of the environment can't be helping." My mother reached for another piece of her artichoke-asparagus pizza. "When did all of this start?" she asked.

"Around the end of last school year," I said. "That's when she started wanting us to call her Fifi and using a water bowl instead of a glass." I sighed. "She actually bit one of her classmates at Green Meadows."

My mother winced. "Ouch."

"That's what the kid said."

She steepled her hands under her chin, much as I had done earlier in the day, and the bangles slid back down her arm with a clank. "How are things between you and Blake?" she asked. "It seems like your auras are a bit . . . cloudy."

I shifted in my chair and reached for another piece of pizza. "Oh, you know," I said. "Same as every marriage." *With a few rather glaring exceptions*—but again, there was no need to discuss that with my mother. She'd be trying to sign us up for yogic vegan Tantric sex counseling, or prescribing a diet of oysters and artichokes. "When you have kids, they're really the focus."

"It's not good for your partnership, though," she said. "Your father and I didn't make our relationship a priority, and I've always regretted it."

I knew I hadn't spent nearly enough time with my mother since she'd arrived—and that I owed her a debt of gratitude for all she'd done for me and the kids—but right now, the last thing I needed was a dissection of my parents' failed marriage. I grimaced and swallowed my guilt. "Shoot," I said, looking at my watch and standing up. "Is that the time? I've really got to run, Mom."

She sighed. "I worry about you, sweetheart."

"I know, and I love you for it," I said, giving her a quick hug. "Thanks so much for your help with the kids. I'll probably be back late. Call me if you have any trouble."

"I've been calling you all day and you haven't answered."

"Oh yeah, that's right. I . . . lost my cell phone."

"Margie, Margie, Margie. How do you keep it all together?"

Keep it all together? I'd met schizophrenics who were doing a better job of keeping it all together than I was. I let out a short, barking laugh and escaped out the back door, thankful to have avoided further interrogation.

Now, as I pushed through the double doors into the coffee-and-hymnal-scented fellowship hall, I felt a twinge of apprehension. It was not assuaged when a circle of depressed-looking women in plastic chairs turned to look at me.

"Hello!" sang the group leader, a plump, chirpy-looking woman with shiny black hair and a bright-red skirt suit. She wore six-inch stiletto heels that made me wonder how she stayed upright. "Are you here for the Warrior Wives group?"

"Um, yeah," I said, edging toward one of the vacant chairs.

"Welcome!" she said with a smile so bright I had to resist the urge to squint. "I'm Barbie Ford, the leader of the Warriors. We were just about to join in our opening prayer."

CHAPTER TWENTY-SIX

I sat down and bowed my head as Barbie launched into the prayer. There was a flowery smell in the room that competed with the scents of old coffee and dusty paper; it made my nose itch.

"Dear God," she intoned, the chirpiness replaced by a sepulchral voice that made me check to see whether someone else was leading the prayer. "Please help us to embrace our femininity so that we can lead our husbands from the path of sin, and help them break their ungodly habits. Please help us help them see that they have been seduced by wickedness, and that the scars of their past can be healed with prayer and by following your path. Please help us as we work to become more attractive, so that we support our husbands as they work to turn away from sinful lusts." She took a deep breath, and concluded, "In Christ's name we pray. Amen."

I looked up, expecting to see expressions of disbelief—or at least disgruntlement—on my fellow group members' faces, but they all looked . . . chastened, somehow.

My mind sorted through the prayer I had just heard. *Path of sin? Ungodly habits? Work to become more attractive?* I'd heard of Throwback

Thursday, but Barbie Ford appeared to be firmly planted in the Middle Ages.

Of course I'd struggled with the idea that I, somehow, had caused my husband to be attracted to men in corsets. Apparently self-blame was common among straight wives; I'd read enough online forums to know that. And of course it had been hurtful to learn that my husband wasn't—couldn't—be attracted to me. But I'd never considered his liking for men "wicked"—nor thought that by wearing stacked heels and Victoria's Secret lingerie and blow-drying my hair I could somehow "convert" Blake to the straight-hitting team. In fact, the main issue I was struggling with was my obvious and glaring lack of judgment when selecting a husband. I'd had absolutely no idea Blake was gay. What else had I gotten wrong? And, presuming I ever even went out to dinner with a member of the opposite sex again, how would I avoid the same mistake twice?

I appeared to be in the minority, however, because as I examined my fellow group members, I noticed a decided slant toward ultrafeminine decor. Everyone but me was wearing a skirt or a dress, and with the exception of one woman in pearls and cashmere, they'd troweled on more makeup than the trannies at the Tuesday Night Drag Queen Showdown at the Rainbow Room.

And three of them were clutching Bibles.

"Now," Barbie began, striding around the circle like a lion tamer. The scent of floral perfume intensified as she passed, making my nose itch. "Let's start by introducing our newest member." She turned on me with an expectant smile.

"Hi," I said. "I'm Margie." I paused, feeling like I'd done my part, but Barbie continued to stare at me expectantly. If she'd had a whip, she would have cracked it.

"And what brings you to Warrior Wives?"

What the heck did she think brought me to Warrior Wives? Did she think that maybe I just was looking for something new to spice up a Wednesday night? "Um, well, my husband's at the Journey to Manhood retreat right now, and he asked me to come to this group." I forced a smile. "So here I am."

"Oh, he's doing Journey to Manhood?" one of the women cooed. She wore a floral dress with a lace collar that was starched so stiff it hovered about an inch above the neckline. "Fred did that a few months ago, and since he came back, I haven't found a single visit to HotHomeboys.com on his laptop."

"That's wonderful news!" Barbie beamed. "Did you check his phone, too?"

"Oh," the woman said, straightening her collar and looking worried. "I didn't think about that."

"I'm sure it's fine," Barbie reassured her. "The program is just magical. Our men, you see," she said, addressing me, "usually are . . . damaged by some tragedy in their boyhoods. Something that prevents them from claiming their masculine identities."

"Tragedy?" I asked, reviewing what I knew of Blake's past and wondering if failing to make the varsity soccer team freshman year qualified. "Like what?"

"The usual suspects. Molestation, abuse, an absent father . . . All of these things tend to make men choose the more submissive, feminine role."

I cleared my throat. "Submissive?" Blake was many things, but submissive wasn't one of them. At least not in my experience.

She nodded wisely. "That's why masculine retraining is so important for them. And why we have to work extra hard to emphasize our femininity."

"I'm confused," I said. "If a man is struggling with attraction to other men, then wouldn't dressing more femininely be kind of . . . counterproductive?"

"But we have to reinforce their roles!" Barbie said. "If they want to watch *Monday Night Football,* the living room is theirs, and we serve them beer and chips. We encourage them to make the decisions around the house, instead of usurping their roles. And, of course, we attend church together—that is just so important in supporting a marriage."

I had a lot of questions for Barbie. Like how watching burly men in tights run around on a field and slap each other's asses was supposed to quell any same-sex fantasies, and how church attendance would magically decrease my husband's attraction to men in satin dresses. On the other hand, I hadn't tried wearing a satin dress myself, so maybe there was something in it. Though in truth, the thought of enticing my husband to sleep with me had all the appeal of trying to seduce a goldfish. But I'd told Blake I'd support him, so I kept my mouth shut.

"Jackie, are there any improvements with Paul? Did your trip to Victoria's Secret help things out in the bedroom?"

Jackie, a slightly round woman in a black sheath dress and painful-looking platform heels, flushed. "I got the push-up bra and garter belt, just like you said, but it didn't go too well." She looked down as if ashamed. "He said he had a headache."

"Hmm," Barbie said. "Well, just try again. Maybe a different color next time?"

"Maybe," Jackie said with a weak smile.

Barbie turned her attention to an older woman in a pink twinset and khaki skirt. Her makeup was tasteful; in fact, she reminded me a little of my mother-in-law, Prudence, only sadder. "How about you, Anne?" the chirpy leader asked.

"Well, I felt very . . . alone for a long time," she said, fingering her string of pearls. "But . . . and this may sound weird . . . my friend's husband just died . . . and the police think he was having some kind of kinky sex. It made me feel like I wasn't the only one in an abnormal situation."

"Sex with other men?" Barbie asked.

The older woman's cheeks turned a delicate pink. "They don't know, but evidently there was . . . urine involved," she said, wrinkling her nose.

I sat up straight, thinking maybe turning up at Warrior Wives wasn't such a bad idea after all. It had to be George Cavendish she was talking about. How many men did you find dead and covered in urine? Even in Austin, it seemed like a fairly unusual way to go.

Anne sighed. "I guess I'm hoping . . . that maybe we can . . . bond over it."

"Did she know he was being unfaithful?" I asked.

"Margie!" Barbie gave a little trilling laugh. "You're asking questions, but we haven't heard your story yet!"

"My story?" I didn't really want to tell it. "It's still a bit . . . raw," I said.

"Better out than in," Barbie said. "We're all friends here!" Something about her tone was less than convincing.

"All right." I took a deep breath. "I found out my husband was sleeping with a transvestite named Selena Sass. He's off at Journey to Manhood, like I said, and I'm here." I turned back to Anne. "But back to you. What a terrible shock that must have been for your friend," I said sympathetically, hoping to prime the pump.

"Thank you for your story," Barbie told me, then clip-clopped back over to Anne. "But as far as your friend is concerned, I'm not sure it's good to confide in her. If attraction to men is an identity your husband is trying to leave behind, it won't help to be reinforcing it in the community. That's why *we're* here! This is a safe space."

"How do you know her?" I asked Anne.

"We've been neighbors for years," she told me. "She's worried about what will happen if the news hits the paper. It will be a real scandal."

"He must have been high up, then," I suggested.

"I shouldn't talk about it," she told me, and I could sense her closing up. "I've already said too much."

"Well, don't say anything else to her," Barbie admonished. "We're here to support our husbands, not tear them down by telling the world about their sins! And now," she said, rounding on me. "Can you tell us a little bit about what you've been doing to affirm your marriage?"

"Well, I haven't kicked him out, so there's that."

There was a titter of nervous laughter.

"I was hoping for something a little more supportive," Barbie said. "Like erotic foot rubs."

"No erotic foot rubs," I said.

"Bible reading together?"

I shook my head.

"You are sleeping in the same bed, at least?"

"Nope. He sleeps in the office." With the exception of last night, that was. We'd clung to our respective sides of the bed as if they were life rafts.

Barbie sighed. "It's a good thing you're here. It's no wonder your husband strayed to the other side. Obviously your marriage needs some serious work!"

Her holier-than-thou tone set my teeth on edge. Safe space? This was about as safe as walking into a den of underfed tigers, from what I could see. "So, what's your story?" I asked pleasantly.

Barbie blinked. "Pardon me?"

"I was wondering about your experiences. Is your husband gay?"

She recoiled as if I'd handed her a snake. "Oh, no! Of course not!"

"Then how do you know that all this stuff—the erotic foot rubs, the football, the push-up bras—works?"

"The program has been well tested," she said. "Even the women here have seen improvements in their marriages since they started walking this path with Jesus." She looked around with an encouraging smile. "Right?"

There were a few wan smiles from the circle.

"Anyway, let's move on to our program for the day," Barbie said, clip-clopping back to the front of the room and retrieving a stack of papers. "Now. Today we're focusing on how to create a harmonious home that is a haven for your hard-working husband."

She distributed something called *The Good Wife's Guide*, which consisted of two xeroxed pages stapled together. The first page featured a grainy photo of a woman in a white dress standing by a 1950s-era stove and greeting her suit-clad husband, with two impeccably groomed children holding hands beside her. Neither of the children, I noticed, was wearing a dog collar.

"I remember this!" Anne said. "My mother gave this to me when I got married."

"How long have you been married?" I asked.

"Forty years," she said.

I looked back down at the list. The only update was item number three, which had originally read, *Be a little gay and a little more interesting for him.* The word *gay* had been crossed out, and *cheerful* was inked in above it.

"Now," Barbie said after she finished distributing the pages. "I know the modern age has completely turned our traditional roles upside down—in fact, I'm sure that's why so many marriages are ending in divorce these days. But there are a few things we wives can do to establish harmony and happiness in our homes."

I skimmed the list. *Gather up schoolbooks, toys, paper, etc. and then run a dust cloth over the tables* was one suggestion. That wasn't likely to happen in my house. Most of the time, I couldn't even see the table surfaces, much less dust them. *Prepare the children* was another chestnut. The article recommended taking a few minutes to *wash the children's hands and faces (if they are small), comb their hair, and if necessary, change their clothes.* Really? It was hard enough getting them dressed once a day, much less convincing them to put on a second set of clothes while I was trying to get dinner on the table.

I looked around to see if the other women were sharing my reaction, but they were all studying their pages intently. I looked back down and read the second-to-last pronouncement. *Don't ask him questions about his actions or question his judgment and integrity. Remember, he is the master of the house and as such will always exercise his will with fairness and truthfulness.* Like paying someone blackmail money to keep his affair with a drag queen secret from me? I wondered. The final bit of advice was the frosting on the cake. *You have no right to question him.*

Really?

If I hadn't questioned Blake, he'd still be cavorting with men in tights and putting a good portion of his salary toward blackmail payouts. Maybe the program came with a time machine that would take us all back to 1955.

I had the urge to get up and walk out. But then I looked at Anne. She knew Cavendish's wife, and I had more questions to ask her. If I left now, I might not have another opportunity. I sat back in my chair, gritted my teeth, and applied a pleasant smile to my face.

It was a very long hour. There was a lot of talk of submitting, and lipstick, and the value of a home-cooked meal. I had no problem with cooking dinner, but again, even if I was able to magically morph into June Cleaver, it still wouldn't solve the fundamental problem. Blake's sexuality had nothing to do with me; I knew that like I knew the sun would rise in the morning. What made me so sad was that the women around me were being told—and seemed to believe—that their husbands' sexuality was somehow their fault.

Finally—*finally*—Barbie wrapped things up. "Did you learn a lot, girls?" she asked cheerfully.

Jackie raised a tentative hand.

"Yes, Jackie?"

"Does this really work?" she asked.

"What man wouldn't want to come home to a home-cooked meal, a neat house, and an attractively clad wife?" she beamed. "And we all know how men are around the house. Completely clueless. We just have to show them the *value* we women have." She turned to the woman with the lace collar. "He's not going to find an amazing housekeeper on HotHomeboys.com, is he?"

Again, I wasn't sure housekeeping was quite what the people on HotHomeboys.com were looking for, but in the interest of interrogating Anne, I didn't mention it.

"Now, for our final prayer," Barbie announced, and we all bowed our heads. She paused for a dramatic moment, and then intoned, "Dear God, please lead us to submit to our husbands. Help us create a haven for our men and show them the value of womanhood. Please help us to guide them to the path of heterosexuality, and help them turn from the path of sin. Amen."

I folded the *Good Wife* handout and jammed it into my purse, then stood up, hoping to follow Anne out into the parking lot. As soon as I stood up, though, Barbie accosted me.

"So glad you could join us," she said, her powdery perfume making my nose twitch. "Have you gotten the workbook for the program yet?"

"Ah, not yet," I said, watching as the pink twinset headed for the door.

"Why don't you just fill out this form, and I'll make sure there's one for you at the next meeting?" She bustled over to her pile of papers and started riffling through it. "I know I've got one here somewhere."

"I, uh, really have to get home," I said, stifling a sneeze. "Maybe there's one online?"

"No. I know it's here . . ." As she spoke, Anne disappeared through the door.

"I really have to go," I said.

"But—"

"Bye!" I said, and bolted after Anne.

CHAPTER TWENTY-SEVEN

I caught up with Anne just as she was opening the door of her Mercedes. "It was so good to meet you," I said, panting with exertion.

She gave me a puzzled look.

"I just . . . It's so encouraging to me that you're handling things so well," I said. "You're just so put-together . . . It's inspiring."

I got a small smile.

"And like Barbie said," I plowed on, "it can be so hard not to talk about this stuff with other people. It's so nice to find people who really understand the situation." I paused. "I wonder, would you be up to having a cup of coffee with me?"

She thought about it for a moment, then shrugged a cashmere-clad shoulder. "I suppose we could."

"That would be wonderful," I said. "How do I get in touch with you?"

She fished a card out of her purse and handed it to me. *Anne Zapp*, it said, with a tony Westlake address. No profession listed.

"Thanks so much. I'll give you a call this week."

"Okay," she said.

"And one last question," I said. It was a ridiculous question and would probably totally freak her out, but I really needed to know. "Your friend . . . What kind of car does she drive?"

"A Lexus," she said.

"Red?" I asked.

"Why, yes," she told me, looking confused. "Why?"

"I'm, uh, working on my psychic abilities," I said, pocketing the card. Red Lexus. Mrs. Cavendish was moving higher on my list of suspects. "I feel terrible for your neighbor—we know just how she feels. Did she have any idea he was being unfaithful?"

She sighed. "She hasn't told me, but I think she did." She gave me a sad smile. "I think we all know, don't we? We just don't want to admit it."

I felt a welling in my eyes that took me by surprise. On some level, yes, I think I had known. I swallowed the lump in my throat and said, "You're probably right." I studied Anne, who seemed so sage, so . . . together. Did she really believe all the stuff Barbie was telling us to do? I had to ask. "What do you think of Warrior Wives?"

She let out a long sigh. "What they teach is what I was raised with, really. I doubt it'll help, but it's worth a shot." Anne's thin face looked worn and tired. "My husband and I have shared most of our lives—it hasn't been wonderful, but it's still better than nothing." She lifted her chin. "I don't want to die alone."

I didn't know how to respond to that. After a moment, I just said, "Thanks for agreeing to coffee. And thanks for talking with me."

"My pleasure," she said.

"I look forward to coffee," I told her. And as I walked back to my car, I realized I meant it.

• • •

Becky was ready to go when I pulled up outside her house and knocked on her door at a quarter after nine. She was dressed all in black—including her eyeliner—and her blonde hair was pulled back into a ponytail. "Let's go," she said. "I told Rick I was going to help you out with a case, but I didn't give him any details." She hollered, "Good-bye!" and shut the door behind her. As we trotted down the front walk to my rental car, she remarked, "Not quite the van, is it?"

"No," I agreed. "It's a bit on the small side."

"Any leads on who did in the van?"

"There are a few possibilities," I told her. I'd been wondering about it myself. Was it Deborah Golden or her husband, Frank? Deborah had caught me out twice, but I just couldn't see her hiring someone with a semiautomatic to shoot up my minivan. Marty Krumbacher, though, was a different story; I remembered seeing him in the back room of the strip club. What had triggered someone to send me a warning, though?

"Maybe Cressida Cavendish was upset that I knocked her husband out of his coffin," I said.

"God, that must have been humiliating for her," she said. "Maybe *she* was the one who shot your minivan."

"I can see why she'd want to, but I think it's got to be someone at Holy Oaks," I said. "The Goldens caught me eavesdropping twice, and Krumbacher saw me at the Sweet Shop when he was having a meeting in a back room.

"So someone at Holy Oaks killed Cavendish, you think?"

"I just don't know yet," I said, thinking of what Anne had said about Mrs. Cavendish's red Lexus. "And maybe we'll find out something more tonight."

Becky opened the car door and wedged herself into the seat. "Cozy—how do you fit everyone in?"

"It's tight, but we figured it out," I said.

"It's kind of refreshing not having McDonald's cups and napkins all over the floor," she said. "And it smells"—she sniffed—"clean!" She adjusted her feet and turned to me. "How did the Warrior Wives thing go, by the way?"

"Awful," I said.

"Really? What did they tell you?"

I pulled *The Good Wife's Guide* out of my purse and handed it to her. "Add in Victoria's Secret underwear, Bible readings, and erotic foot rubs, and you'll supposedly have the cure for homosexuality."

She turned on the overhead light, skimmed it, and wrinkled her nose. "So it was a bust," she said, looking up at me. "I'm so sorry, Margie."

"I really didn't think it would work, anyway. On the plus side, I found out that Mrs. Cavendish drives a red Lexus. One of her neighbors was there."

"What does a red Lexus have to do with anything?"

"Desiree saw one parked outside her apartment the night Cavendish died."

"You're thinking she followed him there and shot him while he was in the wading pool?"

"I can understand the impulse," I said. "But I don't have a lot of evidence."

"Maybe there will be something in his office," she mused as we merged onto MoPac.

"That's what I'm banking on," I said.

• • •

The parking lot at Holy Oaks was deserted, much to my relief. Perky Desk Girl must have had a spare key somewhere; there were no cars that I could see. Security lights blasted the entrances, but the buildings were dark. Both of us had grown quiet as we got closer to the school; I think we were nervous.

I parked on a side street—it felt funny being the only car in the parking lot—and handed Becky a pair of latex gloves.

"What are these for?"

"Fingerprints," I said. "They already found your business card on the body. You don't want them to find your fingerprints in his office, do you?"

"Good thinking," she said, pulling a flashlight out of her back pocket. "But didn't they already go through his office?"

"Better safe than sorry."

She pulled on her gloves. "You have the keys?" she asked as I killed the engine.

I fished in my purse and pulled them out. "I don't know which one is for the door."

"They don't have a security system, do they?" she asked.

"I don't know."

"What do we do if they do?"

"Run back to the car, I guess."

"Maybe we should have parked closer," she suggested, but neither of us turned back. We slunk through the parking lot, looking up for cameras. "And maybe we should have worn ski masks."

"Hard to find ski masks in Texas in the summer," I pointed out.

"Paper bags, then."

"Maybe next time."

Perky Desk Girl had a lot of keys. It took ten tries to find one that turned in the front-door lock. I could hear the bolt snick back, and I held my breath as I pulled the door open.

"I don't hear an alarm," Becky said. "So that's good news."

The security lights blazed through the glass windows; it was almost as bright as day in the front lobby. It only took two tries before we breached the front office door and found ourselves standing in the nerve center of Holy Oaks. It was darker inside the office, and I had to switch on my flashlight. After my experience with Bubba Sue, I'd taken to keeping a flashlight in my purse.

"What do we do now?" she asked.

I pointed to the admissions files. "Find the file for Cherry Nichols, would you?" I asked, remembering the way Mrs. Cavendish had looked at her at the memorial service.

"Why?"

"Just a hunch," I said, and started trying keys in Cavendish's office door.

"Did you see if it's locked?" Becky asked as she riffled through the files.

"I'm sure it is," I said, but tried the knob anyway. To my surprise, it turned easily.

"Told you," Becky said, brandishing a file. "I found her," she said. "What do you want to know?"

"Let's look at it later," I said. "I want to get out of here; I have a bad feeling about tonight." And I did. Did the school have a silent security alarm? I wondered.

I swept the walls of the small office with the light. Diplomas from Duke and Yale hung on the wall, along with a picture of a much younger Mrs. Cavendish on the bow of a boat, her dark hair blowing in the wind and her face full of hope.

"No computer," Becky noted.

"I'm sure the police have it."

"How about I tackle the file cabinets while you take the desk," Becky suggested.

"Sounds like a plan. If you see anything about Golden Investments or the board, grab it."

"Will do," she said.

Any hope I had of finding clues to Cavendish's secret life were quickly quashed. He was not, to my chagrin, a sloppy man; even his pens were lined up neatly in the top drawer, and the rest of the drawers were filled with tidily stowed office supplies. Maybe the police had taken anything incriminating.

"Here's something on Golden," Becky said from the file cabinet.

"What is it?"

"Investment statements, it looks like."

"Grab them," I said as I opened another drawer filled with rubber bands and staplers. "I'm finding nothing."

"Did you check the drawer bottoms?" she asked.

"What?"

She rolled her eyes. "Don't you read Agatha Christie or P. D. James?"

"What's P. D. James?"

"An awesome mystery writer," she said. "Check the drawer bottoms. That's where people hide things all the time."

"In mystery novels," I reminded her.

"Just try it," she said.

I got off the chair and sat down on the floor, training my light on the underside of the desk. "Nothing here," I said.

"Did you pull out the drawers?"

I slid the tray drawer out first: nothing. Not that I expected there to be. But on the fifth drawer, I discovered an envelope taped to the particleboard.

"I need to start reading P. D. James," I told Becky.

She closed the file-cabinet drawer and hurried over to the desk. "What did you find?"

"I don't know. It's an envelope." I slid my hand inside and pulled out a piece of folded yellow legal paper. There were two lines of what looked like code:

Arthur207 C1U2R3R4Y5

Topo66 1S2I3T4N5A6L7T8A

"Weird," Becky said. "What do you think it means?"

"I don't know," I said.

"Maybe they're passwords," she suggested.

"To what?"

Before she could answer, a flash of blue and red lights played across the back wall.

CHAPTER TWENTY-EIGHT

B ecky and I stared at each other.
"Shit."

I flipped off my flashlight and shoved the legal paper in my pocket. "Turn off your light!" I hissed.

Becky shoved her light into her purse and grabbed the files. We almost knocked each other over trying to get to the office door.

There was a cop car right outside the plate-glass windows. "Now what?" Becky asked.

"This way," I said. We sidled down the wall of the front lobby, then I pulled her down the hallway to the elementary wing.

Although it hadn't struck me as long earlier that day, tonight the hallway appeared to stretch the length of three football fields. I could see the faint glow of the moon through the glass doors at the end of it, but it was impossibly far away. We were only to the halfway point before I heard voices in the front lobby.

The closest door was to the boys' bathroom. "This way," I whispered, and yanked her through the door.

A sulfurous smell enveloped us as the door swung shut behind us. "What now?" she asked. It was pitch-black; I reached for my flashlight.

"No window," I said. "We'll have to hide in the stalls."

"It reeks in here."

"It probably reeks in jail, too." I flashed the light over the row of stalls. "Let's take the two at the end," I suggested, "and pull the doors shut."

"Won't they see our feet?" she asked.

"Not if we stand on the toilets."

Becky approached one of the stalls cautiously, as if there might be a wild animal inside, and nudged the door with a foot.

"I'm not going in there," she said as I trained my light on the bowl. They might teach many things at Holy Oaks, but the mechanics of toilet flushing did not appear to be one of them.

At that moment, there was the sound of voices from the hallway. It's amazing what the threat of a night in jail will do. Without another word of protest, Becky launched herself into the nearest stall. I followed suit, clambering onto the toilet seat next door and praying the smell would keep the cops from a close inspection.

We were perched on those toilet seats for a long time, during which I considered bringing up the topic of bathroom-cleaning protocol to the custodian I'd seen the other day. The one who looked like he'd recently retired from gang life, but wasn't quite sold on the career change. I ended up deciding it wasn't worth it; Elsie wasn't going to use the boys' room, anyway. If anything, she was more likely to relieve herself on a tree in the playground.

Ten minutes passed, and I was fervently wishing I'd stuck with yoga, before the door swung open and the lights flicked on. I flinched from the brightness, looked down, and immediately regretted it.

"God. Smells like something died in here," a male voice said.

"At least the urinals are clear," someone answered. "Check the stalls; I've got to take a leak."

A moment later I heard a zipping sound, followed by what sounded like running water. I also heard footsteps.

The first door banged open, and then the second. I cringed, waiting for the third, but it didn't happen. "I hate these security-alarm calls," the low voice said. "Half our time seems to be answering false alarms."

"The front door was unlocked," the other voice said. There were a few last splats, and then I heard the zipper sound again.

"Probably someone forgot to lock it," Low Voice said. "No sign of forced entry anywhere. Waste of time."

"There's a new Kerbey Lane just up the road," the other guy said. "Open late. And gingerbread pancakes are on special this week."

"Too bad the tomato menu went away," Low Voice said wistfully. "That tomato pie was awesome."

"I say we lock up and go check it out."

Low Voice seemed to be in accord with the idea. A moment later, the lights flicked off and the door creaked open and closed again, leaving us in darkness. I waited until their voices had retreated down the hallway before clambering down from the toilet and stepping out of the stall, massaging my shaking quads.

I had just opened my stall door when there was a splash from the next stall over.

• • •

"Becky?"

More splashing, followed by swearing.

"Are you okay?"

"No, I'm not okay!" Her voice was frantic. "I slipped and put my foot in that filthy toilet. Oh my God. These are new boots, too."

I flipped on the bathroom lights and opened the stall door. Becky was hopping on one foot, trying to unzip her left boot. Her jeans were wet halfway to the knee, and the stench was appalling.

"Let's get you rinsed off," I said, offering a hand. "At least you're wearing gloves. And I'm sure the . . . well, I'm sure it will wash out of your jeans, at least."

"I can't wear these. I'm taking them off."

She shook off her boots, then peeled off her jeans, leaving them in a sodden pile in the middle of the bathroom floor. Then she hopped to the sink in her pink bikini underwear and hoisted her foot under the faucet.

"What do we do with your jeans and boots?" I asked as she scrubbed her foot and ankle with pink hand soap.

"I don't care," she said. "Put them in the trash if you want. I'm never wearing them again. What do they feed these kids, anyway?"

"I think it was Frito pie today, actually," I replied.

"That was a rhetorical question, Margie," Becky said. "I think I'm going to throw up now."

"We can't leave your clothes here," I said. "What if someone finds them?"

Becky pumped another cup of pink soap onto her foot. "They're welcome to them."

"We should probably take them with us. Maybe if we wash them off?"

"No way," she said, shaking her head.

I sighed. "I'll go see if I can find a plastic bag." I retrieved my flashlight and edged into the hallway, relieved that all was quiet and dark.

The janitor's closet was toward the end of the hall. I opened the door and flashed my light to reveal a jumble of cleaning supplies: a tangle of brooms and mops leaned up against the corner, and a row of industrial-sized jugs of window cleaner were shoved against the side wall. Rolls of paper towels, napkins, scrub brushes lined the floor-to-ceiling shelves—everything, it appeared, but trash bags.

As I riffled through the shelves, searching for a box of bags, my hand closed on something cold and metallic. I trained the light on it and sucked in my breath; it was a gun.

I pushed the rolls of toilet paper to the side, shining the light on the shelf. There was not just a gun, but also several brightly colored packets labeled *Afterburn*. I picked one up. *For High Times!* the package blared in neon-green letters, under a fuzzy graphic of something that looked like an exploding star. There were a half dozen packets, and one was open. I picked it up and sniffed it, then wished I hadn't; the smell reminded me of the monkey enclosure at the Austin Zoo.

The name "Afterburn" rang a bell, but it took me a moment to place it. I had seen it in the newspaper, I realized with a start. This was the stuff that had killed a few teenagers over the past month or two—some kind of synthetic marijuana. What was it doing in an unlocked janitor's closet at my daughter's school?

Not to mention the gun. Was it loaded? I didn't know how to check, and touching it creeped me out, so I just put the toilet paper back in front of it and kept looking for trash bags. I found a box of bags on the bottom shelf and pulled one out for Becky's clothes, but hesitated before leaving the janitor's closet. What was I going to do? I couldn't just leave those things here—not with my daughter coming to school the next day.

After a moment of indecision, I pulled out a second bag and put the drug packets into it. Then I picked up the gun, shuddering at the touch—even through my latex gloves it felt cold and unpleasant.

Becky was still scrubbing her foot when I got back to the bathroom.

"I got a bag," I told her. "And guess what I found in the janitor's closet?"

"Disinfectant spray?" she asked.

"A gun and some packets of synthetic marijuana."

She stopped scrubbing and looked at me. "What?"

I opened the bag and showed her the contents. "I thought the janitor seemed kind of dicey."

"No kidding. What are you going to do with it?"

"I don't know," I confessed. "I can't leave it here. It's not safe for the kids!"

"Can you put it on the front desk with a note?"

"What if a kid picks it up and the gun goes off?"

"Good point," she said, biting her lip. "Can you leave it in the closet and call in an anonymous tip?"

"There's still a chance it will be here when the kids get here tomorrow," I said. "I think I have to take it with me."

"Speaking of taking it with you, can we get out of here?" she asked, turning off the water and lowering her foot to the floor.

"Let's get your clothes picked up first," I said. "Are you going out in your underwear?"

"Better than wearing those things," she said. "Besides, we can go through the woods. Who's going to see us?"

"If you're sure," I said, clutching the two bags in my right hand. "Ready?"

"Wait," she said. "I can't leave those toilets unflushed."

I rolled my eyes. "Really?"

"They seriously need to reevaluate their housekeeping staff."

• • •

Although my watch said that only an hour had passed since we'd arrived at Holy Oaks, it felt like a month had gone by before Becky flushed the last toilet and we eased the boys'-bathroom door open. "Let's get out of here," I whispered.

Becky started back toward the front lobby, but I grabbed her arm and turned her toward the door at the end of the hallway. "Just in case," I said.

"You think?"

"Better safe than sorry."

We padded down the terrazzo floor of the hallway toward the exit door—me in my sneakers and Becky in bare, very clean feet. "Aren't you cold?" I asked.

"Better than smelling like crap," she replied.

I paused when we got to the door. Opening it would probably trigger the security alarm again; I hoped the cops had ordered their pancakes by now and wouldn't be too inclined to hurry back to the school.

"Ready?" I asked.

"I was ready an hour ago," she said. "Let's do it."

The air outside was hot and humid, which was good for Becky, and what sounded like millions of cicadas and crickets droned in the greenbelt that backed Holy Oaks. "I think the path is over there," I said, sweeping the tree line with my flashlight beam. There was a small gap between two cedar trees. "Are your feet going to be okay?"

"Do I have a choice?" she asked as we hurried across the manicured grass.

"Yeah, but it's a shitty one." Becky snorted, and despite the fact that we had just broken into Holy Oaks Catholic School and she was standing outside in her underwear, we both dissolved into giggles.

"We should get ourselves together and go before the cops get back," I said finally, wiping my eyes.

"Probably. I'll bet they wait until they're done with their pancakes, though."

Unfortunately, once we hit the trees the grass went away, replaced by prickly understory plants, limestone shards, and broken branches. Becky's giggles were soon replaced by muttered expletives. I went first, trying to clear the more egregious sticks out of the path, while Becky followed. "I never should have gotten that pedicure this week," she moaned. "They sanded off all my callouses."

"We're almost there, I think."

"What's that noise?" Becky hissed. I stopped, and then I heard it, too. Footsteps. "There's a light," she said. Sure enough, another flashlight bobbed through the trees ahead of us.

CHAPTER TWENTY-NINE

L et's get off the trail," I hissed to Becky. "Turn off your light."

We both flicked off our flashlights and turned off the path, crunching into the undergrowth. I heard a clunk, then a stifled grunt from Becky, but I didn't dare ask if she was okay. The crunching footsteps grew closer, the light roving through the cedars and oaks. I froze, hoping both of us were out of the flashlight's range.

It wasn't long before the steps drew even with us. The flashlight came within inches of me, and I cringed, trying to stay still so that the bags wouldn't crinkle. I followed the beam with my eyes. Unfortunately, it landed right on Becky's pink-clad rear end.

The footsteps stopped, and the beam lingered. "Get up," a male voice rumbled. Becky turned, looking terrified, and stood up slowly, hands in the air, squinting into the light. "Come here."

She took a step forward, and I panicked. What now? I felt for the bags, trying to find the gun. The crinkling of the plastic drew the man's attention, and the flashlight veered away from my friend, searching for me. My hand closed on the gun just as the beam found me. I pulled it out of the trash bag and leveled it at the man with one hand while I searched in my purse for my penlight with the other.

"Leave her alone," I warned him. I located the penlight and aimed it at his face. It was the janitor, the scar on his cheek looking particularly scary now that we were alone in the dark woods.

"What are you doing here?" he asked.

"Going for a walk," I told him. "What about you? Working the late shift?"

"I heard there was a break-in," he said. "I was coming to check it out."

"Well, go check it out, then," I said.

"What happened to your friend's pants?"

"Bathroom accident," she said. "You really need to do a better job cleaning."

"You broke in," he said in a menacing voice, turning on Becky. His hand snaked out and grabbed her throat. She let out a strangled cry, and I saw his other hand dart for his pocket. "That's against the rules," he hissed.

The gun was heavy in my hand, but I couldn't bring myself to pull the trigger. Instead, I lurched forward and brought the butt of the gun down on his head as hard as I could.

His hand slithered away from Becky's throat, and he fell to the ground like a sack of rocks.

• • •

"Thanks," Becky said, massaging her throat and looking down at the custodian. "That really hurt!"

"That's one scary dude," I said as we both contemplated the unconscious man on the ground. "Thank God I grabbed his gun before we left."

"No kidding," she said. "Although I think most people shoot them instead of using them as blunt weapons."

"It worked," I said, "and we won't go to trial for murder."

"Well, not for murdering the custodian, anyway."

I sighed. "What do we do now?"

"What was he reaching for?" she asked.

I knelt down and poked at his pockets. In his left-hand pocket was a small, gun-shaped object. "I think he was going to pull a gun on you."

"I think we should call Peaches," Becky said as I fished out the gun. We both looked at it; the dull metal gleamed coldly as I shone my light on it. I handed it to Becky and reached for my phone, then realized I didn't have one.

"Can I borrow your cell phone?" I asked.

"It's in my purse," she said, tossing me her enormous handbag as she pointed the gun at the back of the custodian's shaved head. I fished her phone out from a jumble of lipstick tubes and dialed Peaches's cell phone.

"Yeah?" Peaches answered in a gruff voice.

"It's Margie," I said. "I just knocked out the custodian of Holy Oaks."

"You what?"

"We broke in and set off a silent alarm. When we snuck out of the building into the woods, we had a run-in with him."

"Why did you knock him out?"

"He attacked Becky," I said. "I found a gun and some packets of drugs in the custodian's closet."

"What was he doing at the school?"

"He knew we'd broken in. He had a gun on him; he attacked Becky when we were walking back to the car."

"How would a custodian know the security alarm went off?" she asked.

"I don't know," I said.

"I think we need to find out. I'll be right over," she said. "Can you tie him up?"

"Tie him up?" I asked.

"I thought we'd bring him back to the Pretty Kitten and ask him a few questions," she said. "I'm on my way."

"Umm . . . could you bring some spare clothes?" I asked, glancing at Becky.

"Why?"

"Becky fell into a toilet."

"I'm not even going to ask," Peaches said, and hung up.

• • •

The shopping-center parking lot was empty when we pulled into the Pretty Kitten an hour later. I'd attempted to hog-tie the custodian with Becky's wet jeans. By the time Peaches had arrived with a pair of yoga pants and some slippers for Becky, we'd dragged him out of the woods to the side of the road.

Now, the three of us stood a few feet back from the trunk, aiming the two guns we'd commandeered as Peaches prepared to hit the trunk button on her key fob.

"If you have to shoot," she said, "try to get it in the trunk. I just spent three thousand dollars getting the exterior cleaned up."

"Got it," I said.

"Ready?" she asked.

I nodded, hoping my hog-tying job had held, and she popped it open.

Thankfully, the man was still passed out. Peaches handed Becky the keys to the storefront; as Becky unlocked the door, Peaches grabbed the janitor beneath the arms and I took hold of his legs. *We're getting the hang of moving bodies,* I thought. Was that something you could put on a résumé?

"They don't have security cameras here, do they?" I asked, thinking of Wanda—and Detective Bunsen.

"I disabled them," Peaches said.

"Good," I said. I didn't want to know how.

We pushed through the doorway into the darkened waiting room of the Pretty Kitten. I turned right, heading toward Peachtree Investigations, but Peaches pulled to the left.

"I thought you wanted to question him," I said, trying to tighten my grip on his ankles.

"I do," she said, steering the body toward one of the waxing rooms. "Let's get him up on the table in here, and then we can strap him down."

"Strap him down?" Becky asked.

"I've got some tie-down straps in my desk drawer," she said. "They come in handy for lots of things."

We slid him onto the table as Becky hurried to retrieve the tie-downs. "You got a gun?" Peaches asked me.

"Two of them."

"Point one of them at him while I untie him," she said.

"Got it." I fished the gun out of my pocket and aimed it somewhere toward him but away from where Peaches was inspecting my handiwork.

"This looks pretty good," she said, "but you didn't use a square knot."

"How do you know about hog-tying?" I asked.

"I did 4-H as a kid. Plus, Jess has some hogs; I gave him a hand with them a few months ago."

"How is Jess, by the way?"

"Shut up and I'll teach you how to do this," she said. She untied the big knot I'd made in Becky's wet jeans and showed me the proper way to do it. I had just practiced what Peaches had showed me when Becky came back in with an armful of blue straps.

"Are these what you mean?" she asked.

"Exactly," Peaches said, sniffing her hands. "You might need to burn those jeans," she told Becky as she untied the knot, leaving the custodian spread-eagled on the table.

"And you might want to bleach your hands," Becky said, her nose wrinkled.

"Once we get him secured, I will," Peaches said, reaching for a tie. "Man," she said. "This guy's thumbs are like cucumbers." She glanced at his fly. "I wonder if the old saying is true."

"Peaches!" I said . . . and then something clicked. "Thumbs," I said. "When we were at the Sweet Shop, Marty Krumbacher was threatening to set someone named Thumbs on someone else if they didn't do what Marty wanted."

"You think this is him?" Peaches asked.

"Have you seen his hands?" I said. "Still . . . why would he be working as a custodian?"

"A custodian with two guns and a bunch of drug packets," Peaches reminded me. "Who has a gang tattoo and showed up when there was a security breach. Ever thought maybe custodian wasn't his only job?"

Now that she mentioned it, it made sense. "Even so, it doesn't mean there's a connection between him and Krumbacher."

"The good news is, we can ask him all about it in a few minutes," Peaches replied, cinching the guy's hands together under the table. Within moments, she had the custodian completely incapacitated. Not for the first time, I reflected that I hadn't seen a lot of Peaches's investigative techniques in the official private-investigator handbook. I was a little worried about what she had in mind now that she had him laid out on a table. Could we be arrested for kidnapping? He had tried to go after Becky, but . . .

Peaches turned to the sink and scrubbed her hands. As soon as she finished, I squirted a glob of soap into my palms and shoved them under the water, glancing over as my boss flipped the switch on what looked like a little Crock-Pot. An orange light glowed on it.

"What's that?" I asked.

"Wax," she said. "It's still pretty warm; it shouldn't take long to get to temperature."

"Why do we need wax?" Becky said as she picked up her jeans with a wad of tissues and carried them to the trash can in the corner of the room. It was a very serene space, very spa-like, with relaxing bluish walls and a comforting minty scent that almost eclipsed the smell of Becky's wet jeans.

"We're going to use it to convince our friend to tell us what he knows," Peaches said, giving the wax an experimental stir with a small wooden paddle.

"You're going to wax him into talking?" I asked. The bad feeling I had grew abruptly worse. Interrogation with waxing definitely wasn't in the handbook. Was involuntary hair removal a prosecutable offense?

"That's the plan," Peaches said, giving the wax a final stir and turning to the custodian. She pulled up his faded red T-shirt to expose a hairy, muscular stomach. "This guy works out," she said admiringly. "Look at those abs."

"He is pretty ripped," Becky said, staring at the man's stomach. "How do you think he does it? I do all the custodial work at my house, and my abs don't look anything like that."

"You can ask him in a minute," Peaches said. She eyed the wiry hair covering his six-pack abs. "At least we've got plenty of hair to work with. I'll be right back; I just have to go get the smelling salts."

She sauntered out of the room, and Becky and I looked at each other. "For before she waxes him, or after?" Becky asked.

"Let's just hope she doesn't decide to give him a Brazilian," I said, and Becky winced. As the smell of melted wax filled the room, we both turned to look at the unconscious man strapped to the table.

"Is it legal to tie someone down and wax him without his consent?" Becky asked.

I was pretty sure it wasn't, but I didn't know what our other options were. "He attacked you," I reminded her. "Plus, the guy kept a gun and drugs at my daughter's school, in an unlocked closet."

"True," she conceded.

"And more importantly, if we don't find out what happened to George Cavendish, one or both of us may be going to jail for a murder we didn't commit."

She bit her lip. "When you look at it that way . . ."

Peaches bustled into the room with a tiny blue jar. She looked at both of us. "Ready?"

CHAPTER THIRTY

Before we had a chance to answer, Peaches had whipped the top off the jar and jammed it under Thumbs's nose. He jerked awake and started swearing.

"Good morning!" Peaches said in a cheery voice as his head rolled around on the spa pillow. He strained against his bonds, but Peaches evidently had the tying-up thing down pat.

"Untie me, you fat bitch!" he commanded.

"That wasn't very chivalrous," Peaches said, unperturbed, as she walked over to the wax warmer. His eyes followed her, then darted to me. For a moment, he was confused; then I saw the recognition click.

"Hi," I said, giving him a small wave.

"Your kid goes to Holy Oaks," he said.

"Yeah," Becky piped up. "Speaking of Holy Oaks, you need to step it up a bit. The sanitation in the boys' room is disgusting!"

"Becky," I warned her. He'd accused us of breaking into Holy Oaks—and to be honest, why else would we be running through the woods behind the school after dark?—but that didn't mean she needed to spell it out for him.

Peaches pulled a wheeled stool out from under the counter and sat down on it, then rolled over next to him, kind of like a doctor about to examine a patient, if the patient were tied up and the doctor were dressed in a green spandex minidress. "So," she said. "If you're a custodian, why were you racing back to the school when an alarm went off?"

He shrugged as well as he could, considering his arms were trussed up like turkey legs. "I take my job seriously," he said.

"Evidently not," Becky said. "Those toilets were disgusting."

He gave her a confused look. I kicked her to try to get her to shut up.

Peaches stirred the wax. "Do you know Marty Krumbacher?" she asked him.

"Never heard of him," he said.

"Is that why he's a contact on your phone?" she asked. On the way back to the Pretty Kitten, she'd gone through his phone. Krumbacher was definitely a frequent caller.

He snapped his mouth shut, looking nervous.

Peaches pulled the paddle out of the little pot. It was covered with molten wax. "Does the name *Thumbs* mean anything to you?"

His eyes widened. "No," he said quickly, but his face told a different story.

"Are you sure?" she asked.

"Never heard of it." His eyes followed the wax-laden paddle as it drifted closer to his stomach. "What are you doing?" His voice seemed a bit high.

"Oh, just asking questions," Peaches said. "Like, do you know anything about what happened to George Cavendish?"

"The dude died." He stared at the paddle, transfixed. "Get that thing away from me."

"I know he died," she said. "I was hoping to find out a little more than what I can read in the *Statesman*."

"I don't know anything about Cavendish," he said, looking just like Elsie when I'd asked her if she was the one who ate the rest of the marshmallows.

"Last chance," she said, letting the paddle hover his navel for a moment. Becky and I watched, transfixed, as a glob of wax oozed off the end of the paddle. It looked a little like vanilla pudding.

"We'll start with the stomach, I think," Peaches said, and scooped up a big wad of wax and slapped it down just under his belly button, spreading it around like frosting on a cake. "See any cloth strips?" she asked, looking at Becky and me.

"Right here," Becky said, grabbing one from the neat stack on the counter and handing it to her.

"Perfect," Peaches said, smoothing one out over the wax. "I've never done this before, but I'm sure we'll figure it out."

I didn't think it was possible for the guy on the table to look more nervous, but I was wrong.

Peaches smoothed out the cloth and let the wax sit on his skin for a moment. Then she said, in her perkiest tone of voice, "I think it's ready!"

The custodian's voice was husky. "If you tear that off of me, I swear I'll—"

"Here we go!" she sang out, grabbing one end of the cloth and giving it a tug.

He yowled, and then spat out what I presumed were a few curse words in a language I didn't understand.

About halfway through, Peaches stopped. The cloth strip was covered with hair, and there was a bald, pinkish spot on the custodian's flat stomach. "Anything pop into your head?" she asked.

He shook his head. Beads of sweat had sprung up on his temples.

"All righty, then," she said, and ripped off the rest. He yelped. "It's hard to believe people pay for this, isn't it?" she said as she applied another glob of wax a little bit farther south. "Hand me a cloth, Becky?"

"Here ya go," Becky said, handing Peaches another strip of cloth.

"Okay. So, you were working as Marty Krumbacher's henchman. Right? Did he hire you to kill Cavendish?"

The custodian shook his head like a wild animal. "You crazy, lady. Wait until I tell—" He seemed to realize he was about to share classified information, and stopped talking.

"Tell who?"

He swore. Peaches sighed. And then she pulled the second strip.

• • •

By the time he started talking, Thumbs's entire torso was as smooth as a baby's bottom, I had a migraine from the screaming, and Becky was almost out of cloth strips.

"Look," Peaches told him. "I don't really want to give you a Brazilian. You don't really want me to give you a Brazilian. Just tell us what we need to know, and I'll give you an ice pack and a handful of Motrin and we can all go home."

"Oh, God. No," he begged.

"Just tell us who you're working for and what you know," Peaches said, stirring what was left of the wax. "It'll be easier than the Brazilian. That flesh down there is a little looser; I'll bet it hurts like the dickens."

He was quiet for a moment—he looked like Nick when he was trying to hold it until he got to a bathroom—and then it all exploded out. "Krumbacher," he said in a strained voice. "I work for him. I take care of problems."

"Terrific, sweetheart," Peaches crooned. "Margie, can you get an ice pack out of the freezer?"

As I hurried over to the dorm-size freezer in the corner of the room, she asked, "What do you know about Cavendish?"

"Mr. Krumbacher wasn't happy with him," Thumbs said. "He was causing problems. That's why I was working at Holy Oaks—to keep an eye on the guy, let him know Mr. Krumbacher was watching him."

"Were the problems big enough to kill him?"

"No," he said. "I warned him we had pictures he didn't want in the paper. Mr. Krumbacher wanted me around as a reminder. Said the guy was going to pull money out of the business and go to the cops."

"About what?"

"Afterburn," he said.

"The stuff you had in your closet," I said, walking over to him with a blue gel ice pack I'd found on the bottom shelf of the freezer.

He looked at me. "You were in the custodial closet?"

"Yes. I hit you with your own gun," I confessed, then asked, "What is Afterburn?"

"It's like marijuana," he said. "But legal."

"And lethal," I said. "I've seen a lot of articles about people dying from it." Including the article in Cavendish's pants, now that I thought of it.

"They were coming out with a new formula as soon as they ran out of what they had."

"Where was the distribution point?" I asked.

"I don't know," Thumbs said. "I just do what Mr. Krumbacher tells me. I swear," he added, as Peaches gave the wax an exaggerated stir.

"So you didn't kill Cavendish," Peaches said. "Do you know who did?"

"Maybe it was the dude's wife. He was into some weird shit. Women get crazy like that."

"Or maybe you did it."

He shook his head. "No. Mr. Krumbacher never asked me to kill nobody. I've roughed up a few people," he admitted, "but I never offed anyone."

"But Holy Oaks was invested in the drug operation."

"Yeah." He looked wildly at Peaches. "But that's all he told me. I don't know nothing about how the dude died. All I know is I was supposed to scare him."

"Scare him, or kill him?"

"*Scare* him. Let him know Krumbacher was watching him. Jesus, lady. I told you everything I know. Will you let me go now? Please?"

Peaches looked at the wax and at Thumbs's flat, now-hairless stomach. "We probably should. I've never waxed anybody's balls before. I'd hate to rip the skin."

We gave a collective shudder.

"All right," she told him. "Are you ready to do what we ask you to do?"

"Yes." His voice was hoarse. "Anything you say. Just get me out of here."

"My friend here is going to blindfold you," Peaches said. "And then my other friend is going to point a loaded gun at your wiener while I untie you from the table. She's at close range and a pretty good shot," Peaches lied, "so if you like having a sex life, I'd be real careful. Are we clear?"

He turned even paler and nodded.

I pointed the gun in a southerly direction while Becky tied a waxing cloth over his eyes. I couldn't possibly shoot a man in the crotch, but Thumbs didn't need to know that. I tensed as Peaches untied his hands and legs; fortunately, his limbs seemed to be asleep. Everything was going fine until Peaches tried to help him to his feet. That's when he pretended to trip, making Peaches lurch forward. He sprang into action, ripping off his blindfold and lunging for her.

"Margie!" Peaches called. I was still holding the gun, but I couldn't bring myself to pull the trigger. Odds were good I'd hit Peaches if I tried to shoot Thumbs; they were right on top of each other. He was moving to get her into a headlock, but she kneed him in the groin, and he doubled over. As she started to stand up, his arm shot up and his fist sank deep in her stomach.

"That's for the wax, you bitch."

He reared back for another punch. Peaches took a step back, clearing some distance. I aimed at the floor near his right foot and pulled the trigger just as Peaches grabbed the wax warmer and brought it down on his head.

The gun went off a split second after the wax warmer crashed down on his skull. For the second time that night, Thumbs collapsed, unconscious.

"Thanks for not shooting me," Peaches said, surveying both the unconscious custodian and the new divot in the hardwood floor. The walls and ceiling were covered with globs of goo; it looked like someone had tried to make a wax smoothie and forgotten to put the lid on the blender. "That makes things a little bit easier, although I don't know how we're going to explain the bullet hole to Wanda." She looked up at me. "You might keep your kid home from school until they find a new janitor, though."

CHAPTER THIRTY-ONE

The house was dark by the time I pulled into the driveway. I checked the clock on the dashboard: it was past midnight. We'd left Thumbs on the doorstep of Holy Oaks, still unconscious, with his phone shoved into his back pocket. After dropping off Becky, who had scuttled in the back door of her house wearing Peaches's peacock-feather yoga pants and hoping her husband was asleep, I had turned for home.

My adrenaline was still running high, and I considered the bag on the front seat of the car. It still had the gun and the Afterburn packets in it. I grabbed it and stowed the bag on top of one of the garage shelves, tucking it in behind the inflatable Frosty the Snowman. It was still August, so I figured it would be safe for at least a couple of months—not that I planned on keeping it that long. If the custodian said anything to the police—an unlikely prospect, my instincts told me, but still worth thinking about—someone might search my house tomorrow. I'd have to figure out what to do with it—and fast.

I had the urge to tell the police all about what I'd found, but that would be problematic—particularly if they got in touch with Thumbs, and he shared tonight's activities with them. Besides, I'd have to explain why I'd been digging around in the janitor's closet—and Bunsen might make a connection between this afternoon's gunshots at the Pretty Kitten and the security alarm at Holy Oaks. If only I had some sort of evidence to take to the police.

What did I have? I had copies of the bank statements from Golden Investments, although it would be hard to explain how I got that information. Plus I had the piece of paper with the code-like thing on it, which I'd found taped to the bottom of Cavendish's desk drawer. Could I send the info to Bunsen as an anonymous tip? The problem was, although I suspected the Afterburn was being distributed by Golden Investments—or at least by someone in the business—I had no way of proving it. And I was pretty sure Cavendish had been killed by either Thumbs or Marty Krumbacher himself. Even if Marty hadn't actually pulled the trigger, I was sure he had ordered it. If only I had some proof.

I couldn't tell Bunsen that Desiree had seen a red Lexus at the scene of the crime. But there had to be some way to share what we knew with the police—and point the suspicion at Marty.

And the sooner the better. My minivan had been shot at the office this afternoon, and I'd just pissed off a dangerous, gun-toting man named Thumbs. What if he decided to come after me at home? I leaned up against the garage wall, thinking of Elsie and Nick, sleeping in their beds. If anything happened to either of them . . . I couldn't bear to think about it. Should I ask Prudence to take them for a few days, just in case?

I grabbed my purse and pulled out the folded yellow legal paper, studying the strings of letters and numbers. If only I could figure out what they meant, maybe I could break the case open. Would Peaches have any ideas? I reached for my phone before I remembered it was gone. Still with Bubba Sue—just like Elsie's fry phone, which Bubba Sue had been frolicking with for days now. I had to get back there and get that phone.

Tomorrow, I vowed as I let myself into the quiet house, wrinkling my nose at the faint scent of incense. Mom must have been smudging again, getting rid of negative influences.

I hoped it extended to gun-toting, hairless janitors.

• • •

Elsie refused to get out of bed the next morning. I understood completely; I'd barely slept, and felt as if my brain had been replaced with pudding. The fact that Rufus had decided to sleep at my feet and attack my toes every time I rolled over hadn't helped. Not for the first time, I wondered why we'd picked a cat instead of a dog.

At least no one has shot up the house, I thought as I bundled myself into my bathrobe and faced my daughter's fry-phone interrogation. "I'm sorry I don't have it," I told her. "I'm working on it."

"You promised," she said.

"I know," I told her. "And I'm so sorry." Guilt stabbed me.

"No school," she said. "I hate it there."

"It'll get better, honey," I said, stroking her dark hair. "It's a tough transition, I know."

"Oh, just let her spend the day with me," my mother said.

Normally, I'd insist she go to school, but after what had happened at Holy Oaks last night, I gave in. For all I knew, there was a full battery of AK-47s hidden in the gardening shed. Plus, I didn't want her anywhere near Thumbs, particularly while he was recovering from last night's depilatory procedure. How was I going to alert the administration without giving myself away? "Fine," I said. "Just this once. I'll e-mail her teacher and find out what the homework is."

Elsie gave me a brief smile, then turned somber. Tears welled in her big eyes. "Why do you keep forgetting to bring me my fry phone?"

"I'm working on it," I said, wondering what I was going to do to get it back. With everything else that had gone on, I hadn't come up with a plan for Bubba Sue.

"Oh, she'll get it back to you, sweetheart," my mother said. "But we don't need it today, anyway. We'll make fairy houses in the backyard and walk to the library." She turned to me. "You could come with us!"

"I'd love to," I said, "but things are kind of hectic at work." To say the least.

My mother sighed. "I was so hoping we'd have more time together."

"I'm sorry," I said, feeling like not just the mother of the year, but the daughter of the year, as well. "Me too. I just didn't realize this week was going to be so busy. Thank you so much for all of your help."

My mother glanced out the window. "Whatever happened to the minivan, anyway?"

"Engine trouble," I said breezily as I searched the cabinets for something to feed my children. In all the excitement, I'd forgotten to stop by the grocery store yesterday; it looked like another morning of apple slices and oatmeal. My mother had wanted to deep-six the Quaker's, but I managed to salvage it on the basis of its whole-graininess. "It's in the shop."

I poured oatmeal and water into a bowl, tucked it into the microwave, and reached for my laptop to dash off an e-mail to Elsie's teacher. My mother helped get Nick dressed as I doctored the oatmeal with honey—the only Grandma-approved sweetener in the house—and cinnamon. I still didn't have a lunch plan; it looked like another pre-school trip to Subway was in my future.

As I gathered Nick's shoes and began herding him toward the door, the phone rang. I hesitated—it could be Detective Bunsen—and then picked it up.

"Hello?"

"Margie! Are you okay?"

"Blake," I said, putting down the shoes. "Hi. Yes, I'm fine. Why?"

"I've been calling your cell phone for days."

"I, uh, lost it," I said, smiling at Nick and retreating to my bedroom. I wasn't sure I wanted to have this conversation in the same room as my mother and children. "How's the retreat going?" I asked as I closed the bedroom door behind me.

"It's been . . . interesting," he said. "Did you go to the wives' group?"

"It was . . . interesting," I replied. I didn't want to go into the whole meatloaf-and-push-up-bra philosophy of Warrior Wives—or the fact that I'd been shot at, abetted the waxing of a hog-tied custodian, and broken into my daughter's school since his departure—so I asked, "Are you glad you signed up?"

"Yes . . . and no," he said. "It's been a mind-blowing experience."

"Oh?" I asked cautiously.

"I've come to a big decision," he said.

"Ah," I said. "What's that?"

He hesitated. "Um . . . we should probably talk about it face-to-face," he told me. "I've got to run; they're starting the first group session. Love to the kids. I'll see you tomorrow afternoon."

"Blake—"

"Bye, Margie!" he said, and hung up, leaving me holding the phone.

"Margie, dear!" It was my mother. "Nick's calling for you!"

Still preoccupied, I headed out of the bedroom to the kitchen, where Elsie was sitting in the corner with a bowl of the untouched oatmeal. "I love you, sweetheart," I said, leaning down to kiss my daughter's head. She reached out and clung to my leg, pressing her soft cheek into my calf. "Don't go," she said.

"I'll be back before you know it," I told her. "You have fun playing hooky with Grandma."

"You said you left it at the office, but you never bring it home."

"I did leave it," I told her, detaching her arms from my leg and feeling like the worst mother in the world. "And I'm getting it back today."

• • •

Wanda gave me a suspicious look as I walked into the Pretty Kitten forty minutes later—we'd cleaned up the wax the best we could, but there were a few spots on the ceiling we couldn't reach—and let myself into the Peachtree Investigations wing. I laid the yellow legal paper I'd found in Cavendish's office out on the desk and stared at it for an hour, rearranging the digits and trying to make sense of it. *The key to the whole case must be here,* I thought, but I had no idea what the code meant. Defeated, I opened my laptop and started with the search term *pig sedative.* Within fifteen minutes, I had brushed up on my rudimentary understanding of hog-tying—and a plan. I couldn't crack the Cavendish case, but at least I could get my daughter's fry phone back.

The moaning had already started next door by the time I headed back out to the car—apparently, Wanda was occupied with hair removal, so I didn't have to face another withering glare. My first stop was a hardware store, where I picked up a coil of rope and a tarp. My second stop was HEB, where I went through the express lane with a dog bowl and a six-pack of Lone Star beer.

"Rough morning?" the checker asked as she slid the six-pack into the cloth bag I'd brought.

"You have no idea," I told her, giving her a grim smile as I grabbed the bag and headed to the Leaf.

CHAPTER THIRTY-TWO

There was no sign of life at Bubba Sue's place. I parked a few houses down, grabbed the bag with the beer, and once again attempted to look nonchalant as I strolled into the side yard of the bungalow.

The shades were down and there was no Range Rover in the driveway—a good sign, I thought. I could hear the sound of snuffling and low grunting from behind the fence—also a good sign.

I popped open one of the Lone Stars, poured it into the dog bowl, and opened the gate a few inches. "Here, piggy, piggy, piggy!" I crooned, pushing the bowl through the gate and quickly yanking it closed.

The grunting intensified. A moment later, I heard the thud of hooves, and the snuffling sound came closer. "That's a good girl," I said, peering at Bubba Sue through a crack in the fence. She had evidently been wallowing; her coat was covered in dried mud, making me glad I'd thought to bring the tarp. She sniffed at the bowl, then gave it a tentative taste. Evidently beer for breakfast was all right with Bubba Sue; the tasting turned into slurping, and within thirty seconds the bowl was empty. I popped open the second Lone Star and pushed the gate open enough to fit my arm through. She let out a squeal, but the sound of beer pouring into the bowl calmed her quickly. She finished off the second Lone Star in record time, licking the foam off of her muzzle and giving me a hopeful look.

"That's enough for now," I told her, and checked to be sure the gate was closed. Then I gathered my empties and headed back to the car. A half hour later, after stopping for a quick coffee and a review of eHow's page on hog-tying, I returned to Bubba Sue, the rope in one hand and the tarp in another.

I once again strolled to the side yard of Bubba Sue's house, standing beside the Turk's-cap bush and listening. There was no grunting, which was encouraging, and when I peered through the crack in the fence, there was no sign of a pig. "Bubba Sue!" I called.

Nothing.

I eased the gate open and stepped inside, praying that the Lone Star had done its job. I crept to the edge of the house and peeked around it. Bubba Sue was sprawled in the middle of the backyard, emitting a light, whiffling snore at regular intervals.

Next to her, coated liberally in something slimy and brown, was Elsie's fry phone.

With a nervous glance back at the house—I hadn't forgotten that shotgun—I tiptoed out into the middle of the yard, scanning for signs of movement from Bubba Sue—and for my iPhone, which was still MIA. I grabbed the fry phone, which looked miraculously intact, and wiped off most of the brown gunk on a patch of grass. *I should have bought bleach while I was at the store,* I reflected as I tucked it into my pocket.

I grabbed the rope, said a small prayer, and reached for Bubba Sue's rear hooves.

She twitched, and I jumped back, prepared to run for the gate. But her eyes didn't open. Emboldened, I looped a bit of the rope around the hooves and approximated what I'd read about in the hog-tying tutorial.

She didn't move—the beer tip had evidently been right on target—but the tangle of rope around her hooves looked nothing like the pictures on eHow.

She was still asleep, though, and it would have to do. I heaved her onto the tarp and wrapped it around her so she looked like a pig burrito, and then saw the flaw in my plan.

How was I going to get a 150-pound pig out of the backyard and into a Nissan Leaf?

I grabbed the ends of the tarp and tugged with all my strength. She moved about a foot, and grunted softly. I wiped my brow and tugged again. Ten minutes later, I was standing at the gate and looking at the rental car. I was going to have to move it a whole lot closer.

I abandoned Bubba Sue and retrieved the car, pulling it up as close to the gate as I could, and jogged back to the gate. I was about to pull her out of the side yard when a familiar ring came from somewhere in the yard. I dropped the tarp and raced to the back of the house, searching for the source.

A moment later, I found the corner of my phone peeking out of a pile of pig manure. I grabbed it and swiped the screen on the grass before looking at the display.

It was Detective Bunsen calling.

• • •

Maybe it was karma after the week I'd had, but somehow I managed to get Bubba Sue out to the curb without incident. It was only when I tried to lever her into the backseat (there was no way she'd fit into the trunk) that I ran into trouble. I was straining to get her head up onto the seat when a young man with a scraggly beard called out to me from across the street.

"What are you doing?" he asked.

I looked up guiltily, feeling like I'd been caught with my hand in the cookie jar. Or a purloined pig halfway into my rental car, as the case may be. Bubba Sue grunted quietly; was she coming to? Should I have given her a third beer?

"My, uh, pig is sick," I said. "I was trying to get her to the vet. She's pregnant with piglets, and I'm worried about her." Partial truth, Peaches had said, was the best way to go. Bubba Sue *was* pregnant, and I *was* worried about her—primarily that (a) I couldn't get her into the car, and (b) if I did get her into the car, she'd wake up when I was only halfway home and start a one-pig stampede in the backseat.

"I haven't seen you in the neighborhood," he said.

"Oh," I said. "I . . . I'm new to the area."

"Nice to meet you," he said, ambling over. "Can I give you a hand?"

"That would be great," I said, thanking my guardian angel or whoever it was who seemed to be looking out for me this morning. With the young man's help, we levered Bubba Sue into the back of the Leaf. I tucked her snout in and gently closed the door.

"Where are you taking her?" he asked.

"My laundry room," I said without thinking.

"What?"

"She's pregnant," I told him. "The piglets need a safe, warm place when they're born."

"It's ninety-five degrees at night," he pointed out, stroking his wispy beard.

"Yes," I agreed. "Did I say warm? I meant to say cool. Also there are . . . predators here."

"In this neighborhood? We're practically in downtown Austin."

"Um . . . coyotes. Owls."

Wispy Beard gave me a suspicious look. "I didn't know owls were partial to pork."

"Better safe than sorry. No predators in my laundry room." Well, except Rufus, anyway. But I would put my money on Bubba Sue.

"Can't you just put them in the laundry room here?"

"Have to take her to the vet first. Anyway," I said, anxious to end this conversation, and not happy with Wispy Beard's sudden interest in pig husbandry, "I've got to run before she wakes up. Thank you so much. You're a lifesaver."

"No problem," he told me. "See you around!"

I sincerely hope not, I thought as I scurried to the front of the car. Checking to be sure both phones were in my pocket, I wedged myself into the driver's seat and took off before Bubba Sue's daddy got home with his shotgun. As I turned onto South Lamar, I rolled the windows down and allowed myself a small fist pump. I might smell like manure, but I had both phones in my possession—not to mention a pig.

. . .

Bubba Sue had just started to stir when I pulled into the driveway. I rolled the windows partway up and hurried into the house. My mother, thankfully, hadn't gone to the library yet. She and Elsie were at the kitchen table, making crayon rubbings of kale leaves.

"Could you give me a hand with something?" I asked as I cleared the laundry-room floor of baskets, shoes, and detergent bottles.

"What do you need?"

"I need help getting a pig into the laundry room."

My mother looked up at me and grinned. "You got her?"

"Yeah, but now we can't reach the client." I'd called her owner on the way home and left a message, but hadn't heard back.

"Is she cute?" my mother asked, getting up from the table. "I've always wanted to see a potbellied pig."

"Not exactly," I said, leading her out to the car. Elsie trailed behind us, her rhinestone dog collar flashing in the sunlight. To my dismay, a grunting noise issued from the Leaf as we approached, and the car appeared to be quivering.

"Sounds lively," my mother said. As we took a cautious step toward the car, an enormous porcine head loomed up in the side window.

"Jesus," my mother said, forgetting her granddaughter was right next to her. "If that's a teacup pig, I'd hate to see the teapot variety. She looks like a cross between Wilbur and King Kong."

Bubba Sue evidently didn't take well to the comparison, as she began ramming one of the doors with her snout. My mother and I both took a step back.

"Looks lively, too," my mother said. "How did you get her in there?"

"I fed her two beers and hog-tied her," I said.

"I think you need to work on your hog-tying technique," she recommended.

"I followed the eHow directions. Maybe she got loose while I was pulling her in the tarp."

"Got any more beer?"

"Yes," I said. "But it's in the car."

My mother crossed her arms and considered the pig. "That's too bad." We both watched as Bubba Sue squeezed between the front seats and planted her hooves on the dashboard. With every ripple of her muscled hide, large chunks of mud and pig manure fell off onto the upholstery. I didn't want to think about how I was going to explain this to the rental-car company. "How does she feel about scotch?" my mother asked.

"I don't know," I said. "But how are we going to get it in there?"

"A bowl won't work; it'll spill," she mused. Then she clapped her hands together. "Let's try a baby bottle. You still have any?"

A baby bottle? I looked at Bubba Sue's teeth, which glinted in the reflection off the hood. "In the Goodwill box in the garage," I said. "I don't know, though . . ."

"Got any other ideas?"

"It's worth a try."

We headed back into the house. I dug through the box in the garage and pulled out a baby bottle while my mother grabbed Blake's bottle of scotch from on top of the fridge.

"What are you doing?" Elsie asked as I unscrewed the nipple and emptied the rest of Blake's Macallan 15 into the baby bottle.

"Giving the pig some medicine," I told her as I topped it off and put the nipple back on.

"Daddy drinks a lot of medicine," she said, looking concerned as my mother and I headed out to the car.

If the Leaf was quivering before, now it was convulsing.

"What is that pig doing?" Elsie asked.

"It looks like she's trying to rip out the seats," my mother observed. "If I were you, Marigold, I'd get that scotch into her ASAP."

I advanced on the car, brandishing the bottle like a gun, and introduced the nipple into the cracked-open back window. A bit of scotch dribbled from the end of it. Fortunately, the scent was potent enough to distract Bubba Sue from her seat-removal campaign. She snuffled a few times, then turned her head, seeking the source of the intoxicating aroma.

"It's working," my mother murmured as the giant pig shoved herself back between the front seats and lunged toward the window. She latched onto the end of the bottle, sucking hard on the nipple. She'd downed about a third of the scotch before giving the silicone nipple a playful tug that ripped it right off the bottle. About three-quarters of a cup of Macallan 15 sloshed out onto the backseat of the Leaf, which Bubba Sue immediately began licking.

"Shit," I said, then realized my daughter was standing right next to me. "I mean, snit," I said.

"Do you think she got enough?" my mother asked, peering at Bubba Sue through the side window.

"I don't know," I said, watching as she snuffled the stained cloth seat, "but I think we should pull up that hog-tying site again."

CHAPTER THIRTY-THREE

As it turns out, a third of a bottle of Macallan 15 was enough. Twenty minutes later, Bubba Sue was sprawled across the backseat, her head lolling to one side, looking much cleaner now that she'd knocked all the dried pig manure off onto the car's interior. I could really make out the white spot on her snout.

"She's kind of cute when she's sedated," my mother commented as she tugged on Bubba Sue's front legs and I shoved her from behind. I gave one more shove and she slid out of the car and onto the tarp. My mother helped me roll her onto her back, then read the eHow instructions out to me. The final product made her look like she'd tripped on a tangle of rope, but it would have to do; I had no idea when she'd wake up.

"Are you sure you want her in your laundry room?" my mother asked as I gave the rope a final, futile tug. "Wouldn't the backyard be a better option?"

"Have you seen my fence?" I asked. It was essentially a few pickets held up by a mass of English ivy; in fact, I wasn't sure there were any pickets left under the tangle of leaves and vines. "She'd be galloping down MoPac by dinnertime." I stood up. "Can you get the back end? Elsie, will you open the front door?"

"Sure, Mommy," she said, and pushed the door open. My mother and I traipsed through the house with Bubba Sue suspended in her blue tarp, and deposited her in the laundry room. We stood and considered her for a moment.

"Maybe I should untie her," I said.

"I don't know if that's a good idea, but we should at least put a water bowl in here," my mother said. "And what about food? What do pigs eat, anyway?"

"She seems to like phones," I said.

"Phones?"

I glanced back to see Elsie approaching. "Never mind. We should probably leave her tied up for now—I'm sure her owner will be here soon. But water's a good idea."

"But how will she get to it?"

"We'll put it by her head," I said with a confidence I didn't feel. "Elsie, can you get the bowl I left in the car? It's in a bag in the back." My daughter trotted off to retrieve it, and as my mother helped her rinse and fill it, I tossed a couple of seaweed snacks on the floor next to Bubba Sue's head. I figured someone should eat them.

The pig was secured in the laundry room by eleven o'clock. I walked out to survey the damage. The rental car smelled like a cross between a bar and a feedlot, and Bubba Sue had managed to take a few chunks out of the passenger seat, but at least it was pig-free. Did insurance cover livestock damage? I wondered. Could we pass the expense on to the client?

I'd left a message for Peaches posing those questions, and I was about to take a shower and attempt to clean up the fry phone when my mother waylaid me in the bedroom hallway.

"Marigold," she said. "I'm worried about you."

"What do you mean?" I asked.

"Let's go sit on the back porch for a few minutes," she said. "Elsie's building a kale forest, so she'll be occupied for a few minutes."

"Sure," I said reluctantly, reviewing all the unresolved situations in my life as I followed her out to the back porch. The calls from Bunsen I wasn't returning. The attack on my van. The angry, deranged custodian. My husband's predilection for men in dresses. And, of course, Elsie's dog fixation. The only bright spot was that I had the fry phone—even if it was covered in pig manure.

I really didn't want to talk right then, but there was no way around it. My mother had been so wonderful to come and help out with the kids—and Elsie seemed to be blossoming under her care. I owed her listening to a nutrition lecture or two.

I brushed a few months of pollen and dust off the patio chairs and we sat down across from each other. "I'm sorry I've been so distracted the last few days," I said. "I got a friend of mine into some trouble accidentally, and I've been working hard to fix it."

"So it's not always like this?"

"No," I said, shaking my head. "And I haven't told you how much I appreciate your help. Particularly with Blake out of town—you've been a lifesaver."

"I'm glad I can be here," she said, smiling. "But I can tell that things are very out of balance for you."

That was the understatement of the decade. "Oh, it's just been a crazy week."

"My intuition tells me it's more than that. Everyone in the house just seems . . . disconnected, somehow." She waved her arms around, bangles jangling, and smiled at me. "And I still think there's more going on between you and Blake than you're telling me."

"Um . . . We're going through a bit of a rough patch."

She sighed. "I was afraid of that. I don't sense a heart connection between the two of you," she said.

I shrugged. "Doesn't that happen in all marriages once the kids come?"

She gave me a sad smile. "He was sleeping in the office before I got here, wasn't he?"

I looked down at the grass growing between the pavers. "The snoring was keeping me up."

"Hmm," she said, and waited.

Finally, I blurted, "It's complicated."

She reached out and took my hand in hers. "Your father and I went through that. We tried to keep things together for your sake, but in the long run . . ." She shrugged. "I think parting ways was the best thing we ever did."

I wasn't so sure. My father had pretty much disappeared from my life once I hit the age of ten, and it was a hole that no number of homeopathic remedies could fill.

"He made the atmosphere in the house toxic," my mother explained. "You don't remember it that way, but he felt so . . . constrained by family life, even though he loved you. As painful as it was, I believe in my heart that it was better for everyone for him to leave. And I wouldn't have been happy yoked to a man who really didn't want to be with me."

I felt as if she had slapped me. Was it that obvious that Blake wasn't attracted to me?

"I know you're worried about the kids," she said. "And I know how important a stable family is to you. But I don't want you to spend the next fifteen years in misery for their sake." She reached out to squeeze my hand. "It's not good for you—and it's not good for them, either."

"He's trying to work things out," I said. "That's where he is this week."

"I didn't think it was a business trip," she admitted.

"But a stable family . . . It would hurt the kids so much if we split up."

"Elsie's not doing so well right now as it is," she said. "She's a sensitive child. She knows something's wrong. That's why she's retreating into her fantasy world."

"And a divorce would help that?" I asked, running my hands through my hair. "Are you sure it's not just the school?"

"Her dog fascination started several months ago, didn't it?" she asked. "Although, to be honest, it doesn't sound like Holy Smokes a great environment for her, either."

"Holy Oaks," I corrected.

"Anyway, she's a creative child, and Holy Oaks . . ." my mother trailed off. "I just don't know if she'll thrive there. And your aura is so . . . *muddy* right now. I can sense it even on the phone." She twisted the bangles on her arm. "I'm sure Elsie's responding to that; she lives with you."

"I have been kind of stressed lately," I confessed, "but it's not just Blake." I looked up at my mother, who was smiling expectantly. "Remember I told you the headmaster died?"

"Yes? What about it?"

"What I didn't tell you was . . . well, Peaches asked me to help move the body."

My mother jangled as she sat up straight. "What?"

"He was in a hooker's apartment, wearing Aquaman tights and goggles." I didn't mention the urine. "Peaches was trying to help out a friend, and she asked me for help. Anyway, I accidentally dropped Becky's card on top of him, and the police found it."

My mother choked out a startled laugh. "Aquaman?"

"It's not funny," I said. "If I don't get it figured out in the next couple of days, I have to tell the police that I moved the body, and I'll probably go to jail."

"Why were you moving the body, anyway?" she asked.

"He got shot in a hooker's apartment," I told her. "The hooker is a friend of Peaches, and she didn't want her parents to find out what she was doing to pay her way through college."

My mother sat back in her chair. "That's why you've been gone so much. I knew it wasn't just the pig."

"Well, there's been that, too."

"Any idea who did it?"

"I must be getting close, since someone shot up the minivan at the office yesterday."

Her eyes widened. "What?"

"That's why I have the rental. I also found some strange words on a paper hidden in Cavendish's office," I said. "The problem is, I have no idea what they mean."

"That's the headmaster—Cavendish," she said. I nodded. "How did you get into his office?"

"Never mind," I said.

"Is that where you were last night?"

"Maybe," I said.

"Well," she said, "what's done is done. And you did want a job with a bit of excitement. Maybe I can help. I was really good at codes when I was a kid."

It was worth a shot. "I'll go get them," I said. "Maybe you can make sense out of it. Oh—and I got Elsie's fry phone back, but it's covered in pig manure."

"Good for you! I know how to get that fixed up. Three-thieves oil sanitizes everything," my mother said, nodding sagely.

"Are you sure? I was thinking a bleach bath."

"Leave it to me," she said. "Now, go get that paper."

As I went inside to retrieve the legal paper—and a plastic baggie for the fry phone—Elsie looked up at me with a big smile. "Look at my forest!" she said. "I even built a little house." She pointed to a small structure built of seaweed flakes. Her dog collar, I noticed, lay discarded on the table.

"Who lives there?" I asked.

"The kale fairies," she said, as if it were obvious.

I kissed her on top of the head and gave her a squeeze. "You've got quite a forest growing there! Do you need another cookie sheet to expand?"

"That would be great, Mom!"

I gave her a second cookie sheet and another bag of seaweed snacks and glanced at the laundry room. There was a soft grunting noise, but nothing violent. At least not yet.

"Thanks, Mom," my daughter said as I stacked a second bag of seaweed snacks on the table. As Elsie adjusted the roof of her kale-fairy house, I grabbed the legal paper from my purse and headed out to the back porch.

"She looks so happy in there," I said, nodding toward my absorbed daughter. "I never would have thought of making a kale forest."

"It doesn't take much when you've got such a creative kiddo," she said. "Now, let's take a look at this list of yours."

I spread the page out on the table and we both examined it.

"Is it some kind of code, do you think?" I asked.

"*Arthur207*," she said, pointing to the first line. "Hmmm," she said. "What did you say he was dressed as when he died?"

"Aquaman," I said. "Why?"

"What was Aquaman's 'street' name?"

"I'll look it up," I said, retrieving my manure-coated phone from my back pocket and typing it in.

"Arthur Curry," I said, looking at the page. The second word on the line was $C_1U_2R_3R_4Y_5$.

"I thought so," my mother said, eyes glittering. "I'll bet this is a username and password."

CHAPTER THIRTY-FOUR

I looked at my mother; what she said made sense. "They do look like usernames and passwords. The problem is, to what?"

"Let's find out," she said, reaching for my phone. "May I?"

I took the phone out of its case and handed it over. It was slightly dented—probably a tooth mark—but it seemed to have passed through Bubba Sue's digestive system intact. It was a modern-day miracle.

"Let's try the obvious suspects first," she said.

"Like what?"

"Gmail," she said. A moment later, she said, "Nope."

"Yahoo?" I suggested.

Nothing. She went down the list of mail providers, with no luck. I was about to lose hope when my mother said, "Bingo."

"You found it?" I pulled my chair over beside her.

"On Inbox.com," she said.

"What's in the e-mails?"

"Setting up meetings," she said, clicking through his e-mails.

"With whom?"

"Largely a woman named Desiree," she said, "but there's one other here."

"Who?"

"Someone named Cherry," she said.

Hmm. "When did this happen?"

She scrolled through the list. "Looks like last January is when the e-mails started," she said.

"Did they meet?"

"Looks like it," she said. I peered over her shoulder as she read, *"Thank you so much for putting in a good word for me. I'll be extra thankful this Friday night."* My mother looked up at me. "What do you think that means?"

"I think one of the moms was trading . . . favors for getting her kid into school."

"Do you think she killed him?"

"No," I said. "I can't think why she would. She got what she wanted, and it wasn't something he was likely to tell anyone. Let's try the other account and see what comes up."

My mother logged out of Aquaman's account and typed in the next username and password. She was right; Cavendish had two e-mail accounts on Inbox.com.

"Investments?" she said, wrinkling her nose as she clicked on the first few messages. "Why would he need a secret account for investments?"

"Not a lot of e-mails, are there?"

"Only five," she said, pulling up the earliest one. "Second thoughts about investment direction. Cannot afford connection. Please advise soonest."

"What was the response?"

She clicked on an e-mail from Rainbow2348. "Concern noted. When current shipment distributed, will divert funds to lower-risk enterprise."

"Per our meeting, events have become too dangerous. Need to divest soonest."

She clicked on the response from Rainbow2348. "Cannot withdraw immediately. Need four-week lead time."

Two days later, Cavendish sent one last e-mail. "Divest HO within 48 hours, or will be forced to take action."

"And that's the last e-mail," my mother said.

"He was killed the next night," I said, feeling my skin prickle.

"I think you've found the smoking gun," she said.

"Yes. But who's Rainbow2348?"

"That's the question, isn't it?" she said. Though I was pretty sure I already knew the answer. "Is it time to tell the police?"

"Not yet," I said. "Let me talk to Peaches. She may have a better idea."

"I've got Elsie," she said. "You go see what you can find out."

"Thanks, Mom," I said, giving her a big hug. "I don't know what I'd do without you."

"Me neither," she said, eyes twinkling.

• • •

"I've got Bubba Sue," I announced to Peaches as I walked into the Pretty Kitten twenty minutes later, smelling rather strongly of scotch and pig manure despite my change of clothes.

Peaches pushed back from the desk, exposing a few miles of hairless legs. "Terrific! Did the client come and pick her up?"

"I left her a message."

"Where's the pig?"

"In my laundry room at the moment," I said, "but she tore up the rental car. Can we charge that to the client?"

"By tore up, you mean . . ."

"She tried to rip out the passenger seat."

Peaches winced. "Did she succeed?"

"Not completely. But that's not the only thing," I said. "I've got a lead on Cavendish."

"What?"

"My mother cracked the code on the legal paper we found," I said. "It's usernames and passwords to e-mail accounts."

"Anything good?"

I told her what we'd learned.

"Things are coming together. I've got some info, too," Peaches said. "I looked up those license-plate numbers from the Holy Oaks parking lot. Guess who one of them belongs to?"

"Cressida Cavendish?"

"And Marty Krumbacher."

I blinked. "Do you think Krumbacher might have offed the headmaster?"

"It depends on the investments Cavendish was talking about," Peaches said. "What was that company called? Golden Investments?" She typed it into the computer.

"Yeah. Their biggest holding was Spectrum Properties," I said. "Right?"

"Let's look that up," she said. Her fingers flew over the keyboard. "Owned by an LLC, but it doesn't say who's behind it."

"Does it list their holdings?"

"Aha." She grinned at me. "You're going to love this."

"What?"

"They own a lot of bars around town. Including . . ." She paused for dramatic effect. "The Sweet Shop."

"Rainbow2348 talked about a shipment at a shop," I said.

"And Desiree talked about a bunch of boxes in the back of the club."

"Do you think?" I asked. "It sounds shady. If we could get a picture of whatever they're shipping, with a label, maybe we could hand everything we know over to Bunsen, and he'd start looking into Golden Investments and Spectrum Properties."

"Anonymously," Peaches said.

"Probably a good idea," I said. "You think those boxes are at the Sweet Shop somewhere?"

"Only one way to find out," she said. "I haven't had lunch yet. You up for a strip steak?"

"Only if you're driving," I said. I couldn't face another trip in the Leaf.

• • •

The parking lot was stuffed once again at the Sweet Shop, whose marquee blared "FRESH, HOT BUNS: AMATEUR DAY!" Peaches levered the Buick between two SUVs several rows away from the door.

"What's the plan?" I asked, glad I'd changed into a decent pair of jeans and a clean T-shirt after my run-in with Bubba Sue.

"We're going to see if we can get into the back rooms," she said.

"What will you do if Banana Twirl is there?" I asked.

"Hide in a dark corner," she said as we walked up the front steps. Chewy was there again.

"Hey, Peaches!" he said. "Looking good."

"You too, honey," she said. "Hey, is Banana here today?"

"She's off till Tuesday," he said. "You here for Amateur Day?"

"Nah," Peaches said. "Just lunch."

"Too bad. You'd be a hit," he said, giving her an appreciative look. "You should try it sometime." He nodded to me. "Your friend, too."

"Thanks," I said, not quite sure how else to respond, and a moment later I followed Peaches back into the Sweet Shop.

There was no plastic pool this time, although I thought I picked up the faint scent of spoiled milk. Carpet, I reflected, was not the wisest choice for an establishment that specialized in whipped-cream wrestling. Desiree probably could have told them that.

As a woman in three square inches of lime-green spandex writhed on the center stage, Peaches and I headed toward a corner table that was close to the back hallway.

"Should we head back now?" I asked after we'd slid into our sticky seats.

"Let's get a drink first," she said.

"Really, Peaches?"

"I'm still recovering from my date the other night."

"The guy from HonkytonkHoneys didn't work out?"

Peaches looked at me. "He drinks Chelada."

"What's that?"

"Bud Light and Clamato."

"That sounds repulsive. Is it really a drink?"

"It shouldn't be, but it is. He had six of them, and then he tried to kiss me." She shuddered. "When I turned him down, he got on the mechanical bull, and threw up all over the bar. It smelled like Manhattan clam chowder."

I sat for a moment, watching as the dancer stripped off another square inch of spandex, and trying to put the image of regurgitated Clamato out of my mind. "Talked with Jess recently?" I asked.

Before she could answer, the waitress materialized behind us, her tanned, flat midriff—which was about the diameter of my forearm—glowing in the bright-pink neon light. "What can I get you gals?"

"What's on special?" Peaches asked.

"We've got screwdrivers and Screaming Orgasms half-price till three," she said.

"Two Screaming Orgasms," Peaches said, and the waitress smiled and sashayed off to the bar.

"I'll drive," I told Peaches. "Anyway, what about Jess?"

"He still hasn't called," Peaches said.

I crossed my arms. "For God's sake," I said. "I'm trying to work things out with a man who sleeps with drag queens, and you won't call Jess because you argued over ice cream?"

The men at the table next to us glanced over. Peaches shifted in her chair.

"Here's the deal," I said. "I'm going to go to the restroom." I glanced at the back hallway. "And you're going to call—or at least text—Jess, before I get back."

"But—"

"No buts. Do it," I said and stood up.

It was only a few steps from our table to the back hallway, which was lined with doors. All of them were shut. Which one was the storeroom?

I took a deep breath and reached for the knob of the first door. It was locked. I moved down the hallway, trying the next three; they were locked, too. It wasn't until the fourth door that I had any luck. I pushed it open and immediately wished I hadn't.

"What are you doing?" bellowed an extravagantly liver-spotted man flanked by two athletic twenty-year-olds in compromising positions. It was one of the octogenarians who had bought us drinks last time we were here, I realized, recognizing the Darth Vader–shaped blotch on his arm.

"Sorry," I said, averting my eyes. "I didn't mean to interrupt."

"Hey," he said, recognizing me. "I remember you. You and your friend were looking real good in the pool the other day. Here for Amateur Day?"

"Ah . . . no," I said.

"Well, if you're not busy, there's room for a third! I've got enough Viagra to last me all afternoon!" He patted his naked lap.

"I'm good, thanks," I told him. "Sorry to interrupt." I slammed the door closed behind me, wishing I could bleach my eyeballs. Those young women were earning every penny. I just hoped they were putting some away for therapy.

The next door was unlocked, too, but this time I was slower in opening it.

Thankfully, there were no octogenarians—or anyone else—inside. Just boxes.

I closed the door behind me and flipped on the light. There were boxes, all right—dozens of them. I started rifling through them, but didn't find anything incriminating. Swizzle sticks, napkins—there was even a box of pasties. And I didn't want to think about why the Sweet Shop needed an industrial-size box of colored frosting.

I had rifled through almost all of them before I found an unopened box in the corner.

It was light—only a couple of pounds—and the return address was somewhere in Guadalajara. I slit the tape with my keys and opened the box.

It was lined with little black packets, all of which had a blurry star and the word *AFTERBURN* emblazoned on the front.

I snapped a picture of the open box with the packets visible inside, then tucked the box back in behind the frosting. Unless I was wrong, this was the investment that was causing Cavendish ethical heartburn. Spectrum Properties didn't just own strip clubs—it was manufacturing, or at least distributing, drugs that were killing people all across Texas. Heck, Thumbs might even be distributing the stuff to the kids at Holy Oaks. It was a terrifying thought.

No wonder Holy Oaks was making 50% annually off its investments. I had just pocketed two of the packets and was closing up the box when the storage-room door opened.

"What are you doing in here?"

It was Strawberry Shortcake.

"Um . . ."

"The amateurs are meeting next door," she said, saving me the trouble of coming up with an explanation."

"Thanks," I said, shoving the box into the corner with my toe.

"Did you bring something else for the stage?" she asked, running a critical eye over my jeans/T-shirt combo.

"No," I said. "This is my first time."

"Well," Strawberry said, tapping a stiletto heel, "maybe one of the girls can lend you something. Although it might be a little small on you."

"I'll be okay," I said, following her out of the storage room and down the short hallway.

"It's in here," she said, throwing open the last door on the left and ushering me inside.

It might be Amateur Day at the Sweet Shop, but most of the women in the backstage room appeared to have professional aspirations. There were dresses and skirts in a rainbow of sherbety colors, and the material of choice appeared to be pleather.

"First time?" asked a woman in a pink-and-black catsuit with matching eye shadow.

"Yeah," I said, staring at her outfit, which fit her like a too-tight glove.

"Do those jeans have Velcro?" she asked.

"What? No," I said, edging back toward the door. "Just a regular old zipper."

"You should check out some outfits with Velcro," she told me. "This outfit looks like it would take forever to get out of, but one pull"—she grabbed the front of her pants and gave a swift tug, revealing a sequined G-string and a slightly jiggly spray tan—"and it comes right off."

"I'll keep that in mind," I said. "Say. Is there a ladies' room nearby?"

"Nerves, eh?" she asked. "It's right through here," she said, pointing through a door on the far side of the room."

"Thanks," I said, hurrying over to it and letting myself out of the perfume-saturated room—and into freedom. I didn't care whether Peaches had drunk her Orgasms yet—we were getting out of there.

I turned to head down the hallway when a large, muscular figure appeared at the end of it—unfortunately, the end between me and the exit. My stomach tightened: it was Thumbs, with a murderous look on his face. What was he doing here? Abandoning my ladies' room escape plan, I turned and plunged back into the perfumed horde backstage. I was pushing my way toward the other door when Catsuit grabbed my arm.

"Come on," she said. "You're up."

CHAPTER THIRTY-FIVE

B ut . . ."

"I know you're nervous," she said. "But it's better to get it over with. Besides, you don't want to have to compete with all of these outfits. You've got a great"—she paused—"girl-next-door kind of thing going on, but it'll look kind of drab after Pink Squirrel over there." She pointed to a woman dressed entirely in pink satin, except for a bushy polyester tail.

"I'm not here for Amateur Day!" I yelled.

"Just best to get out there," she said. "You'll come alive when those stage lights switch on. I promise you."

And before I could say anything else, she shoved me out through the stage door.

"Please welcome our first contestant for Amateur Day," bellowed the speaker behind me. "Give it up for . . ." There was a pause, during which Catsuit was presumably conferring with the announcer. "Cinnamon Buns!"

As I stood there, staring into the lights, the DJ cued up "I Believe in Miracles." Which, to be honest, felt kind of appropriate. There was a choking noise from the right side of the stage; I squinted into the lights and spotted Peaches, who had just spewed half of a Screaming Orgasm all over herself.

I stood motionless for a long moment, aware of dozens of pairs of eyes locked on me.

"Dance!" somebody yelled from the back of the room. As the music blasted on the speakers, I swayed back and forth a little bit, hoping that this was a nightmare and that I'd wake up. As Hot Chocolate asked, "Where you from, you sexy thing?" the room around me devolved into dissatisfied mutterings, so I attempted to put a bit more swing in my hips and marched down the catwalk. This seemed to help a little, but there were still some noises of disapproval, so I reached down and untied my right sneaker.

"Turn around!" someone called from the back.

I shuffled around a little bit so that I was backward, feeling my face heat up. I glanced to the side; the Holy Oaks custodian was watching me, the scar on his face looking more menacing than ever. What was he doing here? I glanced at his hands—his enormous thumbs were hooked into his jeans pockets.

My mouth turned dry, and I stood up. There was a smattering of boos, so I bent down again.

How the hell was I going to get out of there?

I kicked off the first sneaker and then started on the next, noticing as I looked between my feet that the candy-striped pole was only a couple of feet away. A few seconds later, I slipped off the second sneaker in what I hoped was a seductive manner and shimmied over to the pole, which I grabbed onto like a lifeline. The audience seemed to perk up a bit as I leaned against it. How hard could it be to swing around a pole?

Grabbing it with both hands, I launched myself to the right. It wasn't too bad, I decided after a few turns, and then switched directions. As Hot Chocolate crooned, "I love the way you touch me," the other octogenarian of the drink-buying duo materialized at the foot of the stage, clutching something that looked like a quarter in his veined hand. "Take it off, honey!" he yelled in a high, thin voice. "I got something for ya!"

I let go of the pole and took a surreptitious glance down the front of my V-neck. I was wearing a sports bra. Good coverage, but not, as I understood it, traditional strip-club garb.

"Come on!" somebody hollered from one of the tables. I glanced back at Thumbs, who continued to stare at me through slitted eyelids, and reached for the hem of my T-shirt, still attempting to swivel my hips.

It was just about the last thing in the world I wanted to do, but with Thumbs over by the side of the stage, I didn't see that I had much of a choice. I lifted my shirt as slowly as possible, feeling it still was way too fast. After a brief struggle to get my arms out, I twirled it over my head and tossed it to Peaches, but I missed; it fell on one of the stage lights not too far from the octogenarian.

The sports bra, evidently, was a bit tame for the Sweet Shop; the response was less than electric. I glanced over my shoulder, considering making an exit out the back, but I knew Thumbs would follow me. I unbuttoned my jeans slowly, which was enough to get a few lackluster hoots, and unzipped the zipper. Then, praying the song would end before I finished, I hooked my thumbs around my jeans and began to lower them, exposing the front of my bleach-stained Jockey full-coverage briefs.

The octogenarian went wild. "Just like Mabel used to wear," he hooted, waving his quarter in the air.

I hadn't gotten my jeans halfway down my legs before I understood Catsuit's praise of Velcro. I stood hopping on one foot, struggling to get my left leg out of my jeans. I teetered for a moment, then fell headlong into the quarter-waving octogenarian's lap.

Peaches was there in a flash, disentangling me from his surprisingly firm grip. "What the hell are you doing?" she yelled into my ear.

"I'll explain later. Get me out of here!" I said.

As I grabbed my jeans and yanked them up, the octogenarian shoved the quarter into my sports bra.

"Thanks," I said automatically, and looked up to see Thumbs advancing, a rather unpleasant expression on his face.

"Let's go," I said, eyeing Thumbs.

"I got your purse," Peaches said, tossing a ten at the table and nodding to the waitress, who was staring slack-jawed at the two of us. "Let me get your shoes . . ."

"We can come back," I said.

"But—"

I didn't wait for her to answer. As the octogenarian fished in his pocket for another coin, I trotted to the front door, not daring to look back for Thumbs. Peaches followed me soon after, and as I dashed across the hot parking lot to the car, a few men at a bus stop gave me appraising looks. "Unlock the car!" I yelled as I saw Thumbs emerge from the front door of the club. Peaches was right behind me, huffing hard and smelling like Baileys Irish Cream.

"Shit," she wheezed.

"Let's get out of here," I said as I slid into the passenger seat. Peaches hustled in after me and locked the doors, gunning the Buick into reverse and barely missing Thumbs, who was still advancing on us like a gorilla on steroids. I watched him in the rearview mirror as we squealed out of the parking lot. I had a bad feeling this wasn't our last encounter.

"Amateur Day, Margie?" Peaches asked when we were safely on Lamar Boulevard. "Really?"

"It was an accident," I said.

"We need to get you some dance lessons, girl. You looked like someone rammed a broomstick up your butt. And that's some sexy underwear you've got there," she said. "Victoria's Secret?"

"Give me a break. I don't exactly have an appreciative audience at home," I reminded her.

"All right, you have a point. How did you end up on stage?"

"I was in the storeroom, and somebody found me. I tried to get out, but Thumbs was between me and the exit."

"No wonder you got on stage."

"Yup. And I found this in the storeroom," I said, fishing two packets of Afterburn out of the pocket of the jeans on my lap.

Peaches glanced over at them. "You think that might be the investment Cavendish was having moral qualms about?"

"People are dying from it," I said. "It would give me moral qualms." I buttoned my jeans and wished I had grabbed my shirt.

"I've got a spare top in the back," Peaches offered. She reached back and fished out something zebra-striped and slightly shimmery. I pulled it on, feeling a little like a sausage in a rayon casing.

"Thanks."

"Don't mention it," she said.

It was only when Peaches had dropped me off at the office and I'd gotten into the Leaf that I realized I hadn't heard about Jess.

· · ·

"Nice shirt," Becky said when I ran into her in the Green Meadows Day School parking lot an hour later. I was still wearing Peaches's top, unfortunately. "New stylist?"

"I . . . lost my other shirt," I said.

"I can't wait to hear how," Becky said. "Any progress? I hope so, because Bunsen keeps calling me."

"Sorry about that. I think so," I said. "How about you? Did Rick ask you what happened?"

"He was already dead asleep," she said. "I'm having a hard time explaining why the Austin Police Department is calling me hourly, though."

"What did you do with your boots?"

"I trashed them," she said. "Any luck figuring out that paper we found?"

"My mother cracked the code, actually," I told her. "They were usernames and passwords to some e-mail accounts."

"Were you able to get in?"

I told her about the e-mails, the box of Afterburn I'd found in the back of the Sweet Shop, and my encounter with Thumbs.

"He was at the Sweet Shop? Did he threaten you?"

"I didn't give him a chance," I said, and told her about my first and last foray onto a strip club runway.

"Oh my God, Margie. What was he doing there? Do you think he was just a customer?"

"No," I said. "Krumbacher owns the place, and Thumbs is his henchman."

She glanced at my car, then did a double take. "Margie. Is this the rental? What happened?"

"Bubba Sue," I told her.

"Jesus. Did you get the fry phone back?"

"I did, but it's in pretty bad shape. Got my iPhone, too."

"I'm not sure it was worth it," Becky said, peering at the chewed-up seat. "Is that dirt?"

"Not exactly," I said.

"Gross," she said, wrinkling her nose and stepping away from the car. "Nick's going to love driving home in that."

"I'll keep the windows open," I said as we walked into the school together.

"You'd better hope Mrs. Bunn doesn't ask you for a ride."

I shuddered. The director of Green Meadows, affectionately known as Attila the Bunn, had left me alone since I helped her figure out an embezzlement issue some months back, but I wasn't sure how long the honeymoon would last.

"We spilled half a bottle of scotch in it, too," I told Becky.

"How?"

"Pig sedation. She tore the nipple off the baby bottle, and it got all over the upholstery."

"Baby bottle?"

"It was my mother's idea."

"You got her, though?"

I nodded. "She's safe and sound in my laundry room," I told her.

"Maybe there is hope for me after all," she said.

• • •

We got home just before four, and things were quiet in the house. Rufus had been scarce since the arrival of my mother—he hated when we moved the furniture—but he was still leaving regular deposits. I cleaned up a little pile from the front hall and then headed into the kitchen, wincing at the sight of the flashing answering machine light. I hit "Play," fast-forwarding through Bunsen's two messages. The third was from my father-in-law.

"I wanted to see if we could all get together at Fleming's Steakhouse tomorrow night. I was thinking seven. Let me know if Blake will be back in time." There was an awkward pause, followed by, "Say hi to my grandbabies!"

There was one more message. "She's not answering," someone said—it sounded like Blake. "I tried her cell. Are you sure this is the way to do it?" There was a muffled response followed by a click as Blake—I thought it was Blake—hung up. Weird.

As I puzzled over the cryptic nonmessage, I checked my e-mail and was surprised to see something from Holy Oaks titled *PARENT MEETING*. I clicked on it; evidently Deborah Golden was going to be introduced as the new interim head at six o'clock. I hated to ask, but I hoped my mother was up to babysitting again. I wanted to hear what Golden had to say—and maybe confront Krumbacher about what I'd found in his club. And, if I had a chance, warn Mitzi that she might be married to a murderer. After all, I might not care for her personally, but it wasn't the kind of information I could withhold in good conscience.

"Where's Grandma?" Nick asked as he opened the refrigerator and gazed at the sparse and rather unsatisfying contents.

"She's probably at the library with Elsie," I told him. "Want an apple?"

"I'm tired of apples," he said.

"That's all I've got, I'm afraid. Unless you want to try those seaweed snacks."

He made a face. "Gross."

"An apple it is, then." I glanced at my watch, wondering if I would have a chance to swing by the grocery store before my mother got home. I had sliced up a Granny Smith and started a short mental grocery list when a grunt sounded from the laundry room.

"What's that?" Nick asked, walking over and reaching for the doorknob.

"Don't touch that!" I yelled, hurling myself across the kitchen toward him.

But it was too late.

CHAPTER THIRTY-SIX

The door had hardly cracked open an inch before Bubba Sue rocketed out of the laundry room, squealing at the top of her piggy lungs. I raced over and scooped Nick up from the floor as Bubba Sue gave her hide a mighty shake and turned to face us. The rope I'd used to tie her up with was long gone, and there was a glint in her eyes I didn't like.

"She looks mad," Nick observed.

He had just finished speaking when Bubba Sue pawed at the tile floor and then launched herself in our direction. I leaped onto the kitchen island with Nick in my arms, dislodging the apple along with a packet of seaweed snacks, just as the enormous pig rammed into the cabinet behind the spot where we'd been standing. She lifted her nose and sampled the air, then turned and investigated the apple slices and seaweed snacks that had fallen. As I watched, horrified, she engulfed the apple, then turned her snout to the seaweed snacks. A moment later, the green plastic package disappeared with a crinkle.

"What are those?" Nick asked, pointing toward the laundry room.

I swiveled my head and swallowed hard. Six small black and pink creatures were snuffling around the base of the washing machine.

"I think Bubba Sue is a mommy," I said slowly, wondering how the day could possibly get worse.

"Can we keep them?" Nick asked, looking up at me with bright eyes.

Before I could answer, I glanced up to see Rufus slinking around the corner, rubbing against the side of the kitchen doorway. Bubba Sue raised her head and sniffed, and I held my breath.

"Rufus likes her!" Nick said. He hadn't finished his sentence before Bubba Sue reared back, emitting a loud, threatening grunt.

Rufus froze, his blue eyes glued on the pig. There was a split second of silence, and then Bubba Sue launched herself across the floor, hooves clattering against the tile. Rufus let out a yowl and streaked into the living room with the pig hot on his heels.

I shifted on the island, watching as the piglets emerged from the laundry room and trying to come up with an exit strategy.

"That one just pooped," Nick announced, pointing to a little black one.

"Lovely." As I watched, another one followed suit. "Good thing Grandma and Elsie aren't here," I said.

No sooner had I spoken than the front door creaked open, and I heard my mother trill, "Let's go say hi to your mom!"

Before I could answer, there was a scream, followed by the thundering of hooves. And then silence.

"Mom!" I called, sliding off the countertop. "Stay here," I warned Nick. "Elsie! Are you okay?"

I raced into the living room, worried Bubba Sue had attacked my daughter. My mother and Elsie stood in the doorway, looking out the front door.

"What happened?" I asked.

"Your cat just ran out of the house, followed by a gigantic pig," my mother said. I hurried over and peered out the front door just in time to see Bubba Sue's curly tail disappear around the corner.

• • •

I'd just managed to herd the piglets back into the laundry room when my phone rang. I grabbed it and hit "Talk" without thinking.

"Hello?"

"Hi. This is Janette Hernandez. Bubba Sue's mommy?"

"Oh. Hi," I said, regretting the message I'd left about Bubba Sue.

"I got your message. Thank you so much for rescuing her from that awful man. She's got a delicate disposition, and that . . . that *boor* just doesn't know how to pamper her." She took a breath before continuing. "Is she okay?"

"She's, uh . . . fine," I said. "Look, can I call you back?"

"Oh, no need," she said. "Just give me your address and I'll swing by and pick her up."

"Um . . . I'll call you back," I said, and hung up.

The phone rang again ten seconds later, but I ignored it.

"Who was that?" my mother asked, still clutching Elsie to her.

"Bubba Sue's owner," I said. "She wants to come and pick her pig up."

My mother bit her lip. "How do we get her back? What do we do about the piglets?"

The phone rang again. I set the ringer to silent.

"They're in the laundry room, at least," I said.

"I know that," my mother said. "But what do we feed them?"

I groaned. "I have no idea."

My mother sighed. "Almond milk will have to do for now, I suppose. I'll go get another baby bottle out of the garage."

As my mother opened the garage door, I walked out into the front yard, looking up and down the street. I wasn't too worried about Rufus—he had gotten out before and always made it home, and I was guessing he'd climbed the first tree he came across—but Bubba Sue was a problem.

Again.

How was I going to find her? And what was I going to tell the client if her pig got hit by a car?

At least I had the piglets, I told myself. Plus, I had bigger problems to contend with. Like angry, freshly waxed henchmen and murder cases.

My mother had located another Avent bottle and was warming up almond milk on the stove when I walked back inside.

"The microwave might be quicker," I said.

"It's not good for the milk," she told me. "Do you think we should drive around and look for her?"

"The problem is, I wouldn't know what to do if I found her," I said. "There's no way I'd get her back in the car. Besides," I added, looking at my phone, "I don't have much time; there's a parent meeting at Holy Oaks I want to go to this evening. I hate to ask, but . . ."

"I'll keep the kids," my mother said. "Things sure have changed since you were little," she added. "We always had the evenings at home."

"We didn't have piglets in our laundry room, either," I pointed out as she poured the almond milk into a bottle.

"Maybe Bubba Sue will come back for her babies," my mother suggested. "The maternal instinct is a powerful thing. In the meantime, we should probably look up *piglet care*." She nodded toward my computer.

I Googled *piglet care*. What I found was not encouraging. "We need to get them a heating pad," I said, looking at the laundry-room door. "And they don't do too well without their mother. I hope they had a chance to get a first meal in before she headed out of the laundry room."

"What do they say to feed them?"

"Milk, egg yolk, citric acid, and cod-liver oil," I said. "No almond milk."

"Animal products," my mother sighed.

"I'll run to the store and pick some up," I said. "Can you set up the heating pad? It's in the kids' bathroom."

"I'll set it up," she said. "Think you'll be back in time to make it to Holy Oaks?"

"I'll be back in a flash," I told her as I grabbed my purse and headed out to the driveway.

. . .

The kids were in the laundry room and covered in piglets when I got home. I hadn't seen Elsie so happy in days; there was no sign of her dog collar, and she was talking to the little pink pig in her lap as if it were her best friend.

"They look pretty good," I told my mother as I unloaded the groceries.

"Hungry, though," she said. "They keep trying to suck Elsie's fingers."

"We'll get them fed soon enough," I said, cracking an egg into a pot and measuring milk. "Any sign of Momma Pig?"

"None yet," she told me. "I hope she didn't get hit by a car," she said in a low voice, so that the kids wouldn't hear. I glanced down at my cell phone; four more calls from Bubba Sue's mom. Should I call her and tell her we had the piglets, at least?

I'd give it until after the Holy Oaks meeting, I decided as I added cod-liver oil and winced at the foul smell. It would make a nice dip for the seaweed snacks.

When the concoction had heated to lukewarm, I poured it into the two bottles on the counter and headed into the laundry room, where my mother and the kids nestled with the newborn piglets. One of them had a spot on its snout, just like its mother's.

I handed one bottle to my mother and kept the other. "Can I have a piggie?"

Elsie handed me a small pink one, and as I nestled the small, warm body into my lap, I was reminded of when my own children were infants. It hadn't been that long ago, I reflected as I watched Elsie plant a kiss on the black piglet's head.

I looked back down at the piglet in my lap and offered it the nipple. It latched on hungrily, gulping down the disgusting concoction. I thought of their refrigerator-sized mother, who was doubtless marauding the streets of Austin Heights even now. It was amazing that something so small and sweet could turn into something so massive and ill-tempered.

"It's working," my mother said as the little black piglet in her lap gulped down the milk.

Twenty minutes later, we had a half dozen contented piglets, but there was still no sign of Bubba Sue.

"Can I stay with them until their mommy comes home?" Elsie asked.

"Sure," I said, watching her nestled in with the piglets. As long as she didn't want to keep one, we'd be fine. "Let me put down some paper in case they have accidents."

Once I had everyone settled, I ran into my bedroom, applied some lipstick, and headed for the car. I was just about to back out of the driveway when I put the car in park and ran into the garage. I fumbled on the top shelf until I found the bag with the gun in it.

It was the first time I'd ever gone to a parent meeting armed.

CHAPTER THIRTY-SEVEN

I walked into Holy Oaks just as the program was beginning. I stepped through the door into a lobby that was filled with packed chairs. At the rear of the lobby, near the library, was a table full of Sweetish Hill pastries. I edged toward the loaded table and grabbed a lemon bar and a pecan-pie tartlet to fortify myself, thankful to see food that wasn't green and vegan. At Green Meadows, if you weren't first at the trough, you were likely to go away hungry; at Holy Oaks, I seemed to be the only parent who ate carbs, so there was no worry about missing out on the treats.

"Thank you for coming tonight," Claire Simpson sang into the microphone as I stuffed the pecan tartlet into my mouth and felt around in my purse for the gun. It was still lurking in the bottom of my purse, the metal grip both scary and reassuring. I scanned the room; the Goldens and the Krumbachers were near the front, by the podium. There was no sign of Mrs. Cavendish—not that I was surprised.

The head of the elementary school droned on about all that Cavendish had contributed to the school, and how he couldn't possibly be replaced, and what an upstanding member of the community he'd been. Mention of Aquaman tights or hookers was markedly absent. I did have to give him props for wanting to out the fact that the school had invested in a lethal street drug and trying to back out of it; oddly enough, though, that didn't figure into her speech, either.

I wiped my fingers on my napkin and edged up the side of the room, hoping I could get to Mitzi. I didn't like her, but I couldn't in good conscience not tell her I suspected she was married to a murderer. I would pass what I'd found on to Detective Bunsen, but I wasn't sure any of that evidence would hold up in court. Maybe Mitzi could provide the missing pieces.

"And now," Simpson burbled, "let me introduce our new interim headmaster, who has kindly agreed to take over while we search for a new permanent head. She's a former kindergarten teacher with years of experience in the business community, and I'm sure she'll do a great job keeping Holy Oaks on course. Please join me in welcoming Deborah Golden to the podium."

"Thank you," Deborah said, beaming at the crowd, her veneers flashing in the lights. I glanced at the rest of the front row. Marty Krumbacher leaned back in his chair, looking satisfied, while Mitzi sat beside him, a tight smile on her surgically enhanced lips. Leonard Graves sprawled like a bald lion, his jerky-colored wife adjusting the neckline of her low-cut black dress.

Deborah Golden went on for a while about how a well-run school was like a well-orchestrated real-estate deal, and about how the children, like her clients, would be her top priority, and then went into some extended mixed metaphor about tight ships and armies, which seemed to go on for hours. All the time, my eyes were fixed on Mitzi, who had noticed me and shot me one nasty glare before ignoring me. I drifted back to the snack table and grabbed a few more lemon squares as I waited for her to finish.

"Unusual choice for an interim head, don't you think?"

It was Kevin, who was stacking pecan tartlets on his plate.

"After what you told me at the parent coffee, it's not a huge surprise," I told him. My eyes fell on the door to the boys' room, and I thought of Thumbs; thankfully, I hadn't seen him tonight. "How long has the custodian been working here?" I asked Kevin.

"He started a few months ago," Kevin said. "Vicki tells me he gives her the heebie-jeebies."

"He gives me the heebie-jeebies, too," I said.

"Lupe," he said. "But the kids call him Mr. Thumbs." He leaned in. "Have you seen his hands?"

"Yes," I said, feeling my stomach contract. I hadn't heard from Thumbs since last night, but I suspected I hadn't seen the last of him. "Pretty big." I took another bite of lemon bar and asked, "Did anybody do a background check on him? That scar is a little bit terrifying."

"I imagine so," he said. "They must do background checks on everyone. Too much risk of scandal otherwise."

He had no idea how high the risk of scandal was, I thought as I polished off the lemon bar.

"How's Elsie doing?" he asked.

"It's been a tough transition," I said.

"I'm sorry to hear that; I kind of thought so."

I turned to him, wondering what he knew that I didn't. "Why?"

He hesitated. "Vicki mentioned something to me, and I'm not sure I should pass it on."

"Please do," I said. "She won't tell me anything except that she hates school."

"Well . . . she barks a lot."

Even though I wasn't surprised, my heart seemed to shrink in my chest. "She barks?"

"Yes," he said, leaning in. "And Violet Krumbacher has started calling her Fido."

I glanced up to where Mitzi was sitting. "Fido," I said. "How does she respond to that?"

"She growls," Kevin told me. "At least that's what Vicki tells me." He gave me a sympathetic look. "I'm sorry to tell you, and like I said, it's just what I'm hearing from Vicki. There's more."

"What?" I asked, feeling sick.

"Well . . . Violet tied her to a tree during recess yesterday and told her to stay."

"Tied her to a tree?"

"She used a jump rope," Kevin said. "Apparently the teacher eventually found out about it and released her, but nobody had the guts to tell the teacher it was Violet who'd done it. She thinks Elsie tied herself up."

"Around her neck?"

"Her waist, I think." He paused. "At least I hope."

"That's horrible!"

"I know," he said. "That's why I thought you should know."

"Thanks," I said, meaning it. "I know the transition hasn't been smooth, but . . . wow. I'm glad I kept her home today."

"Holy Oaks can be a tough crowd," Kevin said, glancing at the well-dressed, well-heeled crowd. "And not just the kids."

At that moment, Deborah Golden finished her soliloquy, and there was a burst of polite applause.

"If you'll excuse me," I said, "I need to go talk to someone."

"Mitzi?" he asked, looking worried.

"Yes . . . But about something else. I promise I won't tell her you told me about Violet."

"Thanks," he said. His relief was palpable. "Maybe Deborah Golden will be more open to dealing with bullying, but I doubt it."

"Cavendish wasn't?"

"Not when the big donors were involved," he told me with a wry smile. "Big donors' kids got carte blanche. The Sky High campaign has taken precedence over just about everything."

"Sky High." I snorted, thinking of the packets of Afterburn I'd found in the custodian's closet—and the back room of the Sweet Shop.

"What's funny?"

"I'll tell you later," I said. "Thanks again for letting me know about Elsie."

"Good luck," Kevin called after me as I cut through the perfumed crowd.

Mitzi was standing a few feet away from her husband, who was deep in conversation with the bald hair magnate. I walked up to her and put on a smile. "Hi, Mitzi. I've got something to ask you; mind if I talk to you for a few moments?"

"I'm kind of busy," she said, crossing her arms and inching toward her husband.

"It's about—"

"I said, I'm busy." Her blue eyes were like daggers.

I grabbed her arm. "I know something about your husband you'll want to hear," I hissed into her ear.

She shook me off, but her eyes widened slightly. I watched her consider it for a moment. "Fine," she said curtly. "Just make it quick."

She followed me across the crowded lobby area to the hall leading to the first-grade classrooms. When we were halfway down, she turned to me.

"All right. What is it?" she barked.

I took a deep breath. "I think your husband's a murderer."

Mitzi blinked at me. "What?"

"Cavendish died in unusual circumstances," I told her. "I think your husband might be involved."

"You think Marty killed him?" she asked, glancing down the hall and looking uneasy. "Why?"

"His car was outside the apartment where Cavendish was killed."

"How do you know that?" she asked.

"I just do."

"Even if that were true—and I have no way of knowing if you're telling the truth—why would Marty kill the headmaster?"

"Because Cavendish invested Holy Oaks' funds into your husband's company. Then he found out your husband's company is dealing in an illicit drug that's killed a bunch of people." I glanced over my shoulder. "I have evidence showing Cavendish was having a crisis of conscience and wanted to divest Holy Oaks—and he might have been going to tell the police about it. I think your husband decided to silence him."

"Are you sure his wife didn't off him because she saw him wearing tights in a wading pool?"

"I thought about that, too," I told her, "but it doesn't add up." Then I paused. "Wait a moment. How do you know that?"

The color leached from Mitzi's tanned face. "I . . . Someone must have told me."

Was she in on it? Or had Marty told her what he was doing? All of a sudden it dawned on me. "It was you, wasn't it?" I said slowly.

She had a look on her face I recognized. I'd seen it on Nick's face when I caught him licking the frosting off all the cupcakes for his sister's birthday party.

"You knew about the Afterburn. And you knew Cavendish was going to turn in your husband, and that Marty would lose everything if he was convicted."

"You can't prove anything," she hissed.

"No, but I'll bet Detective Bunsen can," I told her. "Thanks for clearing things up."

I turned to walk back to the lobby, but she grabbed my arm. Her grip was remarkably firm; you could tell she spent some time at the gym. "Wait," she said.

"No," I told her, reaching for my purse.

But Mitzi was way ahead of me. Before I could get Thumbs's gun out of the bottom of my purse, I felt something hard press against my back. "I knew it was a mistake to hire you," Mitzi said, steering me into one of the classrooms.

CHAPTER THIRTY-EIGHT

My mouth felt like cotton, but my palms were sweating. "What are you planning to do?" I asked.

"I'm thinking," she said.

"They'll hear it if you fire the gun," I said, casting about for a way to get out of this situation. Things were hard enough for my kids as it was; the last thing they needed was for me to show up behind Holy Oaks with more holes in me than a colander.

"You're really concerned for my welfare, aren't you?" Mitzi asked.

"I'd be more worried about your kid. The one who thinks she's a dog?"

"And your daughter is a real joy, isn't she?" I asked. The thought of Elsie tied to a tree pissed me off enough to eclipse my fear, at least for a moment. "Where'd she learn to tie people up? Or is that considered a basic skill in your household?"

Mitzi poked the gun into my back harder. "She was talking the talk; maybe Violet decided she needed to walk the walk. Besides," she said, "your kid is weird. You don't see Violet wearing a cheap rhinestone dog collar and pretending she's a Pekingese."

"Oh, I'm sure your kid would prefer the diamond-studded spiked version from Tiffany's," I said. "You knew, didn't you?"

"That Violet tied Fido to a tree?" she asked. "I suggested it. I'm just surprised your daughter didn't pee on the trunk."

The casual cruelty of it stunned me. Mitzi Krumbacher had instructed her daughter to bully Elsie, I realized. I couldn't let this woman kill me. No way was Mitzi going to orphan my children.

"You really don't want to kill me yet," I said.

"Why not?" she asked.

I had to admit I was stumped.

Fortunately, at that moment, Kathleen Gardner bustled into the room. "Oh," she said brightly. "I'm just in here getting a few more of the Girl Scout sign-up forms," she explained, completely oblivious to the fact that Mitzi Krumbacher was pointing a gun at me. Mitzi turned her body away from Kathleen, who was rifling through a drawer next to the teacher's desk. "Ms. Rumpole said she put them in the top drawer . . . Ah. Here they are." She grabbed the forms and turned to me. "So, Margie. Have you given any more thought to—" Her eyes fastened onto the gun in Mitzi's hand. "What's that in your hand?"

"A toy gun," Mitzi said, her voice dripping with condescension. "I was just showing it to Margie."

"It doesn't look like a toy," Kathleen said, walking over to get a closer look. I took the opportunity to take a few steps away from Mitzi, wondering if I could make it to the door faster than she could shoot me. Unfortunately, the answer was likely no; I wasn't exactly a natural sprinter.

"That's real mother-of-pearl on the handle, isn't it?" Kathleen asked. "It looks like a .22. I was considering picking one up for Catriona in a few years, for when she goes to college, just in case. She's just so young and beautiful . . ." A crease formed between her brows as she finally realized what was happening. "Why are you pointing that gun at Margie?"

Mitzi let out a long-suffering sigh. "Oh my God, Kathleen. Really? If I hear another word about your daughter, I might strangle her myself. Now get over there and stand next to Margie," she said, waving her over to me.

"That wasn't very polite," Kathleen bristled.

"I'm holding a gun," Mitzi pointed out. "I don't have to be polite. Now move."

Kathleen put one hand to the neck of her buttoned-up pink blouse. "Me? But all I'm doing is getting the Girl Scout forms."

"Go stand by Margie," Mitzi said. "And shut up about your daughter. I need to think."

So did I. Kathleen came to stand next to me, her round face drained of color. How were we going to get out of there? As much as I had imagined bad things befalling Kathleen, I felt terrible for dragging her into this. How loud was a .22? Would Mitzi shoot us while everyone was in the front room of the school? Or would she wait until later?

Mitzi's blonde head snapped up suddenly. "Let's go," she said, waving us toward the door.

Kathleen held up a Girl Scout form. "But—"

"Shut up," Mitzi barked. "Now move.

Together we walked through the classroom to the door to the hallway. Kathleen went first; I followed, glancing down toward the lobby. Kevin was standing at the end of the hallway, leaning against a wall. "Kevin!" I yelled, waving.

He waved back.

"I said, shut up," Mitzi hissed behind us. "The gun is in my purse, but it's still aiming at you."

I turned away from Kevin, walking slowly down the corridor. Would he get the message that something was wrong?

When we reached the end of the hall, I glanced over my shoulder. Kevin wasn't there.

Things weren't looking good for the home team.

"I really don't think this is necessary," Kathleen said as Mitzi shooed us out the door and into the hot Texas evening. "I don't know what Margie did, but I had nothing to do with it. Where are we going, anyway?"

"Into the woods," Mitzi said. "Shhh."

Although I usually enjoyed a walk along a nature path, I was learning to hate the narrow trail behind Holy Oaks.

"Why are you doing this?" Kathleen complained. "All I did was get the Girl Scout forms. I really don't think pointing guns at people is the kind of modeling we want to do for our children—"

A bullet pinged off a tree to our left, and Kathleen shut up. *So that's what it takes,* I thought. Then I realized that Mitzi wasn't the only one who was armed. I slipped my hand into my purse, feeling around for the gun.

"Kneel down," Mitzi said.

"But . . ." Kathleen said. "My daughter . . ."

"She'll survive," Mitzi said.

Kathleen turned around. "Without a mother? You mean to kill me?"

"I can't wait," Mitzi said. She raised the gun; at the same moment, there was a crashing sound. Mitzi's head whipped around. I threw myself at Kathleen, rolling us both over onto the ground. There was another shot, and then a crack as a broom handle connected with the .22, sending it flying into the underbrush.

I looked up to see Kevin standing over Mitzi.

"What are you doing?" she asked him.

"Keeping you from committing a capital crime," he said. "What is going on here?" He looked at me. "This isn't about what Violet did to Elsie, is it?"

As he looked at me, Mitzi lunged into the underbrush.

Kevin and I reached for her simultaneously, each grabbing a smooth leg and hauling her out of the bushes. Since she weighed less than a hundred pounds, it wasn't a struggle. Kevin rolled her over, and she sat up and glared at him, leaves in her mussed blonde hair. "These two women assaulted me," Mitzi told him.

Kathleen blinked at her. "We did no such thing." She turned to Kevin. "This woman threatened to kill my daughter. All I did was go into a classroom looking for forms, and she waves a gun at us and marches us into the woods. She's a madwoman."

"Seriously, Kathleen?" Mitzi picked a leaf out of her hair. "Killing you would have been a public service."

"What is going on here?" Kevin asked me.

I sighed. "Mitzi killed the headmaster because she was afraid he was going to tell the authorities her husband was a criminal, and then he'd lose his fortune and go to jail."

"A criminal?"

"It seems that one of Holy Oaks' big investments was responsible for the synthetic marijuana that is killing people all over Texas. Cavendish wanted to pull out and was going to go to the police."

Kathleen sat up straighter. "But that's totally against the mission of the school. It's a Christian program."

"You are so fucking naive," Mitzi snarled. For once, I had to agree with her.

"Sky High certainly was the right name for the fundraising campaign," Kevin pointed out, leaning against the broom. "I guess we should call the police."

As I reached in my pocket for my phone, Mitzi hurled herself into the bushes again.

"Shit," I said, going after her, but I was too slow. By the time I got to her, Mitzi's hand was already closing on the gun. As my hand gripped her ankle, there was another cracking sound, and Mitzi went limp.

I looked up. Kevin stepped back, still holding the broom in his hand, and shook his head. "I feel a little bad for saying it, but man, that was satisfying."

"Shall we tie her up to a tree?" I suggested, letting her ankle go and standing up.

"She deserves it," Kevin said, "but it would probably be better to let the police handle it."

I knew he was right, but it sure was tempting.

• • •

"You again," Detective Bunsen said as we walked back into Holy Oaks. The first responders had arrived just as Mitzi came to. She clearly wasn't too damaged by Kevin's expert hit; even as the EMTs shone a light into her pupils, she was batting her eyelashes at the male responder. "These two women just dragged me out here and started threatening me," she told him. "And that man hit me with a broom. All because my daughter is more popular than theirs."

Now, the throng of well-dressed parents looked stunned by the arrival of a leaf-covered Mitzi Krumbacher, whose arm was being gripped by a young policewoman. "Honeybunny!" Marty said, running over to his wife. "What are you doing?"

She flashed him a look of pure hatred, then began to simper. "I don't know why they're holding onto me. Honey, we need to call our attorney right now. This woman tried to kill me, and now they're blaming me!" She pointed a taloned hand at me, and Detective Bunsen raised an eyebrow.

"I can explain everything," I said to Bunsen.

"I certainly hope so," he said.

"That woman tried to kill us!" Kathleen said, pointing at Mitzi. "She would have left my daughter an orphan!"

"And if it weren't for Kevin's shuffleboard skills, she might have succeeded," I said, nodding to my tall friend. "Thank you."

"Glad I could help," Kevin said.

"Are you going to tell me what this is all about?" Detective Bunsen asked.

"You'll never believe it," I said.

"You're probably right," Detective Bunsen said. "But I can't wait to hear it. Why don't you come this way, Ms. Peterson?" He gestured toward the glass doors of the library.

"Talk to you soon," I told Kevin, and followed Bunsen into the library.

"How exactly do you know that woman?" Bunsen asked me as he steered me toward an empty table in the far corner.

"Former client," I said.

He sighed as he lowered himself to a chair. "I should have guessed. Do your clients frequently end up threatening to kill you?"

"Only when I'm about to turn them in for murder," I said.

"Murder?"

"Holy Oaks was investing in Afterburn—that synthetic marijuana that's killing people all over Texas. George Cavendish found out about it, and was going to call the police, so Mitzi—the blonde—decided to kill him before her husband could be indicted. She was planning to divorce him, and didn't want to lose the return on her investment."

"That's quite an accusation." He let out a long sigh. "Why don't we start at the beginning, Ms. Peterson?"

• • •

"You're off the hook," I told Becky on the phone when I finally got back to my car.

"Was it Marty?"

"No," I said. "It was actually his wife—the one who hired me to follow him. She was worried that if Cavendish turned him in, her husband would lose everything, and she'd divorce him and walk away with nothing."

"Nice," Becky said.

"Oh, she's a piece of work," I told her, recounting what I'd learned about Mitzi's daughter, Violet—and Elsie.

Bunsen had quizzed me for a long time; I'd told him about Cavendish's secret e-mail account—one of them, anyway—and what I knew about Golden Investments and what was going on at the Sweet Shop.

"Can you send me that photo?" he'd asked when I showed him what I'd found in the back room.

"Yeah," I said. "But also . . . There's a guy named Lupe—Thumbs—who was working for Krumbacher. He was working as a custodian here, too, and I found a gun and a bunch of Afterburn in the custodial closet the other day."

"What were you doing in the custodial closet?"

"Um . . . looking for a trash bag," I said. "I took the gun and the Afterburn just so the kids wouldn't get hold of it." I fished in my purse and pulled out the gun, handing it to him.

"What's this?" he asked, looking at it.

"The gun I found. I'm telling you, I'm afraid I may have rubbed this guy the wrong way." *To say the least,* I thought, remembering how he'd lunged at Peaches and Becky last night. I couldn't tell him any of that, though, without revealing that I'd broken into Holy Oaks and been party to an involuntary waxing.

Bunsen grimaced. "I hesitate to ask, but could you be a bit more specific about how you . . . rubbed him the wrong way?"

"Ah . . . no," I said. "But I think he may be the one who shot my minivan the other day."

He let out a sigh. "We'll see if we can track him down."

It had been a long two hours, but I'd managed not to implicate myself at all—at least I didn't think so.

"So neither of us is going to jail," Becky said. "That's a relief. What are you going to do about Elsie, though?"

"I'm not sending her back to Holy Oaks, that's for sure. Hey—who do I need to talk with to get her enrolled at Austin Heights Elementary?"

I could hear the smile in her voice. "Zoe will be so excited. We'll go talk to the principal together tomorrow!"

. . .

Even though I got home at eleven, Elsie and my mother were still up. I gave my mother a very edited version of events, and she hugged me. "Congratulations on solving the case!" she said. "I'm so glad Becky is off the hook. And to be honest, I'm thrilled Elsie won't have to go back to that awful place anymore."

"I just have to try to get the tuition back," I said.

"I shouldn't think that would be a problem, considering the circumstances. We'll have to celebrate at dinner tomorrow!"

"Ah, yeah. We're going to Fleming's Steakhouse," I reminded her. "What?"

"You can have the steamed spinach," I said. "Blake's coming, too."

"Hmm," she said, sounding less than thrilled.

There was a squeaking sound from the laundry room. In all the excitement, I'd forgotten about the piglets—and their missing mother. Would we ever see Bubba Sue—or Rufus—again?

"There are the piggies," Elsie said. "I helped feed them tonight."

"Good for you!" I said, and noticed she was clutching her fry phone. "Grandma gave you your fry phone back?"

"She did," Elsie said. "But the buttons don't work."

"I'll work on that," I said. "Sorry, honey." I squatted down and stroked her silky hair. "But I've got great news for you!"

"You found Bubba Sue and Rufus?" she asked.

"Ah, not yet," I said, feeling a stab of remorse. What was I going to tell the client when she called? "The good news," I said, trying not to worry about the rogue sow, "is that you never have to go back to Holy Oaks again."

"Really?" she asked, eyes wide.

"Really," I told her. "We're going to talk to the principal at Austin Heights tomorrow, to see if we can get you into the same class as Zoe."

"Oh, Mommy . . ." She ran to me, throwing her arms around me.

Unfortunately, at that moment, my front doorbell rang. I looked at my mother.

"Who'd be ringing the door at eleven p.m.?" my mother asked.

I didn't know, and was a little afraid to find out. Would Thumbs ring the doorbell? I had a bad feeling I hadn't seen the last of him.

"Why don't you tuck Elsie into bed?" I suggested to my mother. "I'll go answer the door."

She nodded, steering my daughter back to her bedroom as I went to the front door.

I turned on the front porch light and peered through the peephole. An anxious-looking woman about my age, only thirty pounds lighter, was pacing my front porch.

I cracked the door open. "Can I help you?"

Her head snapped up. "Are you Margie Peterson?" she asked.

"Yes."

"Oh, thank God. I'm Janette, Bubba Sue's mom. I'm here to pick her up."

I blinked. How was I going to tell her Bubba Sue was out gallivanting around the streets of Austin Heights?

"It's a little late," I said.

"I know," she told me. "But you weren't answering your phone, and I know my grandpiggies are due any day now. I can't wait to meet them!"

"Actually," I told Janette, "she just gave birth this afternoon."

Her eyes widened. "Oh, my goodness. And I wasn't there for it? Poor, poor Bubba Sue! To have to go through that alone. And she's so sensitive!"

Sensitive was not a word I had come to associate with Bubba Sue, but I nodded and smiled politely.

"Why don't you come in and I'll introduce you to them?" I said. Eventually I'd have to tell her I'd lost Bubba Sue. Maybe it would be easier to absorb the news if she was surrounded by her grandpiggies.

"How many are there?" she asked as she followed me through the house to the laundry room.

"Six," I said.

"Ooh! I was hoping we'd get six," she said as I opened the door.

The laundry-room floor was covered in pig droppings, but Janette didn't seem to mind. "Oh, they're so sweet! And this one has a little dot on her nose, just like her mommy!" She turned to me then, a crease between her brows. "Where is my big girl, anyway?"

"Umm . . ."

I was saved from answering by a terrible bellowing noise, followed by a volley of four-letter words. "Back in a minute," I said, closing the laundry-room door and following the swearing—it had started again—to the living room.

The security light in the backyard was on, revealing a man pressed up against my sliding glass door. A few yards away, an enormous, rabid-looking sow pawed the dirt and scowled at him, a murderous look in her piggy eyes.

Bubba Sue was back.

And so was Thumbs.

CHAPTER THIRTY-NINE

As I stood watching the standoff, the laundry-room door opened behind me, and Janette hurried into the living room.

"My sweet girl!" she said. "There you are. But who is that man?"

"He's an intruder," I said, handing her my phone. "And he's dangerous. Call 911," I told her, regretting having given Thumbs's gun to Bunsen earlier tonight.

"What are you going to do?" Janette asked. "Do you think he'll hurt Bubba Sue?"

"I'd put my money on Bubba Sue, to be honest. As long as she can keep him from getting to his gun."

"He has a gun?"

"That's why we're calling 911," I told her.

"How are we going to save my baby?"

"I don't know," I said. Something nudged my foot; I looked down. The piglets were out of the laundry room and making a beeline for their mother.

"Oh, no!" Janette cried. "The grandpiggies! Come back!" she said, launching herself after a little black porker who was tottering toward the sliding glass door, oinking in excitement.

Bubba Sue's ears pricked up; she now looked both angry and anxious, and I found myself marveling at the range of emotion a pig could convey. Thumbs, on the other hand, seemed wary—or at least that's the impression I got from the way he was backed up against the glass door. Something gleamed in the brownish grass. Another gun. How many did he have?

I shivered; he'd come to get his revenge on me. And the only thing standing between him and his gun was Bubba Sue.

Jeanette scooped up the black piglet who was bumping against the sliding glass door, but the other five had seeped out of the laundry room and begun gamboling around my living room.

As I watched, Bubba Sue lowered her head and charged at Thumbs, squealing with piggy fury. Thumbs dodged to the left just in time, and she rammed full force into the sliding glass door. Janette screamed as the glass shattered with a loud crack, and Bubba Sue hurled herself into the living room.

"Oh, Bubba Sue!" Janette called, hurrying to her side.

But Bubba Sue had no time for her owner; she was fixated on Thumbs. As Janette tried to hug her, she turned and lunged after Thumbs, who was reaching for his gun. He bent over it, presenting an appealing target to Bubba Sue. She lowered her head, charged across the brief expanse of patio, and rammed him between the butt cheeks just as he began to stand up. He yelped and flew up into the air about three feet, sending the gun flying through the air. As it hit the grass, there was a bang and a flash, and the other half of the sliding glass door exploded.

"Oh, Bubba Sue," Janette moaned, but I wasn't there to comfort her. As Thumbs attempted to stand up, both hands cradling his bruised bottom, Bubba Sue rammed him again, this time in the crotch. He doubled over with a moan as the pig pawed the grass again. It had not been a good twenty-four hours for him, I thought as I hurried across the glass-strewn patio to pick up the gun. I turned and aimed it at Thumbs.

"Bitch," he said as he turned to face me. As the sound of sirens filled the humid night air, I clicked back the hammer. "What is wrong with you, lady?"

"Good girl, Bubba Sue!" Janette said behind me. She was struggling to gather the piglets and keep them out of the broken glass, but it was like trying to herd toddlers; as soon as she got two corralled, one of them squirted out and gamboled over toward its mother. "Come here, Bubba Sue," she called. "Let's get our babies inside, away from the glass!"

Bubba Sue snorted and gave me an appraising look that made my insides turn watery. Was she remembering the hog-tying episodes? My intrusion into her yard? Now that Thumbs was down, was I next on her list? I was searching for an escape route and trying to brace myself for impact when she tossed her head, snorted again, and trotted back in to her owner as if she hadn't just been attempting to disembowel Holy Oaks' custodian.

"That's a good girl," Janette cooed as a knock sounded on the front door. "Isn't she sweet?"

"I'll get the door," my mother called from somewhere inside the house. A moment later, two confused policemen walked into the living room. They surveyed the broken glass, the six piglets, and the man clutching his crotch, then turned to me with a questioning look.

"I can explain everything," I told them.

• • •

By the time Blake got home the next evening, we'd cleaned up most of the glass, Bubba Sue and her piglets were safely with their owner, and the reporters had mostly stopped calling. Even Rufus had come slinking back, announcing his return by leaving a steaming pile of poop in the middle of the kitchen floor. Thumbs had been carted off to jail for attempted burglary; I hadn't heard anything about the waxing incident yet, and as far as I was concerned, no news was good news. And Elsie had actually eaten with a spoon!

Things were almost back to normal. Or what passed for normal in the Peterson house, anyway.

"How was your retreat?" I asked my husband, who had put down his suitcase and was staring at the plastic-covered hole where the sliding glass door used to be.

"It was good," he said, glancing at my mother, who had just emerged from the kitchen with a mug of green-smelling tea. We'd cleaned up most of the piglet poop, but there was still a slight livestock aroma in the house. "What happened to the house?"

"It's a long story."

"Margie's a hero!" my mother crowed. "And Elsie never has to go back to Holy Oaks again!"

"What?" Blake asked, looking confused.

"I promise, it's a good thing," I told him as Elsie and Nick barreled into him. He knelt down and hugged them both, giving them kisses on the head.

"We missed you, Daddy!"

"I missed you, too, sweethearts," he said, and looked up at me. "No dog collar?" he mouthed.

I smiled and shook my head. Since she'd learned she was going to school with her friend, she'd taken it off and not even talked about it. She refused, however, to let her fry phone out of her sight. Given my track record with it, I couldn't blame her.

"We should probably talk before Fleming's," he said. "There's a lot to catch up on."

"I wish we could, but we're short on time; we're supposed to be there in twenty minutes, and I haven't changed yet," I said. "Can we talk afterward?"

"I guess," he said, looking pained.

"Great. I'll be out in a few minutes," I said.

• • •

We got to Fleming's only ten minutes late. Prue and Phil were waiting for us. My mother, looking a bit out of place in her turquoise caftan and crystal beads, wrinkled her nose at the smell of meat frying in browned butter.

"Good to see you, Blake," Phil said, clapping my husband on the back. Blake winced, then covered it with a smile. "Make lots of contacts at your retreat?" his father asked, beaming at his handsome son.

"Yeah," Blake said, looking like someone had dumped a cup full of fire ants down his pants.

Elsie saved him from having to say more by turning to Prue and saying, "I never have to go back to Holy Oaks again!"

Prudence looked confused. "What?"

"It's a long story," I told her. I seemed to be saying that a lot lately.

"Once we get seated, I'll take the kids to look at the poor lobsters," my mother said, "and Margie can explain everything."

"I'm going to get to go to school with Zoe!" Elsie said.

"You sound very happy," Prue said, sending me a questioning, worried look. "But we paid a full year's tuition, and school's been in session for only a week!"

"I promise you'll be on board with it. I'll explain in a few minutes," I told her.

Blake looked preoccupied—almost nervous—as we sat down at the table and the waiter took our drink orders. What had happened during his retreat? I wondered. What was it he had wanted to tell me?

"So," Prue said brightly, turning to Blake as Nick began tearing his bread into bits and forming them into a squadron on the white table-cloth. "What was this retreat you were on?"

"It was a . . . personal-development retreat," Blake said. "I'll tell you all about it in a bit."

Prue took a sip of her water, looking stymied. "So," she launched out again, "the new ballet season should be starting soon." She turned to my mother. "Do you enjoy the ballet?"

"I wanna go see the lobsters," Nick announced.

My mother and Prue stood up simultaneously. "Mom," Blake said. "Why don't you stay for a moment?"

Prue sat down, looking ruffled, and watched as my mother hustled the kids off to the front of the restaurant.

"What's going on?" Prue asked me as soon as she was gone.

I quickly relayed a broad-brush summary of what had happened—minus the Aquaman tights, my foray into amateur stripping, and the hour Peaches, Becky, and I had spent waxing the Holy Oaks custodian. It was pretty much the same story I'd told the police.

"That's just terrible," Prue said. "The board was investing in dangerous drugs to fund the capital campaign?"

"No wonder the program was called Sky High," Blake commented.

"The headmaster was killed because he wanted to go to the police," I said. "Mitzi Krumbacher was afraid Cavendish would tell the police about Marty's drug operation, and then her husband would end up going to jail and losing all his assets. She didn't want to lose out on what she hoped to get from their divorce settlement. The Goldens were involved, too."

"I can't believe it." Prue looked shocked. First the headmaster, and now the board of Holy Oaks. It had not been a good year for the Austin social set. "There must be some mistake. They're . . . they're pillars of the community!"

"Were," I said. "Which is why we're moving Elsie to Austin Heights."

"Perhaps we should check Saint Andrew's?"

"I think she'll be happier with her friends, to be honest. Since we told her she's going to Austin Heights, she hasn't been wearing her collar."

"Hmm," she said. "Well, I suppose, for now . . . But we should reassess sometime before high school."

Blake cleared his throat.

"Yes, dear?" Prudence looked at Blake. I realized there was a young man in dark slacks and a white shirt standing next to him. He had very well-groomed eyebrows, I noticed, and his complexion was as smooth as my daughter's. My thoughts suddenly turned to the "news" Blake had told me he wanted to share. I had a bad feeling I was about to hear it now.

"I think we're ready to order," Phil said, looking at the young man. "I'm going to have the prime rib, I think. Rare," he added, casting a glance toward where my mother had disappeared.

"Frank's not a waiter," Blake said. I closed my menu, feeling something twist in my stomach.

"Oh? A colleague from work? Or your networking retreat?" Prudence asked. "Lovely to meet you," she said, extending a hand.

"Good to meet you, too," the young man said. "I've heard so much about you."

"Have you?" she said, her hand jumping to her throat again, but this time to twirl her pearls coquettishly. "All good, I hope."

The young man smiled, but didn't respond.

Blake cleared his throat. "This is Frank," he said. "I met him on the retreat." He looked around the table; I got the impression he was a dinner roll away from throwing up. "I know you've noticed that things between Margie and me haven't been terrific lately. I have to be honest with you." He took a deep breath. "It's my fault."

"It's nobody's fault," Prue said charitably—which was interesting, since she'd been suggesting for the last year that I was failing in my wifely duties.

"What you're experiencing is what every marriage goes through from time to time," Phil said, patting Prue's hand. "We've had our ups and downs, right, Prue? A few sessions with a counselor and you'll be back on track. But what does this young man have to do with anything?"

Blake took a deep breath and looked at his father. "I'm in love with him."

CHAPTER FORTY

I barely remember the next hour, except that it felt like it lasted a year. Phil, after a moment of stunned silence, spluttered that Blake was off his rocker and they'd discuss it in more appropriate circumstances. Prue abruptly turned so white she looked like she'd been sucked dry by a vampire. I wished I'd brought some of Peaches's smelling salts.

And me? I felt as if I'd been rammed in the stomach by Bubba Sue.

Frank squeezed Blake's shoulder and drifted away, which was probably a good thing, as we all digested the news. *I shouldn't be surprised,* I told myself. I knew Blake and I had a problem. But Barbie's words at Warrior Wives kept coming back to me. Would it have been different if I had been more feminine? Was it something I had done that had driven him away from me and into the arms of that young, smooth-skinned man? I felt damaged. Flawed, somehow. As if I had been judged and found wanting.

These awful thoughts were running through my head when the kids came back to the table, giggling about the lobsters in the tank, my mother smiling and looking like a hen with her chicks.

Her smile faded when she surveyed our faces. We must have looked like we were on the wrong end of a firing squad.

"Everyone okay?" she asked.

"Fine," Phil said tersely, his face so red I was afraid he might have a stroke. Thankfully, at that moment, the real waiter came.

We spent the rest of dinner in strained silence punctuated by my mother rattling on about the kids and shooting worried looks at me. It wasn't until we'd gotten home that I had an opportunity to talk with Blake.

"I'll take care of Elsie and Nick," my mother told me. "Go talk with your husband."

"Let's walk," I told him. I couldn't stand to have this conversation in the house.

"Do you want to change?"

"No," I said, even though my dress was uncomfortably tight. "I'll just put on a pair of flip- flops."

Although it was dark, the air was still stifling, as if someone had spread an electric blanket out over the city and turned the setting to "High."

"So," I said after I'd closed the front door behind us. "Journey to Manhood didn't work out."

"I'm sorry," he said. "I tried."

Tears leaked out of my eyes. I didn't want to be with Blake anymore—I hadn't wanted him to touch me for months—but somehow, him announcing he'd fallen in love with someone else felt like a betrayal.

"Oh, Margie," he said, reaching out to touch my shoulder.

"No," I said, shying away. "It's just . . . Couldn't you have told me before dinner?"

"I tried—"

"Not very hard," I said.

"There was no way to put it off," he said. "Frank was already set to show up at the table."

"You've known him for less than a week, and you're in love with him?"

He hung his head, looking like a chastened boy, and for a moment, I could see the pain he'd carried with him his whole life.

"I'm sorry," I said, my voice rough. "I know you didn't mean to hurt me. What you did tonight must have been terribly hard. Facing your parents that way, I mean."

"If I didn't go through with it tonight," Blake said, "I was afraid I wouldn't get the courage again."

We walked on for a while. The cicadas droned in the trees, and lights were on in the windows of the houses around us, looking cozy and inviting. I imagined the families inside, finishing up dinner, reading bedtime stories, snuggling next to each other in bed. My family would never be quite the same again I realized, with a sadness that seeped into my bones. My children would never have the family that I'd envisioned for them, and I couldn't help feeling somehow that it was all my fault. If I'd been a better woman, somehow . . .

Tears welled in my eyes, and everything seemed blurry. I took a deep breath and gathered myself. There would be time to cry later; right now, I needed to figure out what was going to happen next.

"Where do we go from here?" I croaked. "I mean, you and . . . Frank. Are you going to move in together?"

"No," he said quietly. "Not yet, anyway. But I think it's time for me to move out of the office and into a place of my own."

I nodded, wiping my eyes. "Probably," I said. Would I be relieved to have him gone? Or would it just be a reminder of everything I had lost?

"What can I do to help, Margie?" he asked, touching my arm. "It kills me to hurt you like this."

Not enough to not fall in love with another man, I thought bitterly. But in truth, there was nothing left for us. Wasn't it right for him to move on? And, maybe, me? My mind flitted to Becky's brother Michael, but I banished that thought. It wasn't time to think about new relationships just yet. I still had to finish unraveling the old one.

"I don't know," I said, feeling miserable.

"I'll move out this week," he said. "Find an apartment. I'll do anything I can to help. I know this . . . this is all my fault. I've been horrible to you."

I looked at him then. My husband, with his high cheekbones, his sharp chin, his sweep of dark hair. I didn't love him as a husband anymore, but I still loved him.

"I still want to be the kids' dad," he said. "I want to live as nearby as I can. Coach soccer. Help them with homework."

I blinked, surprised. He hadn't done either of those things in the past; was he really going to start now? "What are we going to tell them?" I asked.

"Let's talk to a counselor about it," he said. "For now, we'll just say we're going to live in different places for a bit."

I nodded and wiped my eyes. I didn't want to talk anymore; I needed time to process the huge earthquake that had just hit my life. "We should probably go back," I said.

"Are you ready?"

"I think so," I told him, although I was nowhere near ready. I might never be ready.

But I couldn't afford not to figure things out. My children needed me—and they needed their dad, too. We'd have to figure it all out together, somehow—apart.

We were almost to the door when my phone rang. I looked down at it, but didn't recognize the number. "Go on; I'll be in in a moment," I told Blake, and picked it up as he let himself in the front door.

"Hello?"

The voice on the other end sounded weepy. "Is this Margie Peterson? From Warrior Wives?"

"Anne?" I recognized her voice. "What's wrong?"

She took a deep breath. "I . . . I was hoping I could take you up on coffee," she said. "My husband and I are . . . are separating."

I took a deep, shuddery breath. "Funny you should say that," I said. "I just had the same conversation with my husband. He's moving out this week."

"Really?" she asked, sounding almost . . . relieved, somehow. "I guess Journey to Manhood isn't all it's cracked up to be."

"Doesn't look like it," I said. "So much for push-up bras and casseroles. How about Trianon, tomorrow at ten?"

"Oh, that would be perfect," she said. "Thank you. And I'm so sorry."

"Likewise," I said, feeling a wave of sadness break over me.

I hung up and stood on my front step for a few minutes, trying to process everything that had happened that night. I'd known it was going to happen, I realized. I just didn't realize how awful it would make me feel.

When the wave subsided enough that I felt I could keep my composure, I walked into the house, where my mother was looking at me worriedly.

"The kids are down," she said quietly. There was no sign of Blake. "Are you okay?"

"Not at all," I said, bursting into tears as she held out her arms and pulled me into a hug that went all the way to my toes. At that moment, the doorbell rang.

"Blake?" my mother asked.

I opened the front door. Peaches stood there, resplendent in yellow Lycra, with a cat carrier in her right hand.

"What's this?" I asked.

"Thank-you gift from Bubba Sue's mom," she said. There was a gentle grunting from the carrier.

"It's not . . ."

She nodded. "It is. She's only here to visit for a bit—needs to spend the next few weeks with her mommy. But Janette insisted."

"No," I said, but Elsie was peeking around the end of the hallway.

"Is that one of the babies?" my daughter asked.

"Sure is, honey," Peaches told her. "Say hello to the newest member of the family."

I held up a hand. "But—"

"She is awfully cute," my mother said.

"I've got another thank-you gift for you, too," Peaches said, fishing a box out of her bag. "From Desiree."

I cringed, imagining chaps, or a riding crop. "Do I want to know?"

"Open it," she said.

"But Elsie's here . . ."

"We'll take the piglet into the kitchen," my mother said, and escorted Elsie from the room.

I opened the box; inside was a fifty-dollar gift card to Pottery Barn Kids.

"That's really nice of her," I said. "I know she's on a budget."

Peaches looked at me. "How did the retreat go?"

"Not quite as anticipated," I said. "Blake and his boyfriend showed up at dinner tonight and announced that they're in love." With a twist in my stomach, I added, "I think we're beyond redemption."

If I was expecting condolences, I was wrong. "Hallelujah," Peaches hooted. "It was about damned time."

"You think?"

"I know," she said. "You're too young and cute to wither away without a good man."

"I've got two kids. Who's going to want to date me?"

"Becky's brother, from what I've heard," Peaches said, and I flushed. "In the meantime, there's plenty of business to keep your mind off things. Two more cases came in this afternoon. And when you've got things squared away, Jess's got a friend he'd like to set up. We can double date."

"You fixed things with Jess?"

"He showed up with a dozen red roses and a pair of cowgirl boots," she said, holding out a foot so I could admire her new turquoise footwear. "How could I say no?"

I grinned. "I'm happy for you."

She reached out and squeezed my shoulder. "We've got a bright future, kiddo. Now, I've got to get that piglet back to her momma, but I'll see you at nine in the morning."

"Got it," I said as we headed to the kitchen to retrieve Bubba Sue's progeny, who I was hoping would not be back for a return engagement.

"And Margie?"

"Yeah?"

"You rocked the Holy Oaks case. You're shaping up to be the best investigator I've ever worked with." She cast an eye over my dress. "Even if you do need some help in the wardrobe department."

"You should talk," I said, eyeing her stretchy top. "At least I don't risk falling out of my clothes every time I tie my shoe."

"That's why I wear boots, honey," she said with a wink.

As I followed her into the kitchen, I found myself shaking my head. A year ago, I never would have imagined I'd be a private investigator on the brink of divorce with a new pet piglet. But as I watched Peaches, Elsie, and my mother coo over the little chocolate-colored creature, I couldn't help but smile.

All things considered? I was a pretty lucky woman.

ACKNOWLEDGMENTS

Thanks first to my late mentor, Barbara Burnett-Smith, who encouraged me to write this series in the first place, and to Jason Brenizer (writing buddy and plot doctor extraordinaire) for helping me out of my usual plot dilemmas. Thanks to Cat Adair for help with research, and to beta readers Olivia Leigh Blacke, Samantha Mann, Norma Klanderman, J. Jaye Smith, Ellen Helwig, and Dorothy MacInerney for their thoughtful and thorough reading of the manuscript. (Thanks also to Dave and Carol Swartz for early read-throughs.) And, of course, oodles of gratitude to JoVon Sotak, my fun, patient, and incredibly on-the-ball acquisitions editor; to Charlotte Herscher, developmental editor extraordinaire and My Little Pony connoisseur; to sharp-eyed copyeditor Meredith Jacobson and proofreader (and continuity expert) Michael Schuler for helping me shape the manuscript and for catching my mistakes. I also want to thank Anh Schluep, Alan Turkus, Tiffany Pokorny, Sarah Shaw, Jacque Ben-Zekry, and the rest of the fabulous Amazon publishing team for all of the wonderful things they do!

And, as always, thanks to my family—Eric, Abby, and Ian—for putting up with me. I love you!

ANOTHER SERIES BY KAREN MACINERNEY

Don't miss the Dewberry Farm Mysteries by Karen MacInerney. In *Killer Jam*, a big crime in a small town turns Lucy Resnick's focus from life on a farm to solving a murder.

When Houston reporter Lucy Resnick cashes in her retirement to buy her grandmother's farm in Buttercup, Texas, she's looking forward to a simple life as a homesteader. But Lucy has barely finished putting up her first batch of Killer Dewberry Jam when an oil-exploration truck rolls up to the farm and announces plans to replace her broccoli patch with an oil derrick. Two days later, Nettie Kocurek, the woman who ordered the drilling, turns up dead at the Founders' Day Festival with a bratwurst skewer through her heart and one of Lucy's jam jars beside her . . . and the sheriff fingers Lucy as the prime suspect.

Horrified, Lucy begins to talk to Nettie's neighbors, but the more she gets to know the townspeople, the more she realizes she's not the only one who had a beef with Nettie. Can she clear her name, or will her dream life turn into a nightmare?

A DEWBERRY FARM
Killer Jam
MYSTERY

Karen MacInerney

CHAPTER 1

I've always heard it's no use crying over spilled milk. But after three days of attempting to milk Blossom the cow (formerly Heifer #82), only to have her deliver a well-timed kick that deposited the entire contents of my bucket on the stall floor, it was hard not to feel a few tears of frustration forming in the corners of my eyes.

Stifling a sigh, I surveyed the giant puddle on the floor of the milking stall and reached for the hose. I'd tried surrounding the bucket with blocks, holding it in place with my feet—even tying the handle to the side of the stall with a length of twine. But for the sixth straight time, I had just squeezed the last drops from the teats when Blossom swung her right rear hoof in a kind of bovine hook kick, walloping the top of the bucket and sending gallons of the creamy white fluid spilling across both the concrete floor and my boots. I reprimanded her, but she simply tossed her head and grabbed another mouthful of the feed I affectionately called "cow chow."

She looked so unassuming. So velvety-nosed and kind, with big, long-lashed eyes. At least she had on the day I'd selected her from the line of cows for sale at the Double-Bar Ranch. Despite all the reading

I'd done on selecting a heifer, when she pressed her soft nose up against my cheek, I knew she belonged at Dewberry Farm. Thankfully, the rancher I'd purchased her from had seemed more than happy to let her go, extolling her good nature and excellent production.

He'd somehow failed to mention her phobia of filled buckets.

Now, as I watched the tawny heifer gamboling into the pasture beside my farmhouse, kicking her heels up in what I imagined was a cow's version of the middle finger, I took a deep breath and tried to be philosophical about the whole thing. She still had those big brown eyes, and it made me happy to think of her in my pasture rather than the cramped conditions at Double-Bar Ranch. And she'd only kicked the milk bucket, not me.

Despite the farm's growing pains, as I turned toward the farmhouse, I couldn't help but smile. After fifteen years of life in Houston, I now lived in a century-old yellow farmhouse—the one I'd dreamed of owning my whole life—with ten acres of rolling pasture and field, a peach orchard, a patch of dewberries, and a quaint, bustling town just up the road. The mayor had even installed a Wi-Fi transmitter on the water tower, which meant I could someday put up a website for the farm. So what if Blossom was more trouble than I'd expected, I told myself. I'd only been a dairy farmer for seventy-two hours; how could I expect to know everything?

In fact, it had only been six months since my college roommate, Natalie Barnes, had convinced me to buy the farm that had once belonged to my grandparents. Natalie had cashed in her chips a few years back and bought an inn in Maine, and I'd never seen her happier. With my friend's encouragement, I'd gone after the dream of reliving those childhood summers, which I'd spent fishing in the creek and learning to put up jam at my grandmother's elbow.

It had been a long time since those magical days in Grandma Vogel's steamy, deliciously scented kitchen. I'd spent several years as a reporter for the *Houston Chronicle*, fantasizing about a simpler life as I wrote about big-city crime and corruption. As an antidote to the heartache I'd seen in my job, I'd grown tomatoes in a sunny patch of the backyard, made batches of soap on the kitchen stove, and even kept a couple of chickens until the neighbors complained.

Ever since those long summer days, I'd always fantasized about living in Buttercup, but it wasn't until two events happened almost simultaneously that my dream moved from fantasy to reality. First, the paper I worked for, which like most newspapers was suffering from the onset of the digital age, laid off half the staff, offering me a buyout that, combined with my savings and the equity on my small house, would give me a nice nest egg. And second, as I browsed the web one day, I discovered that my grandmother's farm—which she'd sold fifteen years ago, after my grandfather passed—was up for sale.

Ignoring my financial advisor's advice—and fending off questions from friends who questioned my sanity—I raided the library for every homesteading book I could find, cobbled together a plan I hoped would keep me from starving, took the buyout from the paper, and put an offer in on Dewberry Farm. Within a month, I went from being Lucy Resnick, reporter, to Lucy Resnick, unemployed homesteader of my grandparents' derelict farm. Now, after months of backbreaking work, I surveyed the rows of fresh green lettuce and broccoli plants sprouting up in the fields behind the house with a deep sense of satisfaction. I might not be rich, and I might not know how to milk a cow, but I was living the life I'd always wanted.

I focused on the tasks for the day, mentally crossing cheese making off the list as I headed for the little yellow farmhouse. There might not be fresh mozzarella on the menu, but I did have two more batches of soap to make, along with shade cover to spread over the lettuce, cucumber seeds to plant, chickens to feed, and buckets of dewberries to pick and turn into jam. I also needed to stop by and pick up some beeswax from the Bees' Knees, owned by local beekeeper Nancy Shaw.

The little beeswax candles I made in short mason jars were a top seller at Buttercup Market Days, and I needed to make more.

Fortunately, it was a gorgeous late spring day, with late bluebonnets carpeting the roadsides and larkspur blanketing the meadow beside the house, the tall flowers' ruffled lavender and pink spikes bringing a smile to my face. They'd make beautiful bouquets for the market this coming weekend—and for the pitcher in the middle of my kitchen table. Although the yellow Victorian-style farmhouse had been neglected and left vacant for the past decade or more, many of my grandmother's furnishings remained. She hadn't been able to take them with her to the retirement home, and for some reason, nobody else had claimed or moved them out, so many things I remembered from my childhood were still there.

The house had good bones, and with a bit of paint and elbow grease, I had quickly made it a comfortable home. The white tiled countertop sparkled again, and my grandmother's pie safe with its punched tin panels was filled with jars of jam for the market. I smoothed my hand over the enormous pine table my grandmother had served Sunday dinners on for years. I'd had to work to refinish it, sanding it down before adding several layers of polyurethane to the weathered surface, but I felt connected to my grandmother every time I sat down to a meal.

The outside had taken a bit more effort. Although the graceful oaks still sheltered the house, looking much like they had when I had visited as a child, the line of roses that lined the picket fence had suffered from neglect, and the irises were lost in a thicket of Johnsongrass. The land itself had been in worse shape; the dewberries the farm had been named for had crept up into where the garden used to be, hiding in a sea of mesquite saplings and giant purple thistles. I had had to pay someone to plow a few acres for planting, and had lost some of the extra poundage I'd picked up at my desk job rooting out the rest. Although it was a continual battle against weeds, the greens I had put in that spring were looking lush and healthy—and the dewberries had been corralled to the banks of Dewberry Creek, which ran along the back side of the property. The peach trees in the small orchard had been cloaked in gorgeous pink blossoms and now were laden with tiny fruits. In a few short months, I'd be trying out the honey-peach preserves recipe I'd found in my grandmother's handwritten cookbook, which was my most treasured possession. Sometimes, when I flipped through its yellowed pages, I almost felt as if my grandmother were standing next to me.

Now, I stifled a sigh of frustration as I watched the heifer browse the pasture. With time, I was hoping to get a cheese concern going; right now, I only had Blossom, but hopefully she'd calve a heifer, and with luck, I'd have two or three milkers soon. Money was on the tight side, and I might have to consider driving to farmers' markets in Austin to make ends meet—or maybe finding some kind of part-time job—but now that I'd found my way to Buttercup, I didn't want to leave.

I readjusted my ponytail—now that I didn't need to dress for work, I usually pulled my long brown hair back in the mornings—and mentally reviewed my to-do list. Picking dewberries was next, a delightful change from the more mundane tasks of my city days. I needed a few more batches of jam for Buttercup's Founders' Day Festival and Jam-Off, which was coming up in a few days. I'd pick before it got too hot; it had been a few days since I'd been down by the creek, and I hoped to harvest another several quarts.

Chuck, the small apricot rescue poodle who had been my constant companion for the past five years, joined me as I grabbed a pair of gardening gloves and the galvanized silver bucket I kept by the back door, then headed past the garden in the back and down to the creek, where the sweet smell of sycamores filled the air. I didn't let Chuck near Blossom—I was afraid she would do the same thing to him that she did to the milk bucket—but he accompanied me almost everywhere else on the farm, prancing through the tall grass, guarding me from wayward squirrels and crickets, and—unfortunately—picking up hundreds of burrs. I'd had to shave him within a week of arriving at the farm, and I was still getting used to having a bald poodle. This morning, he romped through the tall grass, occasionally stopping to sniff a particularly compelling tuft of grass. His pink skin showed through his clipped fur, and I found myself wondering if there was such a thing as doggie sunscreen.

The creek was running well this spring—we'd had plenty of rain, which was always welcome in Texas, and a giant bullfrog plopped into the water as I approached the mass of brambles with their dark, sweet berries. They were similar to the blackberries I bought in the store, but a bit longer, with a sweet-tart tang that I loved. I popped the first few in my mouth.

I went to work filling the bucket, using a stick to push the brambles aside, and had filled it about halfway when I heard the grumble of a motor coming up the long driveway. Chuck, who had been trying to figure out how to get to the fish that were darting in the deeper part of the creek, turned and growled. I shushed him as we headed back toward the farmhouse, the bucket swinging at my side.

A lanky man in jeans and a button-down shirt was unfolding himself from the front seat of the truck as I opened the back gate. Chuck surged ahead of me, barking and growling, then slinking to my ankle when I shushed him with a sharp word.

"Can I help you?" I asked the man. He was in his midforties, with work-worn boots and the roughened skin of a man who'd spent most of his life outdoors.

"You Lucy Resnick?" he asked.

"I am," I said, putting down the bucket. Chuck growled again and put himself between us.

"Butch Simmons, Lone Star Exploration," the man said, squinting at me.

"Nice to meet you," I said, extending a hand. Chuck yipped, and I apologized.

"Good doggie," the man said, reaching down to let the poodle sniff him. Usually, that was all the little dog needed to become comfortable, but something about the man upset him. He growled, backing away.

"I don't know what's gotten into him," I said, scooping him up in my arms. "Can I help you with something?" I asked again, holding the squirming poodle tight.

"Mind if I take a few pictures? We're surveying the property before we start the exploration process."

"Exploration process?" I asked.

"Didn't anyone tell you?"

"Tell me what?"

He turned his head and spit out a wad of snuff. I wrinkled my nose, revolted by the glob of brown goo on the caliche driveway. "We're drillin' for oil."

ABOUT THE AUTHOR

Photo © 2008 Kenneth Gall

Karen MacInerney is the housework-impaired author of fourteen books, including the Gray Whale Inn series, the Urban Werewolf trilogy, the Dewberry Farm Mysteries, and the Margie Peterson Mysteries. She lives in Austin, Texas, with two children, her husband, and a menagerie of animals.

For more information, visit www.karenmacinerney.com.